The Many Faces of Family

Joanne Simon Tailele

The Many Faces of Family

Joanne Simon Tailele

Chapter One

Suzdal, Russia

May 1, 2006

The 1ˢᵗ of May celebration in Russia had begun. Fresh strawberry grass and tiny yellow bedstraw sprouted throughout the meadow after a long and frigid winter. They tickled four-year-old Natalia's ankles as she sprinted toward the pigeon lofts to find her grandfather. She peeked from behind each stilt trying to surprise him. Small twigs snapped under her feet.

Yuri Sokolov stopped scooping seeds from the burlap sack. "*Ya slishu tebya,*" he chuckled. "You can't creep up on me."

"Ah, Dedushka, I wanted to surprise you." Natalia came from her hiding place, a steel-gray pigeon with its neck ringed in fluorescent green, perched on her shoulder. She planted a kiss on her

1

grandfather's rugged cheek.

Yuri frowned behind his thick mustache, but his gray eyes sparkled with love. "You mustn't turn the pigeons into your pets. They'll make poor carriers."

"But I love them, Dedushka, and they love me." She reached toward her shoulder, and the bird hopped onto her arm. She stroked his back and cooed into his invisible ears. His soft feathers tickled her fingers. "Hurry, it's festival day."

"Then put Ivan in the loft and make yourself useful. We must work before we can play. Fetch the pail, fill it with seed, and then spread it in the pens. Nice and even, and don't give Ivan any extra. He'll get too fat to fly."

She loved to hear the story of how his birds were descendants of the carrier pigeons that delivered messages for the czar a lifetime ago, how they had won many contests throughout Russia, always finding their way home. Natalia happily followed her grandfather's orders and climbed the steps to the lofts, working her way down the narrow corridor. "I thought you didn't name the pigeons, Dedushka because they're not pets." She giggled.

He furrowed his untamed brows. "Shush, Natalia. Where's your respect?"

She blew him a kiss and moved on to the second of the nine lofts.

He shook his head and turned the hose on the loft floor.

From high in the next loft, Natalia waved to her brother, Nikolai, making his way through the meadow towards her. At fourteen-year-old, his arms and legs sprouted liked the spring grass from clothes perpetually too small. Straight brown hair poked from a

2

navy cap balanced on his head. She could hear him singing as the melody carried across the field. Behind him, the rising sun glistened off the blue and gold dome skyline of the churches and monasteries. From her perch, she could see the small churches where their parents worked, the winter Church of the Nativity of St. John the Baptist with its green, bell-shaped roof and directly behind it, the summer Church of the Epiphany with multiple spires. Papa tended the elaborate gardens, and Mama gave lectures, explaining how the buildings were reconstructed after fires destroyed the earlier wooden structures built in 1739. She could recite the drill in her sleep.

Across the winding Kamenka River, Natalia could see the rambling white Monastery of Saint Euthymius with its high red stone walls and the gold stars on the blue dome of the Cathedral of the Nativity where Nikolai said he would someday be parish priest. It was no wonder people called Suzdal "The City of Churches."

"Dedushka, Golubka, it's time to come home," Nikolai said when he reached the foot of the lofts. "Mama and Papa are waiting for us to go to Mass before the festival. Come."

"Nika, why do you call me *Pigeon*?" Natalia dropped the pail, climbed down the steep ladder of the last loft, and slipped her small hand in his.

He tousled her blond hair with his free hand. "Because you're like a pigeon. You spend more time in the lofts than they do. I'm afraid someday you'll fly away." His voice cracked in mid-sentence, and she watched his cheeks flame red.

"You're silly. I don't have wings. Even if I did, I'd be a homing pigeon like Ivan. I'd always come home."

Together Nikolai, Dedushka, and Natalia followed the rising sun through the meadow and across the wooden bridge. White billows of smoke circled from the chimney of their little red cottage with the gray tin roof that tinkled like music when it rained. The smell of fresh black bread hurried them along.

"There you are," said their mother, Ana. "Nikolai, help your grandmother out the door before we're late."

Babushka sat hunched in the wooden rocking chair, a shawl draped around her sloped shoulders despite the warmth of the room. Across her broad face, a road map of wrinkles crisscrossed and settled at the corners of her thin lips.

"Come, Babushka, time for Mass." Nikolai gently pulled on her flaccid forearms, helping her to her feet, and they made their way over the battered plank floors to the threshold.

Papa held Babushka's arm for the short walk to the Church of the Nativity while Natalia skipped alongside her mother. The family joined a handful of tourists in the confines of the chapel while the Deacon prepared the Eucharist for the Mass. To calm Natalia's fidgety legs during the service, Mama lifted her daughter into her arms. It was so much nicer to be in Mama's arms than standing on the hard marble floor, looking at pant legs and heavy skirts. Mama placed a kiss upon her daughter's cheek. "Be still, my little angel."

Natalia pressed her hands on either side of Mama's face and rubbed her nose in an Eskimo kiss, the way Babushka had taught her.

Ana laughed and squeezed her daughter a little

tighter. "Pay attention to the priest," she chastised Natalia lovingly.

When Mass ended, Nikolai raced Natalia back to the house. Natalia laughed when he pretended to stumble so she could win.

The festival in town was full of games, music, and laughter. Khorovod dancers in their best costumes, twirled in a colorful circle, hands entwined in the intricate ancient Russian folk dance symbolizing the beauty of movement. Tables, adorned in red-checked cloths and laden with pancakes, quail, goat cheese, and chocolate, lined the street. Generous portions of vodka flowed freely to friends and tourists alike.

After the long and happy day, Natalia watched the fireworks light up the sky from her bedroom window. She drifted off to sleep, feeling happy, secure, and loved.

The following day, Nikolai returned to his studies at school, and Mama and Papa resumed their roles at the sister churches. At home, sitting on the low sofa, Babushka helped Natalia with her letters, a tablet balanced on Natalia's lap. Natalia struggled with э (the lower-case *e*) and з (equivalent to *z*).

A loud pop from the kitchen roused Babushka from their concentration over the letters. She struggled to her feet and waddled to the kitchen. "Fire! Run, Natalia. Get Dedushka!"

Natalia heard the panic and fear in her grandmother's voice. She dropped the tablet and rushed out the front door. The stench of burning wood and plastic filled her nostrils. She sprinted across the bridge and through the new grass.

"Dedushka, Dedushka. A fire! There's a fire at the house! Babushka needs you."

Dedushka's snowy head popped through the doorway of the third loft. He peered over her head, the whites of his eyes bulging at the sight of the smoke rising above the treetops.

"Stay here, Natalia. Don't come near the fire." On his arthritic legs, Dedushka hurried past her.

Natalia stared after him. She wanted to follow, but she'd never disobeyed him before. Her heart pounded in her chest; her feet were rooted in place. If only Nika or Mama could tell her what to do. Suddenly her legs found wings, and she dashed toward the house, the black smoke filling the morning sky. The siren of the fire truck signaled that it had pulled away from the center of town.

By the time Natalia reached the cottage, a group of neighbors had gathered as the men tried to douse the fire with hoses. The women circled around her, not letting her see though the heavy curtain of their skirts.

Natalia wailed. "Let me go! I need to find Babushka!"

The fire truck screeched to a halt. "Your Mama and Papa are already here, helping your babushka," said one of the neighbors. "And now the firemen. You stay here where it's safe."

Orange flames licked at the roof and siding and roared in Natalia's ears. "Babushka! Mama!" she screamed.

One of the women pulled Natalia tight against her skirt.

Nikolai had heard the sirens as the fire engines

pulled out of the station but hadn't given them much thought. When the principal called Nikolai from his science project, a cold chill ran down his spine. His feet felt like lead as he followed the Deacon from the Znamenskaya Church and the school nurse into the principal's office. Something awful must have happened.

The principal cleared his throat. "Nikolai, I have some very bad news. You need to be brave, okay?"

"Is it Babushka?" Nikolai asked. *Don't let it be Babushka. She is old and sick.* Mama had prepared him for the worst; someday soon she could die.

The man looked down at his scuffed brown shoes. The deacon sat beside Nikolai and placed a large hairy hand over the boy's soft young one. "There's been a fire at your house."

Nikolai jumped out of his seat. "A fire? We have to help!"

Principal Yegor caught him by the shoulders. "It's out, son. It's all over."

"Babushka and Natalia? They got out in time, yes?" Nikolai could hear his heart pounding in his ears.

For a moment, no one spoke. The men's gazes were trained on the cracked gray tile floor.

"Natalia is fine," said the priest. "Your mama and papa reached the fire before the firemen. They tried to find your babushka. Your mother is in the hospital. She inhaled a lot of toxic smoke."

"And Papa and Dedushka? Are they at the hospital with Mama?"

"Son." The priest patted Nikolai's knee. "I'm so sorry. Your papa and grandparents did not make it out."

7

"What? Are you sure?" *There must be a mistake. Why are they saying these things?*

The priest bowed his head. "They are gone, Nikolai. All of them."

Nikolai backed away, shaking his head. "Nyet, nyet." He wrapped his arms around his middle, bile rising to his throat.

A young woman, who introduced herself as Olga Pavlic, a social worker, drove Nikolai to the hospital. She rattled on about stupid things like the festival and school.

Why wouldn't she shut up? He had to think. He followed her to the ICU unit. Six narrow cots filled the space, three end-to-end on either side of the room. IV bags hung from metal poles at the head of each bed. Someone handed Nikolai a paper mask. The first two beds held old men, covered in faded hand-knitted blankets brought from home. One family member hovered over the man on the left, offering soup he pushed away with a wave of a yellowed hand. A mother clutched a crying child on the next cot.

Mama lay on a thin mattress with an oxygen mask over her mouth and nose. An IV bag pumped nutrients into her body.

Natalia was there with their neighbors, Mr. and Mrs. Butkovsky. Nikolai expected Mama would look bad, but he wasn't prepared for what he saw. Her eyes were sunken deep into their sockets, the color of her skin an ashen gray. Suddenly the room was too hot, the arid smell of burnt flesh too strong, the sound of moaning men and crying children too loud. He gripped the bedrail to steady himself.

"Nikolai, are you all right?" Miss Pavlic asked.

Nikolai nodded, locking his knees to keep from

collapsing. He must be brave in front of Natalia, who cowered behind Mrs. Butkovsky's heavy skirt.

Mr. Butkovsky huddled in the corner talking quietly to a man in a white coat. He handed an envelope to the doctor who nodded. A few minutes later, an orderly brought in an EKG machine and pressed the electrodes to Mama's chest.

Nikolai squared his shoulders, stood erect, and waited for the man to leave. Once Nikolai could see his mother, her blank stare greeted him. He touched her cheek softly. "Mama? Mama?" *Please, God, let her respond.*

Finally, her eyes focused, and she moved a bandaged hand to caress his arm.

Her gentle touch triggered a lump in his throat, and he swallowed hard to fight back the tears. *Be strong.* Nikolai motioned for Natalia to join him beside the bed. "Golubka, don't be afraid. It's Mama. Come here."

She shook her head and buried her face deeper in the fabric of Mrs. Butkovsky's skirt.

He brushed a singed lock from his mother's forehead. "Hello, Mama. Natalia's afraid of all the tubes and wires."

"No, I'm not," Natalia said softly.

But Nikolai knew she was.

Ana gave a slight nod and closed her eyes.

"Мама… Mama!" Nikolai shouted. "Don't go, Mama. Please, open your eyes." He held his breath until she opened her eyes, smiled, and blew him a kiss.

She tried to speak, and Nikolai lifted her mask to hear her. "You must take care of our Golubka now, my son."

Nikolai gulped. "I promise, Mama, I will." He pulled the patchwork blanket over her narrow shoulders. Who had brought the blanket? Perhaps Mrs. Butkovsky?

Natalia crept from behind the skirt and stood beside him.

"See, Golubka," he said. "It's okay. Mama's just very tired."

Tentatively, Natalia reached out and touched her mother's shoulder.

Nikolai lifted Natalia onto the bed, and she spooned in beside her mama. A bandaged hand patted her on the back.

Nikolai breathed a sigh of relief. He reached for Mama's hand. Everything was going to be okay. He stood a long time watching as his mother and sister fell asleep. His mind blurred with images, the way he imagined it happened: the house on fire, Papa and Dedushka rushing into the burning inferno to find Babushka, Mama chasing after them.

He felt eyes burning into him. A woman under a thin gray sheet on the cot across from Mama stared unsmilingly at Nikolai. She looked afraid. He wanted to pull his eyes away, but her stare paralyzed him. Where was her family? Her eyes pleaded at him. For what? A blanket, food, someone to hold her hand?

A loud mechanical screech startled him out of his trance.

A nurse rushed into the room and jerked him out of the way. She scooped up the sleeping Natalia and dropped her into Nikolai's arms.

An orderly ushered them out of the room as while another pushed a cart with a blue machine ahead of him into the room.

What's happening? "Please, Mama. Don't die."

Olga Pavlic took Natalia in her lap on a hard metal folding chair while Nikolai paced the halls, between the patients not lucky enough to get into a room. How would he take care of Natalia all by himself?

Much later, the nurses and doctors filed silently out of the room, wheeling the crash cart with them. A doctor approached them. "I am sorry, but she's gone."

No. That couldn't be. How could they lose their entire family in one day? How was it possible?

An hour passed before they were again led into the room. Nikolai gripped tightly to Natalia's small hand as they said their good-byes to Mama. He gulped several times, trying to dislodge the boulder stuck in his throat.

"Mama, wake up," Natalia wailed.

If only it was that simple. Nikolai turned away from the bed, pulled his sister out the door, and curled into a ball on the floor.

Their neighbors, Varia and Yegor Butkovsky, waited outside the curtain. Ancient and childless, they were the closest thing to living relatives the children had. The social worker was nowhere in sight. Where had she gone?

Mrs. Butkovsky reached a spotted hand to Natalia. "Come, my little one." She wrapped her arm around the child. "The two of you will come home with Yegor and me."

Natalia folded into the woman's broad chest. "Mama, I want Mama," she cried. Her eyes met Nikolai's, pleading, "Nika, I want to go home."

He had to be strong now. He had to be the man

now. Nikolai uncurled his body and addressed Mr. Butkovsky. "We appreciate your hospitality. We won't be any trouble."

They followed the old pair down the long, crowded corridor and into the parking lot as huge gray clouds threatened to break open.

Mr. Butkovsky paused and stared at the sky. "Come, children, it will rain soon. We will go home now."

Nikolai wrapped his arm around Natalia to steady her as she slipped on the thick leather upholstery in the rear seat of the huge old car. No seat belts were in sight. The car sped past their burnt-out cottage.

"Ach, Nika, look at our house!" Natalia cried. The blackened roof had collapsed into the center where one wall crumbled into what was once their living room. The windows were gone, and smoke still rose from the ashes. The brick fireplace and chimney stood intact, towering above the rubble.

"Turn away, Golubka, it's not our house anymore. There's nothing to see. I'll take care of you from now on." Nikolai pinched the bridge of his nose. How was he going to do that? "Mr. Butkovsky, sir, I need to go through some things in there. Will you let me go?"

"Ah, son, what could there be for you there?"

"I don't know, sir. There must be something."

Nikolai and the old man left Natalia and Mrs. Butkovsky at the old couple's home and walked to the smoldering rubble that had once been home. They sifted through the charred remains of bedposts, Natalia's water-logged dolls, Babushka's broken eyeglasses. Nikolai picked up a few scorched

12

photographs, saved by the glass that encased them and brushed away the soot with the back of his hand. Was this it for three generations of life raised here? He forced down the hollowness that filled his stomach and threatened to spill out as a scream. A resolve settled over him. He had to be the man now. Make Papa and Dedushka and Mama and Babushka proud.

Later, after choking down potato soup neither Natalia nor Nikolai could taste, the siblings huddled together on a small single bed tucked in the corner of the old woman's sewing room. A quilting loom and a sinister-looking sewing machine with foot petals and sharp angles took up most of the room, casting eerie shadows on the wall from the moonlight that splayed through the thin linen curtains.

"I'm scared," Natalia whispered into Nikolai's ear.

"It's okay. They're good people, just old, like Babushka and Dedushka. Don't be afraid."

"Nika, Babushka and Dedushka are dead," her high-pitched four-year-old voice quavered.

"Yes, Golubka." He reached out and pulled her close into his arms. "As are Mama and Papa. But I'm here. Go to sleep now."

Chapter Two

Nine months prior to the fire in Suzdal

Chalmette, LA, USA

August 28, 2005

If it weren't for the voodoo curse, Cecile would have made a terrific mother. It was all she ever wanted. She rubbed her hand over the bulge around her middle. *We'll get through this, Junior, not to worry.* Who said a Cajun wasn't supposed to scare easily? Must have been a Yankee. She watched the weatherman on the TV draw spaghetti lines that snaked through the Gulf of Mexico, all heading straight toward the mouth of the Mississippi. They named her Katrina. The die-hards planned hurricane parties. Fire up the outdoor cooker; them mud bugs were waiting for cayenne pepper, hot sauce, and 'taters. *Laissez les bons temps rouler,* let the good times roll.

Mayor Ray Nagin interrupted the weatherman. He issued a mandatory evacuation order. Governor Blanco appeared on the screen next and told anyone refusing to leave to write their names and social security number on their arms in permanent marker so their bodies could be identified.

Seriously? Cecile hunted around the house for a marker. *Don't be ridiculous.* She flipped off the television. Those news people always blew things out of proportion. This wasn't the first hurricane in her thirty years, and it wouldn't be the last. No matter the warnings, she couldn't leave without Armand. He had responsibilities as drilling manager for Murphy Oil Refinery, but he'd be home soon.

She opened the door and stared at ominous dark clouds and things that had no business being airborne. Thousands of mosquito hawks flew in a frenzy, forming a gossamer purple and green funnel. *It's coming ... please let it pass over.* The gray sky turned black, rain pelted in straight arrows, and then suddenly whipped sideways, almost knocking her over, sending loose shingles and small garden tools rolling across yards and down the center of streets. She staggered inside and locked the door.

The phone rang and startled her. She jumped, her nerves as raw as prime rib.

"Come home, CeCe. There's still time," her father pleaded. Home was Butte La Rose, one hundred and nineteen miles northwest, along the Atchafalaya River, safely out of the eye of the storm.

"I'm fine, Daddy, really." She forced her voice to sound steady. "Armi will be here soon." She could hear her grandmother, Mamère Le Bieu, the local voodoo queen, chanting in the background. "What's

15

Mamère doing?"

Her father snorted. "She's in her element. She's beckoning spirits to keep you safe. You should have seen her chase that gecko for her potion. It was hysterical."

Cecile's laugh came out jagged and raw. She pictured the squat fire-plug frame scurrying after the reptile, a rainbow of caftan billowing around her. She stroked the gris-gris amulet around her neck that Mamère made to protect her. "Tell her I appreciate her voodoo and will sleep safer knowing the spirit of Evangeline is protecting me. I'll call later, Daddy, when it's over." If only her mother was still alive to sooth her frayed nerves. At times like this, she missed her the most.

She looked around the sturdy frame house. It was a fortress. Armand had boarded the house so not a sliver of daylight peeked through the plywood sheets. They were prepared. They had filled the bathtub with water, had fresh batteries and flashlights, and the cupboard had enough canned goods to last three days.

By 11:00 a.m., winds reached 175 miles per hour. The sound of a train barreling down its tracks rattled the rafters. The power went out. *Oh God!* Thanks to Armand's diligence, it could have been midnight instead of mid-morning. She felt her way through the eerie darkness for the edge of the kitchen table and slid into a chair. Okay. She was fine. It wouldn't do any good to panic. She stooped to pick up a flashlight that rolled to the floor. "Ah. Whoa there, Junior." The baby kicked hard against her rib cage. She rubbed her swollen belly, soothing the son that wasn't due for another ten weeks. She cranked on the battery-operated emergency weather radio. It warned those still in New Orleans to stay inside. Interstate 10, Highway 39, and Route 61 were deadlocked. Automobiles and gas stations were out of gas. She pointed the flashlight at the battery-operated wall clock. Noon. Would Armand make it home safely? The packed suitcases by the front door mocked her. They couldn't leave now if they wanted to.

Through the boarded windows, she heard large objects slam against the house. *Boom! Crash! Thud!* Each assault made her heart jump to her throat. Was the house going to hold?

She padded barefoot down the hall and felt cold water between her toes. She aimed the flashlight at the floor. "Shit." A small stream weaved through grout lines in the tile foyer toward the thick padding under the front room carpet. Water pooled on concave windowsills and seeped down the wall.

Cecile dialed Armi's cell. *Pick up, pick up, please.* The stilted voice of the machine kicked on, and she groaned as a second pain doubled her over. "Babe, please come home. Things are getting kind of scary here. Water's coming in under the doors and windows. There's no power. And your son's giving me a fit. He doesn't like the storm either." *Beep.* The line went dead. Damn.

She rolled bath towels and shoved them under crevices. The flashlights standing upright on the table cast eerie round circles on the ceiling.

Okay, Cecile, stay calm. He'll be here soon. She wrapped her arms around herself, a chill running down her spine. Relax. There was nothing else to do. Propping her legs up on the sofa, she tried to concentrate on her Lamaze breathing techniques.

Deep cleansing breaths. In and out, in and out. The howling of the wind faded into humming. An eerie, familiar cloud settled in around her as she started to nod off. *No, no, please go away.*

Armand Boudreaux listened to the voice mail from his wife. He had to get home to Cecile. The CEO and operations managers had been in a dead end debate on what to do with the oil tanks for three hours. It was time for him to take control of the situation. "Fill the empty tanks with water so they'll sink. And tie down the ones with the crude oil. Then everyone get the hell out of here. I'm leaving."

Armand patted the dashboard of the high SUV, glad it maneuvered through the rising water that had nowhere to go in below-sea-level New Orleans. Most of the streets were already flooded. The levees would hold the overflow of Lake Ponchartrain and the MRGO, the Mississippi River Gulf Outlet, if the water didn't breach their tops.

Wind and rain beat against the windshield and rocked the heavy vehicle, sometimes tipping it onto two wheels. By the time he reached their home on Ventura Drive in Chalmette, the garage had four inches of water. The front lawn was strewn with debris.

He pushed hard on the door blocked with rolled towels. "CeCe, where are you?"

"In here," Cecile called from the sofa in the front room.

Armand sloshed through the dark kitchen to the front room. Two inches of water covered the thick beige carpet. "CeCe, look!"

She pulled herself into a sitting position, swung

her legs onto the floor, and then jerked her bare feet out of the cold water.

"Are you all right? And Junior?" Armand stroked her stomach.

She managed a smile. "Better ... now that you're home. He's not liking this storm, That's for sure. The curse, Armi ... I saw the cloud."

"Nonsense, there's no curse and no cloud. It's all in your imagination." In take-charge mode, he looked around the room. "We better stack as much as we can." Armand started piling things, the dining chairs atop the table, the ottoman and the magazine racks onto the kitchen counter.

Cecile followed behind him, lifting smaller items out of harm's way.

He kissed her cheek and ran his palm over her silky blond hair. It was damp with perspiration. "We already know what to expect. The storm will pass, it'll get quiet when we're in the eye, then we'll get hit again as it comes around the other side." He rubbed her back. "We'll be okay. Want to curl up on the bed until it's over ... unless?" He gave his best Groucho Mark's impersonation. "You want to do something *else* to take your mind off the storm."

"Oh, no, you don't." She laughed nervously. "Snuggle only, Mr. Boudreaux. Junior is so active you're liable to give him a black eye."

Their nap was short lived. The water kept rising. The water reached knee-high, almost even with the mattress. "CeCe," Armand jumped up. "We've got to go higher."

"Where?" She asked, staring at the rising water. "We don't have a second floor. Should we leave?"

Armand forced open the front door and peeked

19

through the crack as water gushed in. The entire street was a river and the storm had not let up. "Up," he said. "Into the attic. You go, and I'll gather flashlights and batteries."

"Omigod! Don't forget bottled water." said Cecile. "And whatever food you can. And pillows and blankets from the bed."

Armand steadied the ladder as she crawled through the trap door of the attic, her wide girth barely squeezing through the hole. This was not good, not good at all. He pushed water bottles, the battery-operated radio, and everything he could think of through the hole before he pulled himself to safety.

He waited for his eyes to adjust to the filtered light in the small attic. Damn, it must be a hundred degrees in here. The air was stifling. He spread the blankets and pillows on the floor, trying to make Cecile comfortable, amidst boxes of Christmas decorations and old college memorabilia.

"Armi, my back is killing me," she moaned.

"You've done too much. And it's hotter than Hades in here. Try to be still. Practice your breathing." He pushed boxes farther into the eaves, giving at least the illusion of more space. He patted an old electric fan with large black blades in a round metal cage. "Why didn't I buy that generator? I've looked at them a dozen times in the hardware store?"

"It's okay. The storm won't last long." Cecile's wide eyes belied her words. She didn't sound convincing. She curled into a fetal position. "Armi, I think I'm going into labor."

A loud crash pummeled the roof. Armand threw his body over hers to protect her from whatever might come through. When the roof held, he lifted himself off her and stroked her hair. "No, no. it's too early. The stress is causing Braxton Hicks contractions. They'll stop, you'll see."

Her water broke, and a wet spot spread across the blanket. She let out a primal scream and clutched at Armand's shirt. "Omigod! I can't have the baby here."

Armand wiped the sweat from his eyes. Adrenalin coursed through his body. "I'll ... I'll g-g-g-get help." That damn stutter he'd had as child raised its ugly head. He punched numbers into his cell phone. No service. Someone had to rescue them. He needed to get to the roof.

A stack of old boxes sat in the corner. He retained a vague memory of packing them when he left college. There had to be something he could use in them. He tore into them and found a small ball-peen hammer among his college pendant and old textbooks. He pounded on a metal air vent. Sweat dripped from his forehead and stung his eyes. The aluminum vent gave way as the wind grabbed and tossed it away. He reached his arm through the twelve-inch hole, but it was too small to fit his head and shoulders. Rain poured through the opening, and he choked as he pressed his face as close as possible to the vent.

"H-h-help! Somebody?" he sputtered. "Can you hear me? Help! W-w-were in here."

Only Katrina's screams answered.

"Armi, Armi," Cecile shrieked. "Can you see it? The cloud. Why is this happening to us again?"

He shook his head, spraying water over her, not answering. He didn't have time for this nonsense. He gave up the futile call for help and looked around for something to plug the hole. Not finding anything, he tore off his shirt, exposing his dark, furry chest. He loved it when she ran her fingers through those hairs. But not now. What could he do for her?

She moaned.

He rolled the shirt into a ball and stuffed it into the opening. Too small, it dropped onto the plywood floor. He stared at his heaving wife. Maybe they weren't Braxton Hicks after all. Shit. He couldn't deliver a baby. Too early, way too early. He wiped the sweat from his forehead with his arm. "I'm here for you, baby. Tell me what I can do."

Cecile sobbed. "I don't know. He's coming. I can't stop him."

The pains continued every three minutes for the next eight hours—he timed them while forcing small sips of water down Cecile. She was barely conscious from exhaustion and pain. Throughout the night, Armand sat beside her, holding her hand and offering the little support he could muster. The suffocating lack of air, screaming wind, and constant bombardment of flying projectiles hitting the roof lasted through the night. Amid the racket of exploding transformers and a strange creaking sound that strained against the storm, Armand prayed, for the first time since catechism classes as child. *Please, God, spare this child.*

Cecile screamed as the baby crowned. Where did she get the strength? He knelt between her legs as she pushed their child into the world. It was 10:56 a.m., Monday, August 29, 2005. They were in the eye of the storm.

It was quiet. Too quiet. The sudden silence was

as foreboding as the pounding storm. He watched Cecile close her eyes and her body relax. Sleep. Please sleep. Give him these few minutes to deal with this on his own.

His respite didn't last long. She opened her eyes and asked for their son. "Why isn't he crying? He should be hungry."

"Don't, CeCe." He shook his head. "You don't want to see."

"Please," she whispered. "Let me hold him."

He couldn't stop the rivers pouring from his eyes. He had to stay strong for her, even though, inside, his heart was ripping in two. It was over. All those dreams—of tossing a ball with his son, teaching him to fish, sharing "guy" stuff—were over. With a heavy heart, he handed their son to her.

"No, no, no." Cecile clutched their stillborn child to her chest. "Did you see it? Did you see the cloud? The curse took our baby again. It's my fault. I'm so sorry."

"No, CeCe. There is no curse. It's not your fault."

They huddled together on the thin blanket; the child swaddled between them in a beach towel as the back side of the storm hit. If only he had gotten them out of the storm sooner. If there was blame to go around, it was his. Would the house hold against the second onslaught? This could be the end. It had been his job to protect them. He had failed.

By morning, the house was still standing. The storm had passed, but the danger had not. With bare hands and the small hammer, Armand ripped at roof shingles and studs until he had a large enough opening to fit his entire body.

As far as he could see, there was nothing but rooftops and devastation. Along with trees and street signs, bodies of small animals floated by along with bits and pieces of people's lives: a hand-carved wooden cane, a curly haired doll, a soccer ball.

Armand shouted until his voice gave out. Silence. Where was everybody? Where were the rescue boats, the helicopters? He cranked up the emergency radio. Newscasters used the words *total devastation.* Levees had given way, and over ninety percent of New Orleans and St. Bernard Parish were under ten to twenty feet of snake-infested water. Oh, God! How long would it take for the rescue boats to reach Chalmette? They were miles outside of New Orleans. He made a flag out of his shirt, tied by its arms to the end of a broom handle and affixed it to the chimney with bungee cords found in the college boxes. Cecile moved in and out of consciousness, calling for Armand and her mama and mumbling about the curse.

Armand sat on the roof in one-hundred-degree heat, his shoulders blistered by the sun, waiting for someone to find them. Once, a helicopter flew over. He stood, waving his arms and shouting "Come back, come back" as it flew off into the distance.

Cockroaches came next, flying in swarms, swooping in through every hole and crevice, landing on any surface, crawling on their arms, faces, and into their hair. Nothing could kill those bastards. He watched Cecile fight to keep them off the bundle she hugged close to her chest.

By Wednesday, all the food was gone. Armand forced the last swallow of water down Cecile's throat. He gagged on the overpowering stench emitting from the rigid bundle she rocked in her arms. He alternated his time between tending to her in the dank attic and searching for help on the scorching roof.

Finally, two men appeared in a small flat-bottomed fishing trawler. From above, Armand waved them toward him. "Help, please. My wife is inside."

The men threw him a rope and tied up. Thank God! Armand gently pried the bundle from Cecile's arms and helped her onto the roof and into the boat, promising he would return the infant the second she was settled.

Bloated animal carcasses floated by. *Please don't ask about the atrocious smell that's coming from the beach towel.* He couldn't bear to explain. The men spoke few words but agreed to take Cecile and Armand to St. Bernard Parish Hospital. What was there to say? Everything was surreal. Like a sci-fi horror flick. And they were the leading cast.

The boat weaved through flotsam and around snakes knotted together hanging from low-hanging tree branches. Cecile pointed to a little dog paddling furiously, his eyes bulging with fear. Twice he slipped under the water, unable to find a foothold on a tree branch.

"Help him." Cecile cried. "You can't let him drown."

"There's no room for him in the boat and no place at the hospital," said the boatman. He stared, expressionless, as the pup sunk under the water again.

Cecile screamed with all her strength. "No, no! Help him, Armi, please. You can't let him die too."

Oh, damn it. Armand jumped into the rancid black water and swam toward the little dog. At least he could save someone. He grabbed the pup by the scruff of the neck and hauled him to the boat. Tossing the canine over the side of the boat, Armand clung to the hull. "He can have my space."

"For Christ's sake. Get in the boat before you get bit by a copperhead, and I have to save your ass again!" The man pulled on Armand's belt and heaved him over the side, nearly capsizing the small vessel.

The trembling little dog curled up beside Cecile. "It's okay, Neptune, you're safe now," Cecile purred.

"Neptune?" Armand raised an eyebrow.

"Because you pulled him from the sea."

When they reached the hospital they discovered it was also under water, but rescue Air Rescue helicopters were expected to transport people to hospitals out of the flood zones soon. That turned out to be an inaccurate timeline.

Armand found a doctor tending to patients on the rooftop. The doctor briefly examined Cecile, shaking his head. Without medications to sedate her, it was nearly impossible to pry the child from her arms. He spoke quietly to Armand, who strained to hear over the white noise rushing around in his head.

"What is her history?" the doctor said, shaking his head. "The drastic drop in barometric pressure caused women all over the area into premature labor. "The baby … he was too young. If he would have had a few more weeks." His voice trailed off.

"This is her third stillbirth," Armand said.

"She's very weak. Next time you'll lose her too. There can't be any more babies."

Armand reached inside the bundle and stroked the tiny cheek of his son one last time before wrenching him free from Cecile's arms and handing him to the staff. Goodbye, son. We loved you. The body would be transported with the other bodies to the morgue along with patients to another hospital. The doctor was right. This had to be their last child.

Cecile mumbled incoherently, "The potion, must drink the potion."

"What's she babbling about?" Armand asked.

"I have no idea. She's delirious."

Chapter Three

Suzdal, Russia

May 3, 2006

Natalia and Nikolai sat on the stoop outside the Butkovskys' home, the warmth of Natalia's body pressed tightly against him. In the distance, the sun kissed the top of the green bell-shaped roof of Church of the Nativity of St. John the Baptist. Mama and Poppa would have enjoyed the sight if they were not in the pine boxes along with Babushka and Dedushka. Nikolai twisted the cap Babushka had made for him. What were he and Natalia going to do? Right now, just keep from throwing up. Good thing he wasn't hungry anyway. They owned nothing but the clothes on their bodies, the charred pictures, and a few things from his backpack.

"Nika, what's going to happen to us?" Natalia's blue eyes stared up at him.

"I don't know yet, Golubka. I'll take care of you. Don't worry." He pressed his fists against his throbbing temples.

Children's clothing appeared in paper sacks on the Butkovsky doorstep. Sometimes Nikolai saw neighbors quietly leaving them on the doorstep, then creeping away, as if getting too close would bring tragedy upon their families as well.

Nikolai stared at his ankles poking from under his pant legs. He should be grateful for the clothing. Anything was better than nothing. He hoped the boys in school didn't recognize any of the castoffs as their own clothing. That was one lesson in humility he could live without.

He watched Natalia smile at a pink dress with a ruffled skirt and small puffy sleeves. Mrs. Butkovsky tied a wide red ribbon around her waist to cinch it. Against his better judgment, Nikolai couldn't deny Natalia the clothing, even though it looked more like a party dress than something to wear to a funeral.

Mr. Butkovsky gripped Natalia's hand as they followed the four caskets in the funeral procession's short walk from the Church of the Epiphany where the bodies had lain in repose to the Church of the Nativity of St. John the Baptist. Mrs. Butkovsky hung on Nikolai's arm over the uneven steppingstones.

The church bells tolled, somber, mournful tones, high to low. Nicholai's mind was focused on one thing—putting one foot in front of another. *I can do this. I must do this*, he willed himself. Two steps, one toll, two more steps, another toll.

The bearers placed the four caskets in front of the altar.

Nikolai's heart pounded in his ears, in sync with

each woeful bell tone.

Mr. Butkovsky leaned in, explaining the symbolism of bell tolls, "That's to show we believe in everlasting life."

Nikolai nodded. He knew. He'd been an altar boy for almost five years.

Voices echoed off the stone walls in the familiar hymn. "All mortal things are vanity; they do not endure after death. Riches do not last, and glory is left behind. For when death comes, all these things are destroyed."

Nikolai moved his lips with everyone else, but no sound passed the lump in his throat. He stared at the intricate murals covering the walls and ceiling, depicting the saints on cobalt blue backgrounds. He looked any place to avoid the four brown boxes in front of him.

Natalia tugged at his sleeve, and he lifted her into his arms.

Father Vladimir waved the golden wand, spreading incense over each of the burnished wood caskets.

The earthy, bitter scent of myrrh made Natalia's eyes water, and Nikolai wiped them with a clean handkerchief handed to him from someone behind him.

Everyone said in unison; "Blessed are You, O Lord, teach me Your Statutes!"

Mrs. Butkovsky whispered to Nikolai. "Take your sister. It's time to say your final good-byes." Mourners lined up behind them, shuffling in line on the cold marble floors.

Nikolai carried Natalia forward. If only he could make it through the Mass without breaking down or throwing up. He stepped up on a small stool and stared into the first box. Dedushka lay in his best suit, his tie askew, tucked in a pillowy satin bed with a blanket pulled to his waist. His hands cupped a wooden Russian cross. The funeral ribbon rested on his forehead, almost covering the place where his bushy eyebrows should have been. His mustache was gone and had been drawn on with a gray pencil. His skin was too white, his cheeks too red, like Mama's rouge.

Nikolai bent and kissed the ribbon. His lips brushed Dedushka's cheek. Cold. And stiff. So that was why they called them *stiffs*.

"Nika," Natalia whispered in his ear. "Is that really Dedushka?"

Nikolai cleared his throat. "Yes, Golubka, hurry up. Kiss him good-bye."

Natalia shook her head and buried her face deep into his shoulder.

"It's okay, child. Say goodbye to Dedushka," said Mr. Butkovsky, standing behind them in line.

Nikolai lifted her higher so she could bend into the casket, but she wouldn't release the stronghold around his neck.

They repeated the process at each casket. Someone had put a wig on Babushka—it looked nothing like the long gray braid she wore twisted on the top of her head—and pinned a black lace chapel veil to it

Their father's face was turned away with half of his face hidden in the thick pillow. No amount of make-up could fix where his face was damaged. His thick brown hair was completely gone. Did it all burn off or had someone shaved the rest of it? Half of

31

the funeral cloth rested on his temple and bald head.

Nikolai braced himself for the last coffin. Mama looked perfect. Her hair and her skin looked exactly as they should. She was beautiful.

Natalia released her grip on Nikolai's neck and peered into the box. "Mama, wake up. Mama, it's me, Golubka," she wailed, her voice more frantic with each word.

People in the rear murmured. "Poor child." The sound of her weeping almost broke Nikolai's resolve to be strong.

"Stop, Natalia," Nikolai whispered. "You know she can't wake up. Now give her a kiss."

He lifted her higher and leaned her in to kiss their mother, but when her lips met her mother's cheek, Natalia grabbed her shoulders with both hands, almost pulling herself into the coffin.

"Let go," Nikolai pleaded. Natalia and Mama's face blurred through the tears streaming down his face. "Please, Golubka, you have to let her go."

The priest stepped up and unlocked her fingers from the silky gown at her mother's shoulders. "Poor little thing," he mumbled.

A week later, Nikolai stood in the archway to the front room as Natalia peeked from behind Mrs. Butkovsky's skirt at a gentleman standing at the front door. This couldn't be good. The man introduced himself as Ivan Korzhev, Olga Pavlic's supervisor from social services. Beside him, Olga smoothed her simple brown skirt and gripped her imitation leather briefcase. Father Vladimir's car pulled into the driveway behind the tan station wagon.

Mrs. Butkovsky brought coffee and black bread

on a wooden tray and set it on the table in front of the guests who sat, hands folded on their laps, on high-backed straight chairs across from the sofa. "Children, can you join us, please?"

Nikolai took Natalia by the hand, and they sat on the two-seat divan.

When Olga addressed Mr. Korzhev by his full name, Natalia began to cry. "Nika, what happened to Ivan?" She crumbled onto his lap. "What going to happen to all of them?"

"Who?" Everyone turned to look at the children, with puzzled expressions.

"Ivan, you know, Dedushka's pigeon," Natalia wailed.

Mr. Korzhev and Olga exchanged a bewildered look and shook their heads.

Nikolai patted Natalia as she curled into a tighter ball on his lap. "Dedushka's favorite pigeon is called Ivan, like Mr. Korzhev. But Yasha Borelov is taking care of the pigeons. They're safe," said Nikolai. He faced the adults. "Yasha's in my grade at school. He's going to raise Dedushka's pigeons now."

Heads nodded in understanding.

"Natalia…Nikolai," Olga spoke up. "We know Mr. Butkovsky and his wife have been very good to you." She nodded in their direction and gave a slight smile. "But it's a lot of work to raise two growing children, and they aren't young anymore."

Wait for it. A nervous tic fluttered behind Nikolai's eye.

Mr. Butkovsky reached out and took his wife's hand. They stared at the coffee cups on the table.

"What Mrs. Pavlic is trying to say…" Father Vladimir paused. "They're not able to keep you on a permanent basis."

"Where would we go?" Nikolai asked. The tic increased. He wiped his hand over his brow to conceal it.

"Well, *hmmm*," the social worker cleared his throat. "The orphanage here in Suzdal is full, but there is room for you at Orphanage #27 in Vladimir City."

"An orphanage." Nikolai mouthed the words softly. He knew boys from school who were in the orphanage. They looked lost, or angry, or sad all the time.

Natalia whimpered softly and cuddled closer.

He wrapped his arm protectively around her.

Olga Pavlic flashed a plastic smile. "It's quite nice, really. And because it's in such an industrious city, they receive lots of requests from adoptive parents looking for children like you."

"Yes, yes." Korzhev nodded in agreement. "They'll find a new home for you in no time."

"For both of us...together?" Nikolai asked. Not likely. What were the odds someone would want two kids, especially one being a teenager? Russian orphanages were overflowing with children.

"Well, they will certainly try," Mr. Korzhev said, not sounding certain at all.

"When?" Nikolai said, his stomach now keeping rhythm with the tic in his eye.

The Butkovskys hadn't spoken a word. They sat on the green chenille sofa, hands clasped together, concentrating their eyes on the now-cold cups of coffee.

Korzhev stood, his tall frame reaching inches from the low ceiling. "The sooner we get you there, the sooner they can find you a new family."

"I will bless your safe journey and send you in God's embrace." Father Vladimir said. He rested his hand on Nikolai's head, then Natalia's and blessed them.

"Are we going away, Nika?" Natalia's big blue eyes searched for answers.

"I suppose we are, Golubka." Whatever happened, he must protect her.

Nikolai and Natalia gathered their few belongings and followed Mr. Korzhev to the car. Natalia waved out the back window at the old pair. Mrs. Butkovsky was waving a white handkerchief and wiping tears from her eyes.

Nikolai stared at his shoes. If only he could have some of Natalia's innocence, her optimism. They had little to say to anyone on the thirty-minute drive to Vladimir City. The two-story brick building known as Orphanage #27, surrounded by a high fence, was overcrowded with children. The stern-faced director seemed less than pleased to have the children shuffled to him from another city.

Nikolai's heart broke as they dragged Natalia, kicking and screaming to the girls' wing on the first floor. *Don't cry, Golubka.* Already, he was breaking his promise to Mama to look after her.

Nikolai followed the lean silhouette of the director to the second floor, where he was to share a bed with another boy. Beds, crammed together with less than a foot between them, end to end, filled the entire room. *This will never do.* Why didn't they have rooms for siblings, so they could stay together?

They met up again in the playroom, a menagerie of children and toys in an otherwise empty room. At

35

least they were together. He stroked Natalia's head, calming the child who was reduced to hiccups. "*Sh, sh, sh.* You're all right."

"Nika, I'm scared." Natalia huddled next to him, the din of children's voices fighting over toys making him struggle to hear.

"It'll get better." Nikolai patted her shoulders. "We need to get used to it, that's all. And who knows, maybe a family will want us right away."

If only he could believe his own words. If anyone was going to be adopted, it would be Natalia, not him. No one wanted a teenager, unless they needed a work hand.

They hadn't needed to worry about becoming accustomed to Orphanage #27. Within two weeks, an order came from the Kremlin to transport a hundred children from various orphanages in the Vladimir Oblast to the recently opened New Holland Orphanage in St. Petersburg.

Natalia and Nikolai were among two dozen children from Orphanage #27 that joined dozens more designated for transport from surrounding institutions. Before dawn, the director and several caretakers roused the children from their beds and told them to follow the adults to the buses waiting at the curb. Aboard, two tired looking caretakers shepherded children into seats. One dropped a cross-eyed infant into Nikolai's lap. Many of the children cried, others followed numbly, seemingly accustomed to being ordered about with no explanation. The bus moved through town, and Nikolai watched the streetlights zip past in the night. Natalia lay with her head in his lap as he juggled the baby on his shoulder. Two and half hours later, the children exited the bus at the Krupskaya train station and took bathroom breaks.

"Where are we going now, Nika?" Natalia rubbed her eyes and grabbed Nikolai's sleeve as they waited to board the train.

"I don't know, Golubka," Nikolai murmured, shifting the small child in his arms higher on his hip and clasping Natalia's hand. "Stay close to me. Don't wander off." What if he lost her? They would never hold the train to find her. He gripped her hand tighter. Her whimper turned into a howl.

It was daylight by the time the train pulled out of the station, four cars full of children, sandwiched into seats meant to hold half that many adults. A few children cried, but most were silent. Not Natalia. She was wailing at the top of her lungs. *Dear God. Please make her stop.* The caregivers passed out stale rolls and thrust a baby bottle into Nikolai's hand for the infant. He tipped the crying child back, and the infant began to suckle the bottle. He handed a dry roll to Natalia, and she finally quieted down. He rested his head on the rear of the seat. *So tired. Must stay awake.* His eyelids felt like boulders. Maybe if he just closed them for a minute. No, he must watch over Natalia.

Morning turned to afternoon, and the train lumbered forward into a nameless future. If toilet facilities were onboard, the children were too timid to ask. Nikolai pulled his jacket over his nose to block the stench of urine and soiled pants. By the time the train pulled into St. Petersburg eight hours after the journey began, his skin crawled from jagged nerves and his eyes burned from lack of sleep. Thankfully, Natalia had finally fallen asleep on his arm, which was numb from the elbow to his wrist.

Chapter Four

Butte La Rose, LA

September 5, 2005

An Air rescue helicopter finally transported Armand and Cecile to Baton Rouge hospital, but quickly released them as non-emergency victims. Cecile's father picked them up and took them home to Butte La Rose. Armand helped Cecile up the stairs to the guest bedroom and tucked her under the covers.

"Babe, watch this," Armand said, cuddled under the covers next to Cecile. The small TV in his father-in-law's guest room cast a blue shadow around the room. He couldn't tear himself away from the television. The newscaster said the water was receding, and the National Guard had arrived in New Orleans, staving off the looters helping themselves, first to essentials like food and water, then TVs, electronics, and clothing — anything they could salvage or sell.

Cecile buried deeper under the covers, not answering him.

CNN showed packs of muddy dogs roaming the streets and thousands of people waiting in deplorable conditions in the Superdome for buses to transport them God knew where. Fires burned out of control, and the fire department could do little beyond trying to contain them.

"That could have been us," said Armand. "We could be down there; in that stinking pit they call the Superdome. Thank God for your father." Unbelievable.

Armand shook his head, realizing his own parents in Washington D.C. still didn't know he and Cecile were safe in Butte La Rose. He had tried to call, but land and cell service were still out over most of Louisiana.

Eleven days after the storm, Armand's cell phone rang. He jumped as it vibrated in his pocket. Thank God, he had remembered to charge it. At least cellular service had returned. Land lines would take longer with all the downed power lines and debris.

"We need you, Armand," the refinery's CEO said. "A tank breached and leaked 25,000 barrels of mixed crude oil into Chalmette and Meraux when we opened the levees to drain the parish. It's a massive mess, and the EPA are already starting an investigation. If you want to keep your job, you better get your ass down here."

"Yes, sir. I'll be there tomorrow. I've got to take a look at my house, too."

"You live in Chalmette? Don't expect much. You were right to leave when you did. Probably should have left sooner. At least we didn't lose any lives at Murphy."

No, only my son in Chalmette.

Armand wasn't used to gushing expressions of love, especially to men, but he would be eternally grateful to Pop Lafayette for providing a safe haven. Some of their neighbors' only choices had been the promised FEMA trailers which had yet to arrive in Chalmette. It did little to take away the slow, burning ache in his chest. Now, with cell service, he needed to tell his parents they were all right. And the other news.

"We've been worried, son." His father's brusque voice reverberated from the speakerphone. "I was about to send a search party after you. Getting into New Orleans is almost impossible."

"We're fine Father, except … except Cecile lost the baby." His chest squeezed his heart, stealing his breath away as he said the words aloud.

"Oh God, no," his mother chimed in. "She should see my OB-GYN."

"Mother …"

"I can send a private charter to bring her here," his dad said.

Armand ran his fingers through his hair and inhaled deeply. "No, both of you. Really. She's okay. She's resting. This is where she needs to be, home in the bayou."

Chalmette, LA

Armand waited for the insurance adjustor at the house. Would there be anything left to salvage? He hesitated, his hand resting on the doorknob, observing the huge red X spray-painted across the door which meant, "No bodies found inside." *Only because we took him with us*. A slimy brown streak of oil drew a waist-high line of demarcation around the outside of the house showing where the oil had reached when the water receded.

He strapped a white mask over his mouth and nose and pushed hard against the water-logged front door.

The exhausted-looking insurance adjuster followed him inside. It didn't take him long for him to make a decision and tack a "Scheduled for Demolition" note next to the red X on the front door and leave.

Armand stared at the paper, fluttering in the mild breeze. Three years of their lives scribbled away with three words. He returned to the task at hand. Inside, a gray line showed the high-water mark close to the ceiling. Another foot and it would have breached the attic. Then where would they have gone?

Things had shifted in the high water and settled in odd places. Moldy black dots crawled up the walls, and a thick layer of sludge covered everything. In the nursery, the antique mahogany crib, once taking center stage, now wedged itself against the closet door. The other furniture was bunched in a pile by the padded window seat piled with pink elephants and blue teddy bears, now peppered in black mold spots. Armand spotted the rocking horse he'd spent countless hours building by hand for his son and lifted it from the thick blanket of muck. What should he do with it? Tears blurred his vision. He wiped the majority of the sludge from the horse and carried it to the SUV.

A floppy-eared Eeyore stuffed toy rested in a pile of muck in the foyer. He picked it up. Sludge oozed from the once-blue fabric. They had bought it for their second child, Theresa. CeCe would want it. Maybe it could be salvaged. With his sleeve, he rubbed a circle clean on the hall mirror and stared at himself. His countenance matched the sad-faced toy.

Armand set Eeyore aside and dropped a box of heavy trash bags on the nursery floor. He filled the first to the brim with moldy nappies and tiny T-shirts and started on another with receiving blankets, crib sheets and bumpers. Then he hauled the bags down the hall and out the door. He disassembled the crib and changing table, adding the pieces to the growing pile at the curb. He stared blankly at the only order in the chaos; neat rows of refrigerators, their doors removed, lining the street in precision order, like white and stainless-steel sentries. His would be next.

He closed his eyes, trying to force the tightness from his chest, the aching from his joints, the pounding from his temples. Was he really only thirty-seven? He'd gladly give up all these material possessions if he could have his children back. Should he and Cecile rebuild? Where will they go now? Give up his job and move away? What words could he possibly say to make things better? "It's all right, CeCe. We don't need children to make our lives complete. We have each other. That will be enough." But would it?

He leaned against the spotted wall and reflected on the day he first met Cecile. It was 1995. He was hurrying across campus to meet his buddies at a favorite LSU watering hole when he literally ran into her, practically knocking her down on the sidewalk. He grabbed her shoulders to keep her from falling, and her blond head fit perfectly under his chin. Her hair smelled like raspberries. At that moment, he knew he could never live without her.

Armand shook the memory from his head and pulled himself into the present. He looked around the house. Nothing left to salvage. He picked up Eeyore and walked out into the bright sunshine and headed to Butte La Rose.

Butte La Rose, LA

December 2005

It was time to deal with his wife. Four months had gone by. If he didn't do something, he would lose her, too. Since the day of Armand Junior's funeral, Cecile had rarely left the guest bedroom in her parents' home. She stayed in bed with heavy curtains pulled against the light of day and ate scarcely more than a mouthful of food Armand or her father forced down her.

Armand opened the bedroom door and stared at her from the foot of the bed. She was still curled on her side of the bed. She hadn't crossed to his side since before Katrina.

"Cecile." Armand said. "It's Christmas. And three o'clock in the afternoon. Enough is enough. It's time to get up and go on with your life."

"I have no life," she mumbled. "I've tried to tell you. I'm cursed."

The anger boiling from deep in his gut took him by surprise. "Damn it, Cecile. Stop it. I don't want to hear any more about curses." Damn her grandmother and her black magic. "Why would she curse you?" Their marriage was falling apart. What happened to their life together? What about him?

She buried deeper under the covers. Neptune jumped onto the bed and nuzzled his gray whiskers under her chin. "No," she said, "Mamère didn't curse me. She tried to protect me." Cecile stroked the gris-gris at her neck.

Armand pinched his lips, counted to ten and ran his fingers through his dark hair. "CeCe, there is no God-damn curse and that good-luck charm around your neck is crap. I'm not going to let you lie here and die. That won't bring the babies back. We still have each other. I love you, woman. Can't you understand? Now, you have three choices: Get the Sam-hell out of bed on your own, I'll drag you out cave-man style, or I can jump in there and fuck your brains out until you give up all this nonsense." Boy, he was really losing it. He didn't talk like that to her — or to anyone.

Cecile inched up on the pillows and faced him with dull listless eyes. Her hair was plastered to her head, her skin translucent and drawn against hollow cheekbones. She stroked the little dog's head. "Armi, I don't know if I can. I'm sorry."

He gave a curt nod and marched to the window. Okay, if that was the way she wanted it. He pulled the heavy curtains and raised the blinds. A round, full sun surrounded by clear blue skies exploded the room with light. An inflatable Santa rocked in the southern breeze of the neighbors' yard, nodding its approval.

Cecile squinted at the bright light and shielded her eyes with her arm. "Too bright," she stammered. Why did she have to make this so hard? "Because it's the middle of the day and you've been in this cave for far too long. You're done mourning. You're coming out of this room. Today." Pushing the covers off, he scooped her in his arms and carried her to the bathroom with Neptune close at his heels. Armand deposited her on the teak seat in the walk-in shower,

Cecile did little to assist as he removed her gown, washed her hair and sponge-bathed her with a lavender loofah. The scent of her raspberry shampoo between his fingers brought memories of shared showers, laughter, and unbelievable sex. He shook his head to concentrate on the task at hand and not on her beautiful body — or his rising erection.

His soaking clothes stuck to his body, but by the time he dressed her in comfortable warm-ups and white sneakers, there was a glimmer of light in her eyes. "I'm sorry I yelled at you. Do you forgive me?" Armand felt awful. They'd had enough heart ache. He didn't need to add to it.

She reached up and stroked his jaw. "Of course. I love you, Armi. No matter what happens to us."

That evening they sat at the dining room table with Cecile's father and her grandmother, Mamère. They were pleased to see Cecile out of the guest room and dressed.

Poppa Lafayette talked to all the out-of-town grandkids by Skype and wished everyone Happy Holidays. Cecile spoke briefly to her sisters, but Armand could tell they were at a loss for any comforting words.

Armand raised his glass in a toast. "Merry Christmas, baby. To new beginnings."

Cecile offered a half-smile and tipped her glass toward his. "Yes, new beginnings."

Chapter Five

St. Petersburg, Russia

June 2006

A rail-thin woman in a baggy, non-descript house-dress pulled Natalia by the hand to a room where seven other girls between the ages of four and ten years old lived. A strong smell filled the room where someone was mopping. Natalia knew that smell. Mama used PineSol to clean the floor. The woman stacked Natalia's few belongings in a small chest beside a bed and left without saying a word. At least Natalia didn't have to share a bed.

Natalia stood planted in the spot where the caretaker left her. What should she do now? If she closed her eyes, she could pretend she was home and Mama was there, cleaning the floor. It didn't work. She opened her eyes to find the other girls pointing at her and whispering.

A tall girl, a foot taller than the rest, strolled up and greeted Natalia with a finger poke to her chest. The girl was scary. Her forehead was huge, and her eyes looked like black dots drawn on her flat face. "No crying, no getting up in the middle of the night, and no bed wetting, or you'll sleep in it all night. Got it?"

Natalia nodded and chewed on her trembling lower lip.

The other girls watched from where they sat crowded together on two beds.

A dark-haired girl tip-toed from the rear of the room, took Natalia's hand, and led her to her own bed in the corner. "That's Tasha," she whispered. "She's real mean. Stay with me. I'm Petia. I'll show you everything."

Natalia sniffled and tried to smile. She wanted to tell Petia that her brother was coming for her any minute. That she didn't need a friend because they were going to get a new family together real soon. Nikolai and that tall man, Mr. Ivan Korzhev, had said so.

Tasha followed them to the corner and towered over Natalia. "What's your name?"

"Na-Natalia, but my brother calls me *Golubka*."

"Ha." Tasha threw her head back and snorted through her nose. "You're no pigeon. More like a dodo-bird." That's more like it. From now on, your name is Dodo."

"My name is Natalia." She jutted out her chin like she'd seen Nikolai do when some bullies had pushed him on the way to school. She must be brave. She felt a trickle run down her leg.

"Not anymore. I christen you *Dodo*." Tasha

48

poured a glass of water over Natalia's head.

Natalia sputtered and blinked the water off her eyelashes. Could the mean girl see that she was crying? She bit her lip.

"Leave her be, Tasha," said Petia, wrapping a towel around Natalia's shoulders and patting her face dry.

"What are you going to do about it?" Tasha glowered at her.

Petia cowered and slunk away.

Nikolai stood in the doorway of his assigned room. He gazed out the small window at the compound. With the adjoining rivers, he could see they were on a small island. *More like a prison.* How was he going to keep his promise to Mama? "Father," he prayed. "I know you have a plan for us. Help me to see. Was it not your will that I serve you in the priesthood?"

If there was an answer, Nikolai didn't hear it.

Bunk beds lined like soldiers in neat rows on either side of a narrow walkway. The room was immaculate, albeit shabby and sparse. Young boys stared at him from a bare hardwood floor where they played with small, dinged-up trucks and one shiny fire engine they all coveted. One boy had a club foot; another had a cauliflower ear. No one greeted Nikolai. He stood silent, watching the younger boys play, not knowing what to do next.

Three boys about Nikolai's age strutted into the room. One grabbed an apple from a younger boy's hand, took a bite and tossed the apple to the floor. Nikolai watched it roll under a bunk and settle in the corner. The largest of the boys stopped within inches of his nose, openly challenging him. Nikolai stared back at the cold eyes. Don't flinch. Don't show fear. His stomach twisted in knots. The boys cleared the floor, forming a circle in anticipation of a fight.

The tallest of the three boys asked, "What's your name?"

Nikolai sized up the competition. The boy's straight black hair stood on end in a Mohawk, sides unevenly close to his scalp, probably whacked with a pair of kitchen shears. He was a few inches shorter than Nikolai, but from the boy's exposed forearms and thick neck, Nikolai figured the other kid outweighed Nikolai by at least twenty pounds. Could he take him in a fight? Doubtful, but what other option did he have?

"Who's asking?" Nikolai spat out. Did he sound tough? He hoped so.

"A smart ass, huh?" Dimitri slapped the top of Nikolai's head, taunting him.

Nikolai smacked him in return, a little harder. Within seconds they were on the floor, trying to pin each other down.

Shouts rang out. "Get'em, Dimitri. Show him who's boss."

Dimitri had weight on his side, but his moves were amateurish. Nikolai knew what to do. The wrestling moves his father had taught him kicked into high gear. His father had been an Olympic wrestling hopeful until he hurt his back at nineteen. With a quick flip of his wrist, he had Dimitri in a stranglehold, pressing his face onto the splintered wood floor.

"You know I have you," he whispered in the boy's ear. "But I'll let you win this if we come to an understanding."

Dimitri twisted in retaliation and tried to spit into Nikolai's eye. The spittle landed on the shoulder of a small bystander.

"You sure you want to do that?" Nikolai twisted a tighter hold.

Dimitri's face contorted in pain.

"Now, blink twice, and I'll make this look good for you in front of the others."

Stubby black lashes blinked twice.

Nikolai loosened his grip and let the boy take the upper hand. For a moment, he thought his opponent would smash his face into the floor, but he stopped short of any real damage.

Nikolai heard footsteps shuffling across the floor. Scuffed, brown wing-tip shoes appeared in his line of vision. The man pulled Dimitri off him and to his feet. "Enough. Can't we have a single day of peace here?"

The boys scattered.

Nikolai brushed himself off and waited for his punishment.

"Which one of you started this?"

Dimitri didn't speak but glared with open hostility.

"It was me," Nikolai said.

The caretaker shook his head. "You're new here, so I'll give you a break." He raised an index finger. "But that's one." He shuffled out of the dormitory.

"Why'd you do that?" Dimitri blinked. "I'd have kicked your ass and ratted you out."

Nikolai shrugged one shoulder. "New kid on the block. I need an ally. Figured you were the biggest and the baddest ... so, tag you're it."

Dimitri grinned and raised a hand in a high five. Later, in the cafeteria, he lifted bread and fruit from the plates of the younger boys.

"What're you doing?" Nikolai asked as he followed behind him.

"Establishing our domain. Grab that apple." He pointed to a piece of fruit on a little boy's tray.

Now that he knew that he could take Dimitri if he had to, Nikolai let the other boy play the role of leader on the boys' ward. He made sure Dimitri noticed when he lifted the bread, but as soon as Dimitri away, Nikolai returned it with a wink at the younger boys. Someday Nikolai would convince Dimitri of the errors of his ways. He wondered what kind of awful things were happening to Natalia in the girls' dorm.

Bath day, if they were lucky, came once a week. All the boys shared the same water. Nikolai scrunched his nose at the black water. He sure didn't want to be one of those unlucky enough to be at end of the line-up. Sometimes there was a sliver of crude lard soap left but usually not. Dimitri and Nikolai made sure they were always first in line.

Nikolai had only two hours with Natalia twice a week. When he finally got to see her, she looked dirty and hungry and when Nikolai inquired, she admitted to being at the end of the bath line-up. Nikolai saved small shavings of soap and extra biscuits for her and slipped them into her pockets every opportunity he got.

"Nika, I hate it here," cried Natalia. "The other girls are mean to me, all but Petia. They act funny. I miss Mama and Papa. And the pigeons, Nika. I miss the pigeons."

"I know, Golubka." Nikolai said. "You must be brave … and pray. Smile at the grown-ups who come looking for a new child. You're young and pretty. You'll be adopted by a nice family, especially if you're clean. God will give you wonderful new parents and a beautiful home."

"But what about you?" Her lip quivered, and a tear rolled down her cheek. "I don't want new parents. I want Mama and Papa. And Babushka and Dedushka. I want to go home. Please, Nika, take me home. I want to play with the pigeons. I need them."

He took a deep, pained breath and closed his eyes. Her obsession with the pigeons was crazy. It was all she talked about, even more than Mama and Papa. Better she had something to cling to. "Our home is gone, Golubka. You know that. There's no one left but us. And Yasha is taking good care of the pigeons. Be a good girl and find a new family."

"I don't want a new family without you."

Nikolai turned away so she wouldn't see the sadness he couldn't hide from his face. "I'm too old, Golubka. No one wants a boy my age. But soon I'll be old enough to get a job and leave this place. Then I'll look after myself."

"Aren't you going to be a priest anymore, Nika?"

"There's no money left. We used it for the funerals. I'll find a job doing something when I age out."

Her round blue eyes stared up at him with so much faith in him. "And me? Will you take me with you?"

They sat on a bench watching the other children play He kicked at the dirt with the toe of his shoe.

Best that he tells her the truth. "They'll never let me do that. When I'm sixteen, they'll let me go to work, but I'd have to be twenty-one to take care of you. You'll have a new family by then." He kissed her cheek, and they rubbed noses in an Eskimo kiss like Mama and Babushka taught them. "I'll always love you. I'll always be your brother, but we won't always be together. Promise me you'll be happy."

Natalia pulled away and crossed her arms across her dirty dress. "Nyet." She pouted. "I won't be happy, and I won't be good. I'll stay here with you."

Nikolai's chest tightened. He could hardly breathe. He had to convince her that she'd be better off without him. It was the best way he could keep his promise to Mama. "Wonderful families are looking for beautiful little girls like you. You must swear to me that you'll be nice to them."

Natalia didn't answer.

"Golubka, I mean it. Don't disobey me. Swear to me you'll find a family." He held out his pinky finger.

Natalia nodded and linked her pinky in his. "Only if they'll let me see you."

Excited couples came through the orphanage. Nikolai watched child after child leave with a new family, but none asked for him. He knew they wouldn't.

Chapter Six

Chalmette, La.

June 2006

Ten months after Hurricane Katrina wreaked havoc on the area, the new two-story home in Chalmette was under construction. Cecile took little interest in the new house and left all the decision making to Armand. He made the two-and-a-half-hour drive from Butte La Rose to the refinery five days a week, stopping after work each day to check on the progress of the house.

The EPA were still working on the Murphy Oil spill investigation, which had started the huge pay-out of millions of dollars to homeowners for the clean-up. His decisions were under investigation and his job still on the line.

Cecile should be looking forward to the move

home to Chalmette. But Butte La Rose was her home, where she grew up. Why couldn't they stay there in Butte La Rose? She was barely beginning to feel like her old self. She filled her days fishing and tromping through the freshwater bayou. She thrived emptying the crawfish traps alongside her father, the same way she had when she was a little girl. He had filled the plates of the local restaurants as far as Baton Rouge for three decades.

"Armi, look ah dis load." She held up a trap with dozens of red squirming crawfish. "Mmm, we gonna have some good suppa' t'night." She slapped her hand over her mouth, laughing at how her Cajun accent took on a stronger Louisiana drawl when she was in the bayou.

Armand smiled at her as he pulled his body from the car, but his shoulders drooped, and the spring was gone from his step. His shirt clung to his body, and his tie was askew. He looked exhausted. "Those look great, babe. Let me change clothes, and I'll join you in a few minutes." He climbed halfway up the steps, paused, and arched his back before continuing his slow climb to the cottage raised on stilts beside the Atchafalaya River.

Seeing Armi's weariness, the joy from Cecile's catch was short lived. She needed to talk to him. She couldn't keep making him drive those long distances every day. Not if she truly loved him. *Buck up, Cecile. That's what Momma would have said.*

Cecile's grandmother, Mamère Le Bieu, had a huge stainless-steel outdoor cooker bubbling a stone's throw from the picnic tables. "Lordy, dem mud bugs gonna make fine fixins." She threw onions, potatoes, sausage, mushrooms, and green beans in the wire

56

basket along with the crawfish.

"Here, Mamère." Cecile tugged the gris-gris from her neck. "I don't think this is working. Maybe Armand is right. It's only superstition."

Her grandmother frowned. "No, no, don't you tempt the spirits with your blasphemy. I'll make you a new gris-gris."

"I don't need it. There won't be no more babies anyhow." Cecile kissed her cheek and walked away. She secured Neptune to the leg of the picnic table with a leash before she headed for the riverbank. Alligators slithered through the black water, their bulging eyes rising above the lily pads as they stalked blue herons and white snowy egrets that fed along the shoreline. Cecile could imagine Neptune making a tasty lunch.

She ran her fingers over the tangled, grey moss that drooped from the great banyan trees. Closing her eyes, she listened. A frog croaked, a flurry of wings, the small splash of a fish jumping. If only she could stay here, where she felt safe and protected, forever. The twisted roots of the mangrove sprang with life; crawfish, sheepshead and silverfish weaved through the tangled web in the brackish water of the river.

Life would be different this time in Chalmette. They'd start over, with a new house, new dreams. Who said you had to have children to be complete? Lots of women led happy, successful lives without children. She could return to work. She loved interior design. Maybe she should take a few refresher courses at the community college? Would it be open again after the hurricane? She stomped her foot, and a flock of snowy egrets took off in simultaneous flight. Katrina. She wouldn't go there again. Life cannot go backwards. She had to find a way to move forward, Those memories were best left buried. She looked down to see wet circles on her shirt. Where did they come from? She touched her face. Her cheeks were wet. She wiped away the tears with her hand. Tears she must hide from Armand. Did he really think she could ever get over all that happened so easily?

She heard commotion at the cottage. Yvette, her sister from Arkansas, along with her brood of three children and her obnoxious husband, had arrived as planned.

"CeCe!" Armand was hollering for her. "Where are you?"

Begrudgingly, she trekked to the cottage. Her dad fussed over Yvette and tumbled with the boys in the prickly patches of grass.

Armand tossed a beer to Denny, Yvette's husband, and they settled into a heated debate between the LSU Tigers and the Arkansas Razorbacks.

"Aunt CeCe," said six-year-old Devon, climbing on her lap, "was it scary in the hurry cane?" He stroked her arm like soothing a child.

That was an understatement. Cecile forced a smile. "Yes, very. But that's how we got Neptune." She reached down and scratched the pup under his chin. She told them the story of Armi rescuing the pup, leaving out the trauma of childbirth in an attic. She glanced at her sister, hoping she would understand what issues she was dodging.

Devon wiggled out of her lap and joined Dillon and Darwin in the grass playing with the pup. Neptune wriggled and flipped over to have the boys rub his belly.

What was Yvette thinking naming them all with

D's? They were hard enough to recognize, each less than twelve months apart.

"That's enough, kids," Yvette said. "Leave your Auntie and Neptune be."

Cecile and Armand watched as the children moved to more entertaining things, like scuffling over the soccer ball that Denny tossed at them from the trunk of the car.

"I had it first."

"No way, it's mine anyway."

"I never get a turn."

"Kids, kids." Yvette shooed them away. "Please go play over there, away from the picnic table. Pester your grandpappy for a change." She smiled at Cecile.

"See what a pain in the neck they are?" Denny chimed in. "You're the lucky one with all the peace and quiet. Be glad you don't have any kids."

Cecile's heart dropped into her stomach. She turned her face away and focused on the twists in the banyan tree. *Buck up. I know, Momma.* She could get through this. It'll get easier. The stabbing pain in her gut would someday stop. When people stopped talking about babies and Hurricane Katrina. Like that was ever going to happen in New Orleans.

"Oh, God! I'm sorry." said Yvette. "He didn't think. He didn't mean …"

Armand wrapped an arm around Cecile. "It's okay, we know he didn't mean anything by it. How're things in Arkansas, besides those Razorbacks?"

Chapter Seven

St. Petersburg, Russia

July 2006

Nikolai realized that crazy Dimitri, with his wild haircut and offensive talk, was really a decent guy under all that baggage. He showed Nikolai the dozens of catacombs under the ancient brick walls of the orphanage. Some led under the canals to St. Petersburg. Wedged into crevices and corners in the tunnels, they found small artifacts, pottery, and small pieces of armor that Dimitri peddled on the street to the tourists. Nikolai, more interested in finding a pathway to the girls' wing so he could see Natalia, left Dimitri to his treasures. When not with Natalia, he sought the comfort of the Lord in the chapel which he accessed through an entrance from the tunnels. Only God and the saints painted on the walls heard his shattered dreams. He stared up at Jesus, the painted eyes looking to heaven for God's grace. If their Lord and Savior could seek God's grace, why couldn't he?

With Dimitri's connections, Nikolai landed a job outside the orphanage where nobody asked his age. The dark tunnels made travel quick and easy. Head counts at the orphanage were non-existent, and rarely did anyone question his whereabouts. Besides, Dimitri had his back.

Nikolai landed a job at the FCT, First Container Terminal at the Port of St. Petersburg. Thousands of five-high containers came in from the docks. Once unloaded, he had to hose the containers down so the next load could be shipped. Even in the mild summer weather, his body shivered from the freezing water that dripped from the hoses and doused his trousers. The meager cash he was paid, substantially under the normal wage, was slipped discreetly into his pockets on a daily basis. He was keeping his promise to Mama the best way he could, saving every dime for Natalia.

It took several weeks, but he almost had enough rubles to buy a present for Natalia's fifth birthday on the 12th of July. He knew he should save every penny for her future, but he couldn't miss her birthday. This one time, he would buy something with his precious savings. The stuffed pigeon in the window of the department store was perfect. He went inside and asked to see the pigeon. The soft feathers felt real, and when he turned the little key on its stomach, it played "Korobushka," Dedushka's favorite Russian folk song. This was perfect. Natalia was so obsessed with Dedushka's pigeons. Perhaps this would give her some comfort when he was not around, when she was far away with her new parents. A lump formed in his throat. Nikolai counted his money for the tenth time. He was still short two hundred of the 750 rubles needed to make the purchase.

He was out of time. He wouldn't be able to get through the tunnels again until after her birthday. It was now or never. If only he could only sell something, maybe something from the tunnels. Some of it was valuable. They had to be. They were probably hundreds of years old. Dimitri usually found the best pieces, and he wasn't about to share. Nikolai headed down into the dark tunnel. He picked up a broken piece of metal, possibly part of a shield from a battle during the Revolution. About ten centimeters in diameter, it could have been anything. The one thing he knew for sure was that it had to be very old. He slipped it into his pocket and poked his head above ground in an alley on the streets of St. Petersburg. It must have been an escape hatch at one time, now mistaken for a sewer grate. No one around. He pulled himself up and lowered the grate on the opening.

He approached a peddler on the street. "Want a genuine piece of armor from the Russian Revolution?"

The man scoffed. "Where would you get a piece of authentic armor?"

"I have my connections." Nikolai jutted his chin. "I live over the tunnels on New Holland Island. There are tons of treasure down there. See for yourself." He thrust the broken piece of metal in the man's face.

The man grabbed the piece from Nikolai's hand and held it to the light. "Bwah. So, you're one of those orphan kids. This is nothing. Not even worth a single ruble."

Nikolai could feel the heat spread to his cheeks.

"It's real—and old. I'll sell it to you for two hundred rubles."

"Boy, you are dreaming." He tossed it at him.

"Okay, one hundred fifty. That's my final offer." It wasn't enough to buy the pigeon, but it was close.

The man eyed the piece, more interested when the price was right. "One hundred. Take it or leave it."

Nikolai hesitated. Still one hundred short. He knew that the peddler would turn around and sell it for twice that much, but he had to be careful that no one reported him to the police for stealing. He sighed. "Okay, deal."

Nikolai took a deep breath, stood tall, and marched into the store. He would ask to speak to the proprietor. With any luck he would be understanding. When he came out from the back room, Nikolai said a prayer of thanks. The man looked enough like his dedushka to be his brother. Perhaps it was a sign from God.

"Please, sir, the pigeon in the window—will you take 650 rubles? It's for my little sister's fifth birthday. Our family died in a fire, and she loves pigeons. Our dedushka raised homing pigeons in Suzdal. It would make her very happy.

"Ah, yes, Yuri Sokolov. My cousin lives in Suzdal. I went there once to see the pigeon races, and I met your dedushka. He was a good man. If I recall, his pigeons won that race. Sad, sad thing about the fire."

Nikolai's heart lifted. He was finally going to get a break. "Yes, that's him. He had a mustache exactly like yours."

The store owner twisted the tips of his whiskers,

appearing to think through the situation. "I'll tell you what I'll do. I will sell you the pigeon for 600 rubles if you will do one small thing for me."

Six hundred. That would leave him with fifty rubles left over. "Yes, yes. Whatever you want. Sweep your floors? Stock your shelves?"

The man sneered. "Follow me." He stepped into the back room.

Nikolai followed the proprietor through the black curtain that hung between the store and the storage room. A windowless room with shelves of merchandise, a huge box of broken articles, a bare lightbulb hung from a cord. A rat scurried over the filthy floor and ran under a shelf.

The man sat on a high stool and unzipped his fly, his ugly swollen member emerging like a venomous snake.

What did he want Nikolai to do? No, he could not possibly mean that. Beads of sweat trickled down Nikolai's forehead into his eyes. His heart pounded heavily against his chest. Sounds from the other room amplified in his ears. People mulling about. The low voices of people buying goods. The ticking of a clock. Somebody had to stop this. Please, no.

"Please, sir. I can't. Can't I do some chores for you instead?"

The proprietor shook his head. "I don't have all day," he barked. "Do you want the damn toy or not?"

Nikolai stared at the throbbing snake. Could he really do such horrid thing? What choice did he have? He had to get that pigeon for Natalia. Would God ever forgive him? *Please, God, understand I must do this.* He squared his shoulders and dropped to his knees.

When it was over, with the pigeon tucked under his shirt, Nikolai slithered to the alley and threw up. It was the first time he had ever felt real shame. A low moan escaped deep within his soul. He ran through the dark tunnel, falling prone on the cold brick floors in the cathedral. He prayed. *Heavenly Father, I have sinned. I am not worthy to be your servant. Save me from this life of hell and perversity.*

Natalia's birthday passed without any fanfare. It was two days later before Nikolai could give her his present.

"Ooo," Natalia squealed and clapped her hands. "A present." She unwrapped the pigeon from the plain brown butcher paper. "A pigeon. I will name him Ivan, like Dedushka's favorite. I love it, Nika."

"Golubka, turn the key." The "Korobushka" played, and she danced around the room, the pigeon tucked between her chin and her shoulder. He tried to forget the taste that lingered in his mouth. Or was it only in his mind? He swallowed bile. "You're welcome, Golubka. I love you too."

Natalia hugged the toy pigeon to her chest.

Nikolai kissed her cheeks. "You must keep it forever and ever. When we are apart, it will remind you of me. Be nice to the new mamas and papas."

Chapter Eight

Butte La Rose, LA.

August 2006

It was time. Armand had practiced what he would say until he could recite it in his sleep. They weren't getting any younger, and sometimes it took months, even years, to go through the adoption process.

He watched Cecile as she swatted the first of the twilight mosquitoes on her arms that emerged from the swamp. Her honey mane partially obscured his view of her face. But he knew every detail by heart. The curve of the tip of her nose. The way her eyes turned emerald-green when she was happy and the dark green of moss when she was sad. God, he loved her.

Everyone's stomach was full, and all the swamp stories told for the hundredth time. Mamère was cleaning the table, and Pop Lafayette filled his cheek full of snuff and settled into the bentwood rocker.

Armand took Cecile's hand as they walked under the old oaks draped in gray moss, along the murky Atchafalaya River. Neptune followed close at their heels.

"Go home, Neptune." CeCe pointed to the house.

The little dog's ears drooped, and he tucked his tail between his legs. But he obeyed.

"It's not safe for him by the river." She pointed across the brackish water at an alligator dozing in the last sliver of sunlight on the opposite bank.

"Right, babe." He took a deep breath, praying his timing was right. "I've been thinking ..." He squeezed her hand.

"Uh oh." She returned his squeeze. "That could be dangerous." Her eyes danced with mischief.

There were those emerald eyes. God, he loved it when she smiled. He swallowed. *Go for it, you coward.* "The new house is done. It's time to go home. And I've been thinking about adding to our family."

Cecile stopped and stared into the brackish waters. "Armi, you know what the doc said. I can't have no more babies."

"I know. But, well, there're lots of babies out there looking for new mommas and daddies. Maybe one of them is waiting for us." A gush of cool air rushed through his fingertips as she pulled her hand from his and wrapped her arms around herself.

"We talked about this before... after Theresa. I wanted our own baby, not a throwed away one."

Armand reached for her, brushing a blond strand from her damp forehead. He could smell her raspberry shampoo. "But we have to look at other options now. Who says those babies were thrown

67

away? What if they lost their mommas and daddies in an accident? Those little ones are as broken-hearted as we are. They deserve to be loved, just like we do."

He felt her breath close to his ear, her body coiled within herself.

"I don't know, Armi. What if I don't have the strength? The house, Chalmette, going back there. The memories. I don't know if I can handle more than that."

He held her away from him by her shoulders, bending down to force her eyes to meet his. They had changed to the color of moss. "CeCe, Chalmette is our home. You know I should be close to the refinery. I can't keep making this drive. I know this is hard for you. Life has dealt us some raw deals. But this could be our chance, a chance for a whole family."

"Well, even if we did consider it, all that paperwork, hoping and believing for years that we could have a family. What if our dreams get dashed again?"

"Adoption doesn't have to be that hard. There's an easier way. I've done some research. There are orphanages in Russia overflowing with children. Their wait time is half what an American adoption would be. Will you at least look at the websites?" He held his breath.

"Ouch. You're hurting me." She pulled away from his grip on her shoulders.

"Oh, God. I'm sorry, CeCe." He let go, not realizing that he had been squeezing her shoulders. "You know I'd never hurt you on purpose."

She walked ahead of him down the narrow path, then stopped so quickly he almost ran into her. She was staring at a tortoise sitting by the bank, a baby tortoise resting on its back and nodded. "Okay, I'll look, but I'm making no promises."

"Really?" Oxygen rushed into his lungs. Bubbles of joy welled up in his chest. "CeCe, that's all I ask. Don't close your mind to it. Let's go home." He kissed the top of her head, wrapped an arm around her waist, and turned her toward the house. Things were going to turn out well. He was sure of it.

Cecile sat in the car staring at their new home. It had little resemblance to the one lost in Katrina. From the street, it looked like a one story, except for the three dormer windows that protruded from the tile roof. He had promised her a second story this time. A long wide porch spread across the entire front of the house. She shuddered at the memory of the roof tiles slamming into the house when—no, she wouldn't go there.

She looked around at the neighborhood, where the real estate consisted of empty lots where houses once stood, or blue tarps that still covered hundreds of roofs of homes that somehow were still standing. The sludge was gone, and intermittent sprouts of green grass tried to add color to the brown yards, adding specks of normalcy. Would normal ever return? The city of trailers loomed in the distance. How long would the hundreds of FEMA trailers that housed other families stay there?

She waited for Armand to come around and open her car door.

"Ready?" he asked, his hand extended.

Gallant. He really was her knight in shining armor. At the door, he swept her up in his arms and carried her over the threshold.

She shook off the memories and laughed. It felt good. "Hey, it's not our first home or our honeymoon, old man." Those milk chocolate eyes she fell in love with almost melted all her fears.

"It could be. The bed is all made up for us." He gave her those Groucho-Marx eyebrow arches.

She swatted at his arm. "Stop. Put me down. Let me see what you did here. Where did you get this flair for decorating?"

He shrugged as he set her down so she could walk around. The house was furnished with an entirely new décor, with modern, sleek lines, monochromatic colors, stainless-steel appliances. A chrome umbrella stand stood by the front door where her favorite terra cotta planter once rested.

Cecile had to admit it was nice. In this modern marvel, she could almost forget she was in Chalmette, until she looked out the window at the sea of blue tarps. She angled the plantation shutters to let in the light but block the ground level view.

Up an open staircase, a balcony looked down into the great room, and a wide hall serviced three bedrooms, each with adjoining baths. The first room was empty except for the padded window seat nestled in the dormer. The second was identical except for a rocking horse with a golden mane in the center of the room. A sad-faced blue Eeyore sat on the painted seat, looking a little worse for wear, but waiting for his ride.

Cecile gasped and stepped into the room. "I thought everything was lost." She picked up the stuffed toy and tried to wipe away the brown stain that partially covered his face.

"This was all I could salvage. I sanded down

Junior's ... I mean, the rocking horse and put a fresh coat of stain on it. The dry cleaners did the best they could with Eeyore."

Cecile swiped away a tear and nodded. "Thank you."

The master bedroom looked more familiar. Armand had done his best to replicate the room that held the secrets of their most intimate times together. The color scheme was the same soft hues of teal and brown. The king-sized oak headboard had a slightly different curve, but the high bureau was such a close match that she had to think hard about the details of the old one.

"You did a wonderful job, Armi." She should have helped him, not sulked in her own misery in Butte La Rose. It must have taken him weeks to pick everything out, to sand and stain the rocking horse, to try to duplicate the one place she had always felt safe.

"Do you like it? You can change anything you want. If the colors aren't right, I can re-paint. I didn't know about the modern living room. We can ex-change things if —"

She pressed her fingers over his lips. "It's per-fect. I wouldn't change a thing. Have I told you lately how much I love you?"

He pulled her into his arms. "As a matter of fact, no, you haven't. Just how much do you love me?"

She pulled him down onto the *almost* identical comforter of their king size bed.

Cecile sat at the computer and stared at the blank monitor. She typed "Russian Adoptions" into the browser. Several international adoption agencies and some private organizations displayed their web addresses. Clicking through them, adoring little faces with sad eyes pleaded for her to rescue them. A newborn was not an option.

She looked at the hopeful eyes of her husband and knew she could not deny him. Neptune wiggled at her heels, his oversize tail throwing his back-end side to side. Maybe they could have a family. "Okay. What do you think, Neptune? Should we give it a try?" A flicker of hope warmed her from deep in her belly as Neptune danced rings around her ankles.

After endless hours searching through the multitude of sites, they agreed on Hope International Adoption Agency in New Orleans. The information was clear and welcoming. Cecile pressed her hands together in a silent prayer as Armand dialed. He winked at her from across the table and hit the speaker button.

"Hope International Adoption Agency. Lu Anne speaking. How may I help you today?" The voice echoed with optimism.

"Yes, my name is Armand Boudreaux, from Chalmette. We, that is, my wife and I, would like information on adopting a child."

"Wonderful, Mr. Boudreaux. Would this be your first adoption?"

"Yes, w-we have tried for years to have a baby of our own."

Cecile frowned. Did he have to bring that up first thing, like they were failures? They did have children, but they all died.

Armand realized his mistake and squeezed her hand.

The kind voice on the other side of the line filled

in the awkward silence. "Let me put you through to Martha Schwab, our director of Family Services. She'll help you get started. Can you hold, please?"

Cecile smiled and returned his squeeze.

"This is Martha Schwab. Thank you for calling the Hope International Adoption Agency. Why don't we start by letting me tell you a little about Hope, and then you can tell me a little about you?"

Ms. Schwab highlighted the benefits of Hope and briefly covered the steps to adoption. "We can send you an application. When you have it filled out, we'll set an appointment for your initial interview where we'll get a chance to know each other better. I'll introduce you to the entire staff and walk you through the process of adoption. The next step would be the beginning of the Home Study Program, which takes approximately a year to complete. From there we work on your dossier and start the placement process to find you a child. How does that sound?"

"That sounds great." Armand said. "We're anxious to get started. We'll fill out the application right away. Do we mail it or bring it with us to the interview?"

"Why don't you email or fax us a copy prior to your interview so we have a chance to review it beforehand. Is that something you can do?"

Martha Schwab reminded Cecile of the grandmotherly type, and she wondered if she was picturing her correctly in her mind. Martha's calm, quiet demeanor soothed Cecile's frayed nerves while Armand answered a few basic questions about their situation. Martha was easy to talk to. By the end of the twenty-minute conversation, contact information had been exchanged to receive the application.

Within a week, a brown envelope arrived in their mailbox. Most of the forms were straight forward: legal information, social security, insurance, tax information, employment history. The medical forms would take more time, especially for Cecile. They took the forms to Dr. Teekell, who assured them that Cecile's past medical problems should not preclude her from being a healthy mother. He gave them a raving personal recommendation. One line asked about mental conditions such as depression or anxiety. Cecile wrote, "None."

Armand raised his eyebrow but kept silent.

Chapter Nine

Chalmette, LA.

December 2006

Cecile Lafayette Boudreaux drummed her fingers on her leg while Armand drove to the Hope International Adoption Agency in downtown New Orleans. Were they really going to do this? The city was still a shamble after Hurricane Katrina, but it was obvious that work was going on, trying to bring it back. "What if they don't like us, or we were too old, or they don't have any matches for us?"

"Don't be silly." Armand said. "They aren't going to run out of children. They're going to love us. You'll see."

First, they met Dorothy Schwab. Exactly as Cecile had imagined, Dorothy was matronly, with a wide girth and a warm smile. Cecile's nerves calmed a notch. Then Dorothy introduced them to the Family

Coordinator, Miranda Fisher. Miranda embraced them with a warm hug.

She looked much too young to have a job with that responsibility. Freckles peppered her nose and hair the color of sand fell in a straight waterfall over her petite shoulders.

"It's such a pleasure to meet you." Miranda said. "I've been going over your file. I'm sure we can find a child for you." She gestured to a small round table with three chairs. "Please, may I get you some coffee or a cold drink?"

Armand shook his head and pulled out a chair so Cecile could sit, then did the same for Miranda. "No, thank you, ma'am."

"I'll have some iced tea, if you have it, ma'am," Cecile said.

"Yes, of course. Please, call me Miranda," she said with a toss of her sandy mane. She retrieved a can of sweet tea from a small refrigerator next to her desk. "Let me tell you my story before we begin. I'm sure you're curious how a woman as young as myself ended up across the table from you."

Cecile felt the heat rise above the collar of her dress. Was she that transparent?

Miranda pushed aside the manila folder on the table and folded her hands in front of her.

"Twenty-two years ago, I was born Ariel Motkov, in Moscow, Russia. When the doctors told my biological mother I would never be a normal child, she left me in a basket on the doorstep of Baby House #5 in Moscow. Born with a cleft pallet, I was considered undesirable. If the Hope Agency hadn't brought my American parents to me, who knows where I would be today?"

Cecile caught Armand's glance. He raised an eyebrow.

"My adoptive parents, Benjamin and Caroline Fisher, saw past the deformed upper lip and missing upper palate. I had emotional issues as well, but they saw me for who I was as a person. By age five, I had a new name, a new palate and upper lip, and new parents in Charleston, South Carolina." She touched the small scar on her lip. "I became Miranda Fisher. My parents loved me unconditionally. Growing up, I asked my father to tell me the story of my adoption over and over. He told me that when his eyes met mine, he knew I was meant to be his.

"I graduated from the University of South Carolina and wanted to head straight to New Orleans and the Hope Agency. I wanted to be a part of the organization that saved my life." She glanced down at the file in front of her. "I see you've lived in Louisiana all your life, so you understand all about Hurricane Katrina."

Armand and Cecile nodded. She fought down the lump in her throat as Miranda continued.

"It destroyed a good part of the agency, and the employees had to be relocated. I spent six months in Dallas at their other branch until this office re-opened."

Cecile clutched Armand's hand. "That's awful that your mother would throw you away like a piece of garbage. How lucky of you to meet your new parents. Do all the children at the Russian orphanages have living parents that gave them up? Are they all … umm … do they all have …?" She didn't know how to go on.

"Do you mean health issues?" Miranda laughed.

Cecile rapped her thumb against her leg under the table. "I'm sorry."

"It's fine, really. Children in orphanages in Europe and Asia are like children everywhere; some have lost their parents due to tragedy, others because of financial issues, and some with stories like mine. It is true that most children in international orphanages have some sort of health diagnosis, simply because of being institutionalized. They don't receive the same stimuli as a child in a safe, loving home, so they are often delayed in their physical or mental growth."

Armand gave Cecile's hand a slight squeeze under the table. "We didn't mean to offend —"

"No offense taken." Miranda waved a pretty, manicured hand in the air. "These are honest questions, and if we're going to make this work, we need honest questions and honest answers. You can ask me anything."

"How long does this process take?" Cecile asked.

"It takes a little over a year. First, we run through the basics on your application, finances, background checks, doctor evaluations. Next, we'll schedule your home study. Normally, that would be with another person in our office, but since Katrina, we are short staffed, so I'll be doing your home study. We do multiple home visits and file reports with the country of interest. Then you'll make two trips, bringing your child home with you on the second trip."

Armand scribbled furiously on a notepad, trying to absorb everything.

Miranda reached out and patted his hand across the table. "We'll walk you through each step as it happens. Let's simplify it. On your first visit, you'll meet your child, accept him or her, and petition the court. The second visit is all about the paperwork, birth certificate, passport, adoption decree. You don't have to remember any of this. We'll walk you through it step by step.

Cecile and Armand walked out into the southern sunshine. Cecile tucked a packet of information into her bag and asked, "What do you think?"

He grinned at her. "It's a lot of steps, but a year isn't that long to wait. Just think, we could be parents by this time next year."

January. 2007

Every corner of the house gleamed. Cecile had worked her fingers raw scrubbing the house from top to bottom. It had been over a month since they had filed their initial paperwork, and today they were about to receive their first home visit from the adoption agency. Cecile looked at her simple shirtwaist dress and wondered if she should change again. Was it too dressy, not dressy enough? She'd already been through three outfits, piled her hair on top of her head, combed it out and put it in a ponytail, then finally left it loose on her shoulders.

"You're going to wear that shirt?" Cecile frowned at Armand.

He looked down at his blue chambray button down. "What?"

"It's old and faded. Can't you find something nicer?"

"CeCe, this isn't an inquisition. She needs to see us how we live. It'll be fine."

Cecile applied a fresh pink coat to her lips. "I want everything to be perfect. I feel like we are on trial."

"Don't be silly. She's not looking for reasons to turn us down. She wants us to have a child."

The doorbell rang, and Cecile rushed down the stairs.

"Good morning," Miranda said. "This must have been a beautiful neighborhood before Katrina." She nodded toward the rows of homes with blue tarps still adorning the roofs.

"Yes, it was. But it's coming back." Cecile said.

"Maybe a little slower than we would have liked." Armand greeted her at the foot of the stairs with a handshake. "We started over. Our house was too far gone. I didn't want Cecile anywhere near potential mold problems, and we didn't need the memories there." Armand gave Miranda a tour of the house, chatting casually about the neighborhood and how it was improving.

Armand was right. There was no reason to be nervous. Following the tour, they sat around the kitchen table getting better acquainted. Miranda asked about their experience with Katrina. Deep breaths. Thank God, Armand did most of the talking.

"You lost a child during the storm?"

"Yes," Cecile said. "The barometric pressure caused women all over New Orleans to go into labor. I was seven months. He didn't make it." The old feeling of despair worked its way into her gut. "The doc said I couldn't have any more children."

Miranda squeezed Cecile's hand. "That's why I'm here. We're going to make sure you have a wonderful child."

Really? Was that really going to happen?

By the second home visit, they were both feeling a little more relaxed. Miranda asked about where their child would sleep. They showed her the room with the rocker and stuffed animal that would someday be their child's room.

"We'll be getting all new furniture for her or him ... and toys and clothes ... everything. It was all destroyed in the hurricane." Cecile said. "All but the horse and this." She picked up Eeyore. "Is it wrong to keep something for a child that we lost?"

Miranda put her arm around Cecile. "Of course not. It's wonderful that you were able to save something."

"Armi made the rocking horse by hand. And he worked really hard to clean it up after the storm."

Miranda turned around and took in the full scope of the room. "It's a wonderful room, great light. I love the window seat tucked in the dormer. I know it'll be perfect for your child, and he or she will love the horse and Eeyore."

"How about some coffee? Wait, I remember, you are a tea drinker," Armand said.

"Coffee is fine," Miranda said as she followed him down the stairs.

He placed three steaming mugs of coffee on the round, white-painted wood table. "What are the children like in these orphanages? You mentioned last time the words *health issues*?"

"That's a good question, Armand. It's something I wanted to discuss with you in more detail. As I said, children that have been institutionalized typically are behind in the growth cycle of a child in a family environment. The caretakers at the orphanages work hard to keep the children clean, clothed, and fed, but they don't have time to give a hundred or more children the personal one-on-one affection and nurturing children naturally need."

"Those poor little babies," Cecile said, sipping on her coffee.

"They do the best they can. These children need the patience of loving parents to bring them up to speed. The majority have normal or even excellent IQs, but they lack the opportunity to develop normally."

Armand nodded. "We can do that. Sounds like all they need is someone to love them."

"It's true they need love, above everything else, but it's not as simple as it sounds. The child you adopt could have RAD, Reactive Attachment Disorder, which means he could avoid eye contact, be hyper-active, have a difficult time connecting emotionally, or have poor impulse control.

"Wow... I don't know." Armand rubbed his forehead. "Maybe we aren't ready to take on a child like that. What are the odds that our child would have RAD?"

Cecile fidgeted in her seat. *Omigod.* She wasn't sure she could handle a child like that. What were they thinking? This was a mistake, a big mistake. Was it too late to back out? Cecile hoped Armand would read her thoughts and cancel this whole thing.

"The children institutionalized at a very young age, typically those under two, are at the highest risk of RAD. Babies, like I was. These children have no memory of a normal loving home. They are hard-wired to expect adults—and even other children—to be perfunctory and give them nothing but the most basic of needs. They don't understand or relate to emotional attachments."

"You were a RAD child? You seem so … so …" Cecile was at a loss for words.

"Normal? I'm not comfortable with that word. What is normal? But my adoptive parents spent a long time turning me around, or so I'm told. I don't have any memory of not being happy in my parents' home."

Cecile smiled. "Well, that makes me feel better. If you made it, then it's not impossible."

"So," said Armand, "we would have a better chance of a normal child —" He stopped, feeling heat work its way into his cheeks. "Oh, I'm sorry, a child without RAD … if he was older and had not spent his entire life in an orphanage. Is that correct?"

"Yes, the odds would be more in your favor if the child is older. But that is not a guarantee."

Later that evening, Cecile said, "I'm still not sure we're doing the right thing, Armi. What if we can't get through to her, make her love us?"

"Her? Are you saying you want a little girl?" He slipped an arm around her shoulder.

"I think so. Would that be terribly disappointing after losing Junior?"

"Babe, if you want a girl, then a girl it will be. I just want us to have a family. We'll just love her until she comes around. We're talking about a small child here. We're the adults. We'll get through to her. Don't worry about it. You're going to make a terrific mother."

Cecile was almost asleep when the old familiar cloud settled around her. *No, no. Go away.*

Before the home study was complete, Miranda met with both Armand and Cecile separately, giving her a chance to uncover any concerns they may have had that they felt uncomfortable discussing with their mate.

Armand had no problem opening up to Miranda. "If we aren't one hundred percent sure the first child is right for us, will that hurt our chances for a second child?"

"Not necessarily. If, after your visit, you are sure that you don't want to accept the child, we'll look for a better match for you. That would delay the process, and you would have to make an additional trip for your Meet-Greet-Accept visit. And — we would have a long discussion about whether you are really ready to adopt. What scenario do you see that wouldn't be a fit?" She wrote something in her notebook that Armand could not see.

"That's the thing. I don't know. I can't imagine turning down any child, but this is so new to us. Cecile is afraid of the whole RAD thing, that we won't be able to get through to the child, that she'll never love us. And I'm not even sure if I am asking the right questions."

Miranda closed her notebook. "I understand. I want you to know that I am here for you for the long run, not only until the child is in your home. I'll be here for you for you for as long as you need me. There are no questions too small or inconsequential."

"Thank you, Miranda. We'll keep that in mind."

Cecile met with her next. If only she knew what questions to ask.

"Who had the idea first to adopt a child?" Miranda asked.

"Armand." Cecile hesitated. "I had a hard time getting over losing the last baby. It took me a while to get back to my old self."

"Cecile, no one expects you to be the same, especially after a tragedy like that. Different is okay. We all grow with our life experiences, good and bad. We at Hope want to make sure that this is something you want as much as your husband. This is a life-changing decision, not to be entered into lightly."

"Oh, no." Cecile answered, alarmed by Miranda's serious tone. "I'm not taking it lightly. Please don't get me wrong. I do want a child. I'll be a good mother. I promise." *I hope.*

Miranda smiled. "I don't doubt you want a child, Cecile. But are you ready to take on the challenges of an adopted child?"

Cecile pressed her hand hard down on her knee to stop her drumming thumb. "Is anyone ever ready? All I can do is my best."

"That is all anyone can ask, Cecile."

Chapter Ten

St. Petersburg, Russia

January 7, 2007

Nikolai woke to the sounds of the Christmas Day church bells pealing across St. Petersburg. Rubbing the sleep from his eyes, he peered out the window at the white blanket of snow. Normally, this was his favorite day of the year. He would have been busy serving as an altar boy at all the Masses, helping with communion and running between their cottage and the Church of the Nativity with the freshly baked bread Babushka made to give as colorfully wrapped packages to neighbors and tourists. But all that was over. No altar boy at Mass, no bread, no Babushka.

Nikolai was sure God didn't want the likes of him in His house anymore. He avoided Mass and never went to confession or took communion. No one at the orphanage noticed his absence. Only Natalia begged him to attend Christmas Mass with her.

"Please, Nika. It's Christmas. Mama and Papa would be mad if they knew you were not going."

"Golubka, you're too young to understand. I can't go to Mass. Maybe never again. You go and sing like an angel. I will see you afterwards. I'll have a Christmas gift for you."

She bit her bottom lip. "I don't have a present for you."

"I don't need a present," Nikolai said, plastering a smile on his face. "If you find a family, that's all I would need."

She followed the rest of the girls into the chapel, turning once to raise her little hand in a wave.

Nikolai sprinted toward the tunnels. Why did he promise her a gift when he had nothing? *I need to find her a gift.* Dimitri had a stash of special finds, but he wasn't likely to share. Deeper in the tunnels, it was frigid. The candle, which lit his way and assured him fresh air was coming from somewhere, blew out. He regretted not bargaining with Dimitri for a flashlight. Three times he stopped to relight the candle with trembling, stiff fingers. *What if I get lost down here?* Would anyone ever find him? No one knew he was there. But he couldn't return without something for Natalia. The temperature dropped the deeper he went. He lifted the candle to the wall, looking for anything, a piece of silver, a small shard of pottery.

When his fingers traced the shape of a small cross, he couldn't believe his luck. The light was poor, and he couldn't tell what the cross looked like, but it had to be something good. He shoved it deep into his pocket and turned to find his way out.

A breeze from deep within the tunnel blew the candle out again. It was pitch black. He couldn't see his hands in front of his face. *Don't panic.* Despite the cold, his hands were suddenly clammy, and the matches would not light. He wiped his hands on his pant legs and tried again. Feeling inside the match-box, he counted the matches. One…two…three… three small wooden matches.

Nikolai struck the first one on the side of the stone tunnel. *Psst.* The light flashed, and then fizzled out.

Breathe, stay calm. His body trembled as he felt in the darkness for the next match. His stiff fingers fumbled with the two sticks in the little box. He pinched his fingers around one. Once it was out of the box, he dropped it into the darkness. "Damn, damn." The words echoed off the walls.

Kneeling on the cold stone floor, Nikolai felt around for the small match. What else might he come across? *Rats? Spiders? Bones? Stop. Don't be ridiculous.*

Seconds felt like hours. How long had he been down there? Giving up on finding the match, he pawed against the wall to a standing position.

Follow the wall until you are out. Okay, he could do that. Was he going in the right direction? Had he gotten turned around when he dropped the match? What if he was going deeper in instead of out?

He was completely disoriented and shaking uncontrollably. He rubbed his hands over his arms, clad only in a thin sweater. He gulped for air. The air was getting thinner. *No, you're panicking. The air is the same. You are not turned around. Go forward.*

What was that? His own thoughts or God directing him? Of course not. It was only his fear. God

88

had long given up on him. Either way, he was going forward.

Things became clearer. His heartbeat returned to normal. He still had one match left and the candle in his pocket. He'd saved it for an emergency. "Ha!" He laughed out loud at his own joke. *This isn't an emergency?*

Hand over hand, feeling his way along the wall, he made forward progress through the dark. He wished he had paid attention to how far or how long he had traveled into the tunnel.

Surely soon he would see a glimmer of light from the entrance. What if it was night already? There wouldn't be any natural light. He could be down there until morning. He'd have to pick up the pace to make it out while there was still daylight. Should he use his last match?

He raced forward as fast he could, maintaining contact with the wall. He stumbled and fell, picked himself up, and continued. Stopping to catch his breath, he heard a sound.

A voice, coming from far ahead. He stood still and listened.

"O-lay, O-lay."

Was someone saying Nikolai? He called out. "Here! I'm here."

"Nikolai? Where are you, man?" Dimitri hollered.

"Here! Dimitri… Is that you? I'm here."

At last, Nikolai saw a light getting brighter with every second. Brighter than a candle. A spotlight. When the light flashed in his eyes, it blinded him. "Whoa, my eyes."

Dimitri turned the spotlight on his own face. His

blond spiked hair created a silhouette on the tunnel wall of exaggerated pointy stalactites. "Who the hell did you think it would be? What are you doing way back in here? Scared the shit outta me. Lucky for you I give a rat's ass what happens to you."

Nikolai didn't know whether to laugh or cry. He reared his head and said a silent prayer. *Thank you, Father, for this obnoxious jackass who cared enough to look for me. You send strange angels to watch over me.*

He wrapped Dimitri in a huge bear hug. He pulled away. Awkward.

"Hey, let's get the hell out of here," Dimitri said.

"You got it. Lead the way, my man."

By the time they were on the main floor of the orphanage, everyone knew Nikolai had been missing. The staff was furious, thinking he had run away. The younger boys thought he was some kind of hero. Natalia was crying.

"What do you have to say for yourself, young man?" said Master Kovak, the headmaster of the boys' dormitory.

Nikolai faced the headmaster, with his stooped back and bad comb-over. Before he could answer, Natalia barreled toward him and jumped into his arms. "Nika, Nika. I was so scared. Where were you?"

"I...I wanted to go to town to get you a Christmas gift. I'm sorry, Golubka, I didn't mean to scare you."

"You can't leave the grounds without permission," the headmaster boomed. "Now I have to punish you on Christmas Day. Do you think that's what I wanted to do on the birthday of our Lord?"

Nikolai had no idea what he wanted to do on

this day. But he was sure it didn't include scouring the countryside looking for a wayward orphan.

"Sorry," Nikolai mumbled, not the least bit sorry.

Master Kovak shook his head, huffing and puffing before settling into a calm. "All the rest of the children are in the dining hall. Go now. I'll think of what kind of punishment to give you."

Nikolai led Natalia by the hand to the dining hall. The noise was deafening, children laughing and shouting to each other, anxious for their one gift. Nikolai hated the idea of receiving charity from the toy drive at the Cathedral of Spilled Blood. He was too old for toys anyway. If only he had understood that when he felt so self-righteous doling out gifts to the children of the Suzdal orphanage last year. Life certainly looked different from the opposite side of the charity.

He watched as red, green, and silver-wrapped packages were handed out. Paper ripped open and flew as eighty-three children tore into their treasures.

"Look, Nika." Natalia squealed. She held up a Barbie doll, dressed in cowgirl boots and a fringed skirt.

"Nice, Golubka." Nikolai smiled. He patted the cross in his pocket. Once he was alone, he'd look at it in the light, clean off the dirt, and give it to her.

"What did you get, Nika?" She looked expectantly at her brother.

Nikolai looked at the wrapped package in his hand. "Here, you open it." He handed the small round gift to her.

She pulled the paper off and oohed at the glass snow globe. Shaking the ball, snowflakes floated down on a tiny cottage with red sides and a tin roof. "Look, it's our house."

The globe reminded Nikolai of what they had lost. He forced a smile. "You keep it, so you don't forget where you came from." He had a gift for her after all. He'd see if the cross was valuable enough to keep or pawn for cash.

"I'll never forget, Nika. I promise."

Nikolai ducked into the bathroom to take a closer look at the cross. Privacy was always an issue, so he rinsed it off quickly at the sink and ducked into a stall. Beneath the dirt and grime, the most beautiful thing he had ever seen rested in his hand. He held it tight between his fingers, afraid he'd drop it into the commode. About seven centimeters tall, the Orthodox cross appeared to be pure gold, encrusted with diamonds, rubies, and emeralds. The backside had engraved markings, too faint for him to decipher and at the top, a small, looped clasp created a way to hang it from a chain. If this was as old as he thought it was, perhaps it was from Peter the Great himself. It could be priceless. What should he do with it? How could he explain how he got it? He couldn't give it to Natalia right now. The snow globe would have to do. The cross could be security for Natalia's future for the rest of her life. For now, he would hide it. But where? Unwilling to put it in the dorm room where someone could find it, he stuffed it in his pocket. He kept it there for weeks, afraid to have it out of his sight, and terrified he would be caught with it.

January 19, 2007

The Theophany Feast was upon them. Nikolai lay in his bed, struggling with the one sense of hope he knew. In Suzdal, they called it *The Frosts of Baptism.* If he joined the hundreds in St. Petersburg to wash himself in the icy waters of the Neva River, would God wash away his sins in the purification ceremony? The water temperature was -26C (-7.6F). In the past, Nikolai had watched others take the plunge in the Kamenka River in Suzdal, while he stayed bundled in a down-filled coat, assisting the priest with blankets and towels as the cleansed souls rose from the river. Father Vladimir would have expected this of Nikolai this year. Did he have the faith to make the plunge?

He walked to the other end of the dormitory where the only clock ticked loudly on the wall to the displeasure of the boys that slept below it. 7:10 p.m. The blessings by the cleric would only last until 8:30 p.m. The line was most likely long. He'd have to hurry if he was to make it on time. He didn't own swim trunks. Simple things like that had not been replaced since the fire. *I'll take a dry pair of trousers.* He tucked them under his coat as he headed for the door.

"Hey, man." Dimitri stopped him at the door with a hand to his chest. "Where you headed? Got a piece waiting for you? Does she have a sister?" he said with a laugh.

Nikolai brushed his hand away, matching his laugh. "Not one that would want you. Got some business on the streets."

"Sure, man. I'll cover for ya." He reached for something in his trunk beside his bed. "Here, take my flashlight this time. It's freezing out there. I don't want to save your sorry ass again."

Nikolai took the flashlight and patted his chest, his spare trousers warming him under his coat. "Double layers. Later." He made his way down the back stairs, through the furnace room, and into the small, obscured door to the tunnels.

Nikolai could smell the incense the priest waved over the chasm in the ice. A hundred spectators watched the thirty or more people standing in line, wrapped in long coats and furry hats they would shed seconds before dropping into the tri-bar, cross-shaped cavity cut into the frozen river. He looked at the faces of the people as they climbed from the abyss. Even with red skin and clothes instantly frozen on their bodies, each face radiated joy and absolution. Nikolai joined the end of the line, rubbing his hands together to warm them, and then shoved them deep into his coat pockets. Through the coat's liner, through his pant leg, he felt the small shape of the cross. Imagined or real, a warmth traveled up his extremity.

Bouncing on one leg, then the other, he made his way toward the front of the line. He lowered his head in prayer, pleading with God to grant him the courage to plunge into the gash in the solid silver river. Only two ahead of him. Behind him, a young woman repeated her prayer, "Lord Jesus Christ, Son of God, have mercy on me, a sinner," on each knot of the chotki, the prayer rope of yarn made into ornate knots and a cross. He nodded at the young woman, remembering his own chotki had been consumed in the fire.

He stepped forward. Next in line.

"I'm sorry," said the priest to the woman behind him. "This is the last. It is past time to end the immersions."

"But I've waited so long," the young women wailed, her face crumbling.

The priest shook his head.

"No, I need the blessing. Please, please." She dropped to her knees on the hard-frozen ground. Her tears instantly froze on her cheeks. "Mercy Father, please show me mercy."

The priest lifted the woman to her feet. "My child. I do wish to show you mercy. But it is already past time. And this young man is in front of you."

"No, Father," Nikolai spoke, stepping out of the line. "Let her take my place. Give her the last spot."

The woman clutched his arm. "Thank you. Oh, thank you. If you only knew…"

Nikolai let her move to the edge of the water. He held her coat as she stepped off the edge without hesitation.

She burst through the icy water, crossing herself, shouting "Halleluiah" in Russian.

Nikolai turned and headed back to the tunnels. Did he do an unselfish act to give joy to someone else? Or did God prevent him from absolution because he was unworthy? If only he knew the answer, but God was silent.

Chapter Eleven

St. Petersburg, Russia

February 2007

With Petia's help, Natalia crossed off the months on a calendar that one of the parents-to-be had left in the recreation room. They had been at the orphanage for eight months. Nikolai's fifteenth birthday came and went, and all Natalia could do is wish him "Happy Birthday."

"Natalia," said Petia. "Many of the children here have no idea what day they were born, so the orphanage doesn't celebrate birthdays. Be glad you know when yours and Nikolai's are."

It didn't make Natalia feel any better. Why did Mama and Papa have to die? She pressed her eyes shut tight and tried to remember their faces. It was getting harder every day. She remembered Mama's smell, like fresh baked bread. Sometimes she thought she heard the pigeons cooing in Dedushka's lofts. But that couldn't be. She was far away from Suzdal.

She tried to be brave in front of Nikolai, but in her room, she cried into her flat pillow so no one would hear, especially Tasha. Even after all those months, she was still afraid if she wasn't with Nika or Petia. Some of the girls were mean, even the very young ones. She watched them as they huddled over a cardboard puzzle, never inviting her to join in. The other older girls were nicer to the younger ones when Tasha was not in the room. But the minute she returned, they pushed them out of the way and took over the project.

Petia told Natalia that a family wanted to adopt her. Natalia cried for a week. Petia had been her only friend.

"What will I do without you? Nobody else wants to be my friend," wailed Natalia.

"No one wants to make friends because they'll be sad when they leave," Petia said.

Natalia tried to understand but watching the huddle of other girls didn't convince her. If only Nika could stay here with her. She wouldn't care if nobody wanted to be her friend.

Another family adopted Tasha at the beginning of the New Year. Things were quieter after she left, and a few of the girls began to talk to Natalia.

"Tasha said you had bugs," one of the girls said.

"Do not!" Even if she was the last one into the black bath water each week. *They check my head every week, just like everyone else.*

A month later, Tasha returned to the orphanage. "They didn't like me, so they sent me back. Who cares? I didn't like them either."

"Why, Tasha?" Natalia asked. "Why would they send you back?"

"They wanted a maid, someone to do their laundry and wash all their stinking clothes. When I refused to work, they beat me."

Natalia gasped, cupping her hands over her mouth. "They beat you?"

Tasha waved a hand in the air. "It was nothing. A slap with a fly swatter. I could've handled that, but I wasn't going to be their slave. Sometimes that's all they want, you know. They aren't all nice. Some only want kids to work for them, be babysitters for their own kids, do laundry, work in the fields... or worse."

Natalia didn't know what the "worse" was, but she was afraid to ask. "Then I don't ever want to be adopted. I'll stay here forever."

"Don't listen to Tasha." One of the other girls spoke up. "Most of the families are good. I bet she was mean to their kids like she is to us. That's probably why they returned her."

Who was telling the truth? At least she knew what to expect at the orphanage. She had food, a bed, Mass on Sunday, and most of all, Nikolai. If someone adopted her, she didn't know what she'd get.

Chapter Twelve

Chalmette, LA.

February 2008

Cecile arms were in dishwater up to her elbows when the call came. She dried one hand to reach for the receiver. "Hello?"

"We have a child for you." Miranda's jubilation spilled through the phone.

"What?" Bubbles on Cecile's arm floated into the air. Seriously? Was this for real? "Say again?" The call they had waited for eleven months had finally come.

"A little girl." Miranda said. "We have a little girl for you. Are you ready to take a trip to Russia?"

"Ah! Omigod." Cecile dropped into a chair. "Yes, yes. I mean, I think so. I have to call Armi at work. Omigod! Miranda. Tell me all about her."

Miranda laughed into the phone. "I know. Exciting, right? Well, she's six years old. She's been in the orphanage for two years. As I told you, it's a closed adoption, so I don't have a lot of details prior to her coming to the orphanage. But I understand she lost her entire family in a fire, all but one older brother. I'll mail the portfolio to you to take on your trip, but I can email you a photo right now if you want."

"A photo? You can send me a photo? Yes, yes? Omigod, yes. Send it right now." Cecile powered up their PC and waited for the email to come. Then, there it was. The inbox said Miranda Fisher, Hope Agency. Cecile clicked on the attachment. And there she was, their future daughter.

The first photo was a recent snapshot taken at the orphanage. It showed a little girl with platinum blond hair and far-away looking eyes. She was not smiling into the camera. She looked lost. A second photo showed a younger child with a yellow cap pulled over her hair and a bright purple coat. Her eyes danced with laughter. She was holding a gray pigeon in her hands. The edges around the photo looked singed. The photo showed a note handwritten in Russian and translated into English paper; it read *copy of original found in ashes.* Cecile stared at the contrasting photos.

Would they be able to make her that happy again?

Chapter Thirteen

St. Petersburg, Russia

February 2008

The three-hour flight from Louis Armstrong New Orleans Airport to JFK in New York was uneventful. With a short layover, Cecile and Armand boarded the huge Boeing 767 at 8 p.m. for a ten-hour flight to Sheremetyevo Airport in Moscow. Per the flight schedule, the overnight flight would cover 4,646 miles.

Armand dozed in his seat while Cecile stared into the black night, anxious over the possibilities that lay ahead, clutching the portfolio of their child to her chest. Natalia Varyshnikov, six years old, in the system for almost two years. One sibling, a brother, Nikolai, sixteen years old. According to Miranda, he would age out of the system into his own care without being adopted. Because of Russia's closed adoption policy, they would never know much more about this child…their child…their daughter. It sounded foreign to even think it.

It was important to Cecile that they had a child with no living relatives. But the agency chose this child for them. What if she fell in love with this little girl and then lost her? Could this older brother present a problem during the ten-day waiting period? Did he have any legal rights to her at all since he was still a minor?

Cecile leaned her head back and pictured what their life would be like. She saw tea parties on a blanket in the yard on warm spring days, drinking Kool-Aid from tiny plastic cups. Her daughter would love her, and she'd smother her in kisses. She'd smell like baby shampoo and have soft little hands that fit perfectly into Cecile's when they took walks in the park. But as she drifted into a twilight sleep, another vision took hold. Visions of a tormented child, screaming at her in a language Cecile didn't understand, hurling toys and shoes with strong little arms. She awoke with a start. Would there be a language barrier? Neither Cecile nor Armand spoke a single word of Russian. Why didn't they think of that before? There had been time to learn some Russian so they could communicate. Why hadn't they? Now it was too late. They weren't prepared at all. This was insane. What if she was a RAD child? How would they cope?

When they arrived in Moscow at 6 a.m. New York time, 1 p.m. the next day by Moscow time, Cecile was exhausted from battling her inner turmoil through the flight. She was slightly irritated that Armand was rested and alert. Why wasn't he suffering from the same doubts? They grabbed a quick bite to eat at the Moscow airport before changing planes for a short flight into St. Petersburg. She scrutinized her husband as he settled into the seat beside her for the final leg of their journey. He looked perfectly at ease. His eyes shone with excitement and anticipation.

He caught her staring. "What? Why are you looking at me like that?"

She couldn't tell him her fears. "Nothing. I was thinking how happy you look."

He leaned over and snapped her seat belt across her lap. "Aren't you? We're about to meet our daughter. I know she's going to be amazing."

Would she? "I'm a little nervous. Do you really think she'll like us?"

"Of course, silly. What's not to like?" He closed his eyes.

Omigod! He was going back to sleep. Did he have nerves of steel?

Cecile pressed her nose to the window. As the plane flew low, she could see the beautiful countryside and cities with magnificent churches with gold and blue domes, ornate crosses, and beautiful architecture. *My, this is a beautiful country*. Why hadn't she ever thought of Russia like that before?

Upon landing, they grabbed a cab to the St. Petersburg's branch of the Hope International Agency, a small office housed in an ancient building of stone and alabaster.

The social worker, Anastasia Ianova, met them with a warm embrace. "Welcome to Russia." She had a heavy accent, but she was easy to understand. "Have you found accommodations here?"

"Yes," Armand answered. "We have

reservations at the Four Seasons Lions Palace."

"The Four Seasons is a wonderful place, rich with history and opulence. Take some time to enjoy your stay there. You won't regret it."

"Will we be going to the orphanage today? Will we meet Natalia?" Cecile drummed at her pant leg.

Anastasia offered a warm smile. "Yes, of course. I'll make the introduction and stay in the room with you for the first time. Natalia understands English, but sometimes, she's a little shy. She may not be very talkative. Let her get used to seeing you. I know she'll open up. We'll keep it short today and come again tomorrow after you have had a chance to adjust to our time zone."

Whew! Natalia speaks English. That's one hurdle they wouldn't have to cross.

Unlike the view from the air, the close-up of St. Petersburg was an eye opener, offering a totally different perspective. Although the buildings were impressive, either ultra-modern with lots of glass and sharp angles or regal sixteenth century charm, all had dirty, homeless children begging on every corner and sleeping in alleys and train stations. My God. So many of them. How did they live? Armand clutched Cecile's hand a little tighter and hailed a cab to take them to the New Holland Island Orphanage #5.

Butterflies fluttered in Cecile's stomach. She bit her lip, crossed and uncrossed her legs. Were they really doing this? Will their child love them? Will they love her?

Armand pinched her knee. "Breathe, CeCe. You're going to hyperventilate. I didn't bring my brown paper bag," he said, laughing.

She could see the excitement in his eyes. Could he see the terror in hers? "What?" she said, her voice coming out squeaky.

"Calm down, girl. It'll be fine. She'll love us. Trust me."

The driver weaved through the heavy traffic and crossed over a bridge. In broken English, he explained that Peter the Great built the New Holland Island in 1730. "Originally, it was a shipyard and military port, fashioned from Dutch architecture with the red bricks. Later, a fortress, then a prison. The man-made island sat abandoned, vacant for over a hundred years, until the city of St. Petersburg opened it as Orphanage #5 after the Russian Revolution. Three sides are a moat surrounding the nineteen acres, connecting to the Moika and Kryukuv Canals."

Anastasia greeted the receptionist in Russian and showed Armand and Cecile to a room behind the offices. Four straight-backed chairs surrounded a round table. A play area with a braided rag rug and bookcase of toys sat under a massive window that overlooked one of the rivers.

"The rivers and moat shut the children out as much as they protect them from the rest of the world," Armand whispered to Cecile.

Exiting the cab, they were greeted by a tall, older man, extending a wrinkled, aged-spotted hand. "How do you do? I am the director here at Orphanage #5. My name is Alex Tankov." He was well-dressed, except for the plastic pocket protector bulging with pens and his tie, a red and green monstrosity the tail of which hung three inches below his belt. His English was crisp, with a British accent.

Anastasia explained. "Mr. Tankov and I will give you a tour of the grounds, so you can get an idea what life has been like for your future daughter the last two years."

They passed a corridor of rooms with desks and computers. Beyond that, a huge room with high ceilings had rows of long wooden tables with benches. Against the wall, more infant highchairs than Cecile could count were lined up like little soldiers.

"This is the cafeteria." Tankov said. "Currently eighty-three children and forty-six infants live here. They eat in shifts, the girls first, then the boys. "Breakfast is over, and the noon meal just ended for the first group."

They followed Anastasia and the director into a huge courtyard, surrounded by buildings. Playground equipment in fresh spring grass waited for children to use them. A small section of the area had a concrete pad and a netless basketball hoop. "The boys love basketball. Even in the winter, they shovel this clean so they can play," Anastasia said. "The fresh air is good for them."

Armand pulled his light jacket tighter as a sudden wind pushed them forward "What is that building?" He pointed to a round structure that rose several stories higher than the others.

"That holds the Baby Houses. There are two here, with children ranging from infants to three years old. At four, they move to the boys' or girls' dormitories, in those building on either side," said Tankov.

Cecile leaned closer to Armand. "If there are so many babies, why couldn't we get an infant?"

Anastasia heard her and answered, "Russia

does not allow adoption of infants to Americans. It is complicated." She seemed rather defensive.

Cecile blushed, feeling like somehow she had done something wrong. "Is Natalia in one of those?" she asked, her voice suddenly scratchy, giving away her nervousness.

"Not right now," said Anastasia. "She's in pre-school, over there." She pointed to another set of buildings to the far left.

"This is a huge facility," Armand said.

Mr. Tankov nodded. "Yes, twelve acres in all. I'm going to take you to the girls' dormitory first, then we'll return to the office. You'll meet Natalia in the greeting room."

They crossed the courtyard to a rectangular three-story building to the left of the round Baby House. They climbed the wide stone steps to the second floor, passed a playroom with toys stacked neatly in rows and lined along the wall, a computer room with workstations and video games, with books filling a low bookshelf.

Not too bad. It was very clean, albeit a little sterile looking. What was noticeably missing was anything personal. Ten of this, five of that, nothing a child could call their own.

Tankov stopped at the third bedroom. Eight low metal beds lined either wall. The metal headboards were painted in different colors to make the room more cheerful. Most of the beds had identical quilts, but a few had hand-made covers, perhaps heirlooms from a lost family. They stopped at a bed under a drafty window at the end of the room. A blue-painted headboard with a pink and red plaid quilt, exactly like most of the others, covered a thin mattress. Then

Cecile saw it. *A pigeon.* On the flat little pillow, a toy pigeon with gray feathers and a green florescent neck, exactly like the real one in the photo. This had to be Natalia's bed.

Anastasia picked up the toy and held it out to Cecile. "Natalia's been here since she lost her parents and grandparents in a fire. Her brother gave her that pigeon for her fifth birthday, shortly after they arrived here. She takes it everywhere with her. She'd take it to school if the rules allowed."

Cecile caught the frown that Mr. Tankov gave to Anastasia.

Cecile voiced her concern. "Aren't you concerned about splitting the siblings up?"

"Well, naturally, we would love a family to take both of them," said Tankov. "Unfortunately, that doesn't happen often. Nikolai will most likely age out of the system without finding a family. The most we can do for him is to give him the skills to survive on his own. He's already showing aggressive behavior, getting in fights, disobeying the rules."

Any fleeting thought about taking both of them and keeping them together vanished from Cecile's mind. Taking one child would be hard enough, let alone a boy with behavior issues.

In the conference room, they waited with Anastasia while Mr. Tankov retrieved Natalia from the pre-school.

Cecile beat her thumb against her leg until Armand steadied it with a firm press on her hand. Finally, she could see a bit of nervousness in him. He stood and paced the length of the room while raking his hand continually through his hair.

Finally, the door opened, and Natalia followed

the man into the room. She didn't look at either of them but stared across the room at the window. Then she backed away into a corner.

Omigod! There she was. Their daughter. Blond pigtails, much longer than in the photo, hung on either side of her shoulders. Even with her head bowed to her chest, Cecile knew the child was beautiful. She looked tiny for six years of age, but what did Cecile know? Her sister's boys were brutes, sucking from Denny's gene pool. And her nieces in Texas were already teenagers, so she had no bar with which to gauge Natalia.

Anastasia encouraged them. "Get down on her level. Armand's a pretty daunting frame for someone her size."

Cecile sat cross-legged on the rag rug by the bookcase.

Armand squatted on his heels. "Hello, Natalia. My name is Armand." No reaction. He looked at Anastasia. "Does she understand me?"

"Yes, she understands English. She's a little shy. Why don't you pull a book from the shelf? See if she'll look at the pictures with you."

Cecile found one with birds, hoping Natalia would connect it with the pigeons. What was the story of the pigeons? Perhaps the girl would tell Cecile one day. She handed the book to Armand. Thumbing through the pages, he pretended to read the words, but because it was written in Russian, he made up a story to match the pictures.

"One day there was a little bird trapped in a golden cage …."

Cecile watched in silence. Then Natalia lifted her eyes and looked at her. Cecile's heart caught in her throat. "Hi, sweetie. Want to come over here and sit by me?"

Natalia's eyes darted away. They spent the next twenty minutes with Armand making up stories to the Russian storybooks while Natalia never moved from the corner, her arms crossed over her chest, her eyes cast to the floor.

A caretaker arrived, and Anastasia gave a nod. The caretaker said something to Natalia in Russian, and the child scooted quickly out the door without looking back.

"That didn't go very well." Armand unfolded his six-foot frame from the floor.

"Actually, that was quite good," Anastasia said. "You didn't press her, and you stayed down on her level. Very good. If they don't go screaming out the door on the first visit, we consider that a victory. You'll see, tomorrow will be better."

Cecile's only conversation had been one sentence. But Natalia had looked her straight in the eye. What had she been thinking? Did she like what she saw?

Cecile admired the calm Armand demonstrated and his persistence with the stories. "You're good at this. A natural at being a father." She smiled at him.

"I don't know about that. She didn't respond to me. I was just as nervous inside as you were."

Impossible.

Chapter Fourteen

St. Petersburg, Russia

February 2008

The lobby of the Four Seasons Palace Hotel was shrouded in elegance. Cecile spun in a circle staring at the beautiful inlaid ceiling, supported by massive granite columns. Their footsteps echoed on the marble floors, and a porter showed them to the elevator taking them to their suite. She couldn't help but feel guilty about treading past homeless children in the streets to get there.

"Armi, can we afford this?"

He smiled, tucking his arm in hers. "We deserve this. Who knows when we'll get to do something like this again once we are raising children and saving for college tuition? Enjoy it while you can, my princess."

Cecile gawked at the spectacular room with its twenty-foot ceiling, heavy satin curtains framing floor-to-ceiling French doors, and a full living room adjoining the colossal bedroom.

After a luxurious soak in a Roman bath fit for a queen, she lounged with a glass of wine on the private terrace overlooking the lights of St. Petersburg. She rested her head on the satin chaise. "What did you think of today? Of our girl?"

Armand took a sip of the best Russian vodka he could afford. "She's beautiful. I think I'm in love."

"She was afraid. I'd be scared, too. Knowing somebody could take me who-knows-where, without any say-so." She shuddered at the thought.

"I know. I'm not sure how to make this a happy transition for her. CeCe, do you think she is the one for us?" Armand asked. "I felt a definite pull at my heart the minute I saw her."

She was certainly adorable. But where was that motherly instinct Cecile was expecting to feel? "I don't know. Maybe I need more time."

Armand tossed a pillow at her, laughing. "What? Twenty minutes didn't make you fall in love with her?"

Was he kidding? Should it be that instantaneous? Cecile didn't know.

On day two of getting-to-know-you, Armand and Cecile sat together on the rug, hoping Natalia would join them. She stayed planted in the corner for the entire hour. They left disappointed, feeling their visit was again unsuccessful. They'd yet to hear her speak.

Anastasia tried to be positive. "For some children, it is easier if they aren't in their environment. Let's try taking her into the city tomorrow." Anastasia would pick them up at the hotel on the third morning in her own car. The plan was to take Natalia to St. Petersburg to do some shopping and have lunch.

Mr. Tankov brought Natalia to them in the lobby, not in the conference room. "How would you like a trip to the city for some ice cream and shopping?"

Anastasia bent and looked at the somber little girl pressed tightly against the wall.

Natalia shook her head and smoothed the crisp fabric of the yellow jumper that matched her hair.

"Well, we're going to give it a try." Anastasia reached out to take the child's hand.

"Nyet. Not go. Not go." Natalia screamed at the top of her lungs, waving her hands so Anastasia couldn't touch her.

Cecile jumped back in shock. Well, at least they knew she could talk.

"Natalia," Anastasia said. "We're going to do this, so let's not fight it." She reached again for Natalia's hand. This time Natalia let Anastasia escort her out the door and buckle her into the booster seat in the rear, a pouty lower lip leading the way.

Cecile looked at Armand. Oh, boy.

He shrugged his shoulders. "Now we know the trick, be firm."

Cecile doubted it would be that easy, but the trip went better than expected. Natalia followed along, submissive but unattached. She still didn't speak or look directly at either Armand or Cecile. She gave one-word answers in Russian to Anastasia about what she wanted to eat or the flavor of her ice cream, chocolate. The closest to any connection was a giggle when Armand pretended to push the ice cream cone in Cecile's face.

At the end of the visit, they needed time to talk to Anastasia alone. "Is this normal? Her shunning us?" Cecile wanted to know.

"Yes." Anastasia assured them. "She's leaning on me because I am familiar to her. We'll try one more visit before you leave, with you alone with her. I think when she sees that no one is around to communicate for her, she'll respond to you. She understands English, so don't let her convince you she doesn't."

"Do we go ahead with the adoption even if she doesn't respond to us?"

"Of course, the final decision is yours, but she's not doing anything different than what every child in here would do... better than some. You must be prepared for an adjustment period. It could take a few weeks — or a few months."

"Nika," Natalia cried. "A family wants to adopt me." She clung to his arm.

"That's great, Golubka," he said with a smile that didn't quite reach his eyes. "Have you met them?"

Natalia sniffled. "Yes, but I didn't talk to them."

"Natalia." He turned so she had to look at him. "Remember what I said? We want you to find a family. You need to tell them you want to go with them. What if they choose someone else?"

"I don't want to go, Nika. I want to stay with you." She wiped tears with the soft fabric of her toy pigeon. Why couldn't she stay there with Nika?

"I can't take care of you. You know that. Is this a Russian family?"

"No, they are Americans. Is America far away?"

Nikolai let out a deep sigh. "America is very far away. But Americans are rich. You'll have a wonderful home. Were they nice to you?"

"Yes," she whispered. "The papa is funny."

Nika smiled. "See? This is good." His voice wavered. "When? Do you know when you'll leave?"

"I don't know." Natalia collapsed in another flood of tears. "Why can't you come too?"

Nika squared his shoulders and stood. "I told you. I'm too old for anyone to want. It'll be fine. I'm sure we'll have time together first. Remember, I'll always love you and be your brother. I promise. We will see each other again. I promise." If only he knew how that would happen.

Natalia was called from pre-school again the next day. Did that mean they were taking her away already? She hid under the table, her arms wrapped around her knees.

"Come out from there," her teacher prodded. "This is the last day for you to visit with your new momma and poppa. They're going back to America today. Be a good girl and come out."

They were going away. She could breathe again. She crawled out from under the table. Did they not want her? Nika would be very upset. She let the teacher lead her to the conference room.

"There you are," the man smiled at her. "Do you remember my name? I'm Armand. This is Cecile." He nodded toward the woman.

Natalia nodded, slipping into a chair at the table beside them. She knew who they were, and she remembered their names. She still didn't meet their eyes.

"That's better, Natalia," Armand said. "We think you're a very special little girl. We would like you to be our little girl. Do you understand that?"

She nodded, looking at her hands folded on the table.

From the corner of her eye, she saw Cecile glance at Armand. She reached out and patted Natalia's hand. "When we return, we're going to take you on a big airplane to our house in America. Won't that be fun to fly in a big plane?"

Natalia pulled her hands into her lap.

"We have a little dog," said Cecile. "His name is Neptune. We adopted him, too. Do you like dogs?" She pulled a photo of the three of them in a Christmas photo, red caps on each head, even a tiny one over the dog's ear. She set it on the table in front of Natalia.

The little dog looked silly. Natalia almost smiled.

"Do you have a favorite color? We'll paint your bedroom any color you want."

She was not about to answer them.

"Natalia," Armand said. "We understand that you're afraid, and that's okay. We won't let anything bad happen to you. You'll have a wonderful life with us. We'll love you and be your new mommy and daddy."

Natalia curled into herself, wrapping her arms around her middle. She didn't want a new momma and papa.

"Can I give you a hug, Natalia?" Cecile pleaded.

Would it make them go away sooner? She raised one shoulder in a slight shrug.

Cecile lifted Natalia out of the chair and sat her gingerly on her lap. Her lap was nice. It had been

116

so long since anyone had held her, but it didn't feel like Mama or Babushka. Cecile gave a small squeeze and pressed Natalia's head against her chest with her hand.

No, let me go. Natalia jerked her head away.

Armand shook his head. "Too soon."

Cecile loosened her grip, and Natalia squirmed off her lap and back into the chair.

"It's okay, Natalia," Armand said. "There's lots of time for hugs when we get home. Is there anything you want to ask us?"

She shook her head. Would they leave now?

Chapter Fifteen

Chalmette, La.

March 2008

The phone was ringing as they walked through the door. Cecile ran to answer it.

"Well?" Miranda asked. "What did you think of her? Is she as adorable as her picture?"

Cecile laughed at her enthusiasm while trying to calm Neptune who was dancing around her, glad to be home from the kennel. "She's beautiful. But she won't talk to us."

"That's understandable. Don't worry about it. All in good time. I want to know everything you did, how she reacted, what you thought of the orphanage."

"Let us get some shut eye first. We have some serious jet lag. How about getting together Saturday?" Cecile said.

"Great. See you then. I'll bring coffee cake."

Cecile smiled to herself as she hung up the phone. Miranda was quickly becoming more than a family coordinator from the agency. She was their friend.

"The issue of her brother bothers me." Cecile said over coffee the following Saturday. "Do you think he can cause a problem during court?"

"He's only sixteen," said Miranda. "He's not old enough to be legal guardian. He's nothing to worry about."

Armand shook his head. "Maybe not legally, but losing her brother could be very hard on Natalia. Is it right for us to separate them?"

"She's young. Not that she will forget him, but she'll adapt. They always do—or most of the time. Do you think you could handle two children?"

Cecile shook her head. "I'm not sure we can handle one," she said with a nervous laugh.

"She'll be fine," said Miranda. "What did you think of Russia?"

Cecile and Armand spent the next hour telling her about their experiences. They loved the old Russian architecture, but the homeless children on the streets really tugged at their hearts. "Why aren't those children in orphanages, if they don't have a home?" Cecile asked.

"Most of them do have a home, but it is so unstable or violent, they choose the streets. Many Russian parents are alcoholics or addicts. Russia's fight with addiction is worse than America's. If their families can't afford to feed them, some children get left on the street. They think the institutions will pick them up. But without their papers, the street is their only choice. It's very sad."

"They're almost always in groups, like packs of wild dogs," Armand said.

"That's true. They form very tight groups and protect each other from adults that want to harm or abuse them, from the police, even from other gangs of children."

Cecile drummed her fingers on the side of her coffee mug. "So sad."

The ten-day waiting for the final decree dragged on at a snail's pace. Cecile was beside herself with anxiety. What if a different family member emerged and protested the adoption? They would lose her forever. What if they didn't? Would she be a good mother? Ten days came and went with no call.

On the twelfth day, they received the call. "It's approved," said Miranda. "No objections. Natalia is yours."

Cecile could almost see Miranda beaming into the phone. "Omigod! Armi," Cecile shouted to him with the phone held to her cheek. "It's approved! She's ours. She's really going to be ours."

Armand raced into the room, lifting her off her feet, twirling her around. Neptune started yipping and running through his legs. He understood the excitement.

"Hello? Hello?"

Cecile forgot all about Miranda hanging on the line. "Oh, I'm sorry. We're so excited."

Miranda laughed. "Congratulations. Now, go fill that room with things for your little girl."

Armand grabbed the receiver from Cecile's

hand. "Miranda, thank you so much. We'll try to be the best parents ever."

"I know you will. You'll need to book another flight. Fly into Moscow. You'll need to get a new birth certificate for her with her new name, Boudreaux, and a passport from the U.S. Embassy. And her visa. Plan on staying in Moscow three days. Then go to New Holland and pick up your daughter."

"Our daughter!" Armand said reverently. "We'll get our daughter." Then he let out with a huge "Whoopee!"

They had so much to do in such a short time. Superstitious as she was, Cecile refused to buy one thing for Natalia's room until they knew for sure the adoption was final. Now, they had to buy furniture, paint the room, shop for clothes and toys. So much to do…so little time.

Cecile changed her mind on the paint color three times before Armand finally put his foot down. "Pick one, for God's sake." But his eyes revealed laughter. Cecile's dad came from Butte La Rose to help paint while Cecile shopped for little girl clothes and Armand scoured Toys R Us for anything they thought Natalia would like. Armand's parents sent their best wishes from Washington, D.C., and money to fund their return trip with their daughter.

Finally, Cecile looked around the room. It was perfect. She noticed Theresa's Eeyore on the top shelf where Armand placed it after the dry cleaner had cleaned it up. She pulled it down and crushed it to her chest. "You're getting a new sister." She spoke to the ghosts of little Armi, Theresa, and Mariella. "I hope you'll love her, too." She placed the doll on the top shelf in Natalia's closet.

Armand wandered into the room, surveying the results. "Good job, Mom." He kissed her on the cheek. "A perfect room for a perfect little girl."

Cecile crossed her arms. "What do you think about giving her an American name? I was thinking maybe we should change her name to Natalie. Natalie Boudreaux. What do you think?"

"I don't know, CeCe. What's the difference?"

"I think she should be an American. I'm not trying to wipe out her heritage, but don't you think she'd fit in better at school if it didn't stand out that she is adopted. Miranda received a new name when she was adopted."

Armand's eyebrows furrowed together. "Natalie or Natalia, what's the difference? CeCe, are you ashamed of her being adopted instead of your own biological child?"

"No, no." She retaliated. "I only want it easier on her." Was she ashamed she wasn't her birth child? No, of course not.

Chapter Sixteen

St. Petersburg, Russia

March 2008

In the greeting room, Nikolai and Natalia sat melted together into one entity, almost like conjoined twins. At least they'd been given some private time to say good-bye. Nikolai repeated the mantra to himself over and over. Be strong. *This is God's will. This is for the best. Best for Natalia.* That was all that mattered.

"Please, Nika, don't make me go." Natalia sobbed, her little arms like vises around his neck. How did she get so strong? He peeled her arms away and made her look at him. "Golubka, don't be afraid. They'll take good care of you. This is a good thing."

Natalia flung herself around his neck, burying her head deeper into her brother's shoulder. "I don't want to leave you."

He fought the tears that pooled in his eyes.

He could feel her heart pounding against his chest. "Golubka, I'll always be with you in your heart." Pulling her away again, he tapped her chest. "In here. Someday we will see each other again. I promise you."

"How?" She sniffled. "How will I see you again if I go to America?"

Nikolai pinched her chin. "I don't know how yet, but it's a promise. Have I ever lied to you?" *This may be the first time.*

Natalia shook her head, her tears now dissolved to hiccups. She was breaking his heart. Even losing everyone in the fire didn't hurt this bad. That had been out of his control. But this, this was different, like he was giving her away.

"You must believe me. I love you, Golubka. Momma and Papa would want this. Be good...and be happy."

The social worker, Anastasia, stood in the doorway. "It's time, Natalia."

Fresh tears coursed down Natalia's little cheeks.

The lump in Nikolai's throat made his words stick. When he finally could speak, they cut like glass and came out jagged and raw. He pried her arms from around his neck. "It's okay. Remember, I love you. When you get sad, squeeze Ivan, your pigeon, and I will feel it—like a hug, wherever I am. It's time now, Golubka, go with the lady." He stood and briskly walked out the door without looking back.

On the other side of the closed door, he pressed his hands into his face, steeling himself to walk away, to move on without her. Only then did he let it out. Blinded by tears, Nikolai choked on strangling sobs. He slid to the floor, burying his head between his knees. This was good. This was right. He repeated the mantra over and over in his mind, willing himself to believe it.

Natalia held Ivan tight against her chest. *Can you feel it, Nika? I'm hugging you.* Her entire body was shaking so badly she couldn't move, no matter how much Anastasia prodded her along. The couple that would become her new momma and papa was in the director's office, waiting to take her away. What if they didn't like her after all? Or she didn't like them? How would she ever return to Nika?

Anastasia picked her up and carried her the rest of the way. "It'll be okay, sweetie. You're going to be very happy in your new home."

How could she know that? Had she ever been to America? Natalia bit her lip, the tears drained from her face. *Tasha said her family was mean and sent her back. Maybe mine will send me back too.* She squeezed Ivan a little tighter.

"Hello, Natalia," said her new papa. "We are so happy we'll be a family. We have your room all ready for you at home."

Momma Cecile bent down and took her hand. "I know this is scary. But we'll try to make it easier for you." She reached to stroke the pigeon in Natalia's arms. "Is your bird ready to fly in an airplane? It's much too far for him to use his wings."

Natalia jerked the pigeon from Cecile's touch. Ivan would have been able to fly that far if he were real. He was a homing pigeon. He'd find his way home.

The new, complete Boudreaux family waited in

endless long lines that snaked through roped walkways to enter the huge plane. Natalia followed beside Cecile and Armand but refused to be held or touched. As they entered the security area, the guard tried to take the toy pigeon from Natalia's arms and put him in a plastic bin to go through the X-ray machine. She let out a blood-curling scream that hushed the long line and made everyone strain their necks to see what was happening.

"Nyet, Nyet, Ivan." She grabbed him out of the hands of the guard.

Cecile pleaded with the man. "Can't she carry it through the scanner? This is very traumatic for her." Whispering closer to his ear, "She's our newly-adopted daughter, and this is all new and scary for her."

The guard nodded and showed Natalia how to stand in the machine. She followed his instruction, her hands raised above her head and Ivan clutched between them. The alarm went off as soon as she entered the x-ray machine. The guard ran her hand scanner over the child. Nothing. Then she ran it over the stuffed pigeon. Loud beeping emitted from the device. She frowned and asked for a supervisor.

With great effort, they pried the toy from her fingers as she screamed and set it in the x-ray machine. Several guards examined the findings.

"It's the music box inside." The supervisor shook his head, examining the irregular stitching on the belly of the bird. "What shoddy workmanship. Probably done in some sweat shop in China." He handed the toy to Natalia with a huge sigh.

Cecile tried to console Natalia and wipe her eyes and runny nose, but she pulled away. Cecile handed her the tissue. "It's okay. Here, sweetheart, do it yourself."

Natalia wiped her nose and hiccupped through her tears.

Through the long flight, Cecile watched her new daughter sleeping. She wanted to scoop her out of the chair and cuddle her in her lap, but neither the air stewards nor the child would have any of that. The poor thing must have been exhausted from all the trauma. In her sleep, she cried out in Russian. What was she saying? Cecile could only guess.

New Orleans to Chalmette

They stepped off the plane at the Louis Armstrong New Orleans International Airport, with Cecile tightly griping Natalia's hand. The smell. It was the first thing Natalia noticed. America smelled funny. She pulled her hand from Cecile's but followed close beside her. What was that smell? The aroma tickled her nose. She rubbed Ivan's belly under her nose and stifled the urge to sneeze. Posters lined the walls of the corridor, black people with musical instruments, scary looking masks, and bright neon-colored writing. People rushed by, bumping and pushing her along with the crowd. Everything was big, loud, and smelly.

"Come on, Natalie," Cecile said. "We're almost home."

Natalia... my name is Natalia! She looked up at her new momma between the maze of pant legs and swaying hips. Home? This didn't feel like home. She dragged her feet and stumbled forward when the rubber soles of her new Mary-Janes caught on the tile floor.

"Whoa there, Little Bit." Papa Armand scooped her up. She could see down the long corridor to the wide double doors that led out of the terminal. It was better being able to see, but his big arms didn't feel like her Papa or Dedushka. She squirmed to be let down.

Through the outside doors, a hot blast of air hit her in the face. *It's hot in America?* It had been cold when they left St. Petersburg. So many new things to get used to.

A young woman stood on the sidewalk with a grin and a big poster that read, "Welcome Home, Natalia."

"Ahh, you made it!" the lady said excitedly. She gave a big hug to Momma Cecile and reached to pinch Natalia's cheek. Natalia backed away. Papa Armand grinned at her.

"It's Natalie now, Miranda, not Natalia." Cecile corrected her.

The lady made a frown face at Momma Cecile for a second before she smiled at Natalia.

"It's been a long flight, but we're glad to have our girl home." Armand planted a kiss on Natalia's cheek.

She flinched and turned her head away.

"Give her some time," Miranda said. "This is a lot for one little girl to take in all at once. She'll be fine, won't you, Natalia?"

"Natalie!" Cecile corrected, not too pleasantly.

Natalia buried her eyes behind the toy pigeon and didn't answer.

Miranda ushered everyone to a big white car for the ride from the airport to Natalia's new home.

The luggage was piled in the trunk; Papa Armand sat in the front with Miranda while Momma Cecile strapped Natalia into a booster seat beside her. Cecile talked the whole trip, too fast for Natalia to understand everything she was saying. And her words sounded different here, not like the English Natalia learned in school. Momma and Papa talked the same as the Miranda lady, English but different. Did they talk like that in St. Petersburg? Natalia wasn't sure. She tried not to listen when they talked to her there.

Natalia stared out the window at the roads that twisted on top of each other, going every which way, like the trains that run above the city in St. Petersburg, but not the same. Soon the roads got smaller and flat on the ground. Everything looked strange. No rolling hills with beautiful gold-domed churches. Even the cold brick building of the orphanage felt more familiar than this. The landscape was flat, with little color, the ground the color of sand, with only a few green patches here and there. The car turned into what looked more like a village. A lot of houses had big blue curtains on top of them. Natalia wanted to ask why, but she bit her lip and kept quiet. Other houses were falling apart, like they had been thrown in Babushka's mixer. There was grass in front of some of the houses, but the streets all looked alike, with a mixture of new-looking houses and others with the big blue curtains over them. Natalia looked around for a meadow or a stream, like in Suzdal, but she couldn't find any.

"We're home." Cecile clapped her hands as they pulled up to a red brick house. A low, slanted roof supported a wide front porch that ran across the front. Two small windows poked out of the roof.

Cecile, Armand, and Natalia tumbled out of the car.

"I'm going to give all of you some time to get better acquainted without me." Miranda stayed seated behind the steering wheel. "I'll be back once you're settled." The big white car pulled away leaving them standing in the driveway.

"Look, Natalie." Cecile pointed toward the top left window. "That's your window—in your very own room. No more sharing with other little girls."

Natalia, not Natalie. Did the woman not even know Natalia's name? She looked in the direction Cecile pointed, but she was trying to remember her home in Suzdal. She searched hard in her mind. What did the window look like? How did the room she shared with Nika look? The walls were blue; no, they were green. Nika had posters of the Church of the Nativity over his bed, and she had Evgenia Obraztsova, the Russian ballerina in a pink gown. She was balancing on one toe with her other leg up beside her head.

Armand struggled with the suitcases, and Cecile grasped Natalia's hand and pulled her up the wide wooden steps to the front porch.

Natalia looked left and right. Everything looked too perfect. Perfectly positioned flowerpots, evenly spaced along the railing, three white rocking chairs that matched the white swing at the end of the porch. A distant memory surfaced of mismatched stools and weather-beaten red siding on a cottage in Suzdal. *This could never be home.* She wiped tears away with the her fist.

"It's okay, sweetie," said Cecile. "You're going to love it here, I promise. Give it a little time."

Natalia pulled away. Momma Cecile didn't

know that.

Cecile held the door so Natalia could step inside. A little gray bundle of fur with an overly long tail jumped up and licked her in the face.

"Oh, that's Neptune," said Momma Cecile. "He loves everybody. And he's so glad to meet his new sister."

Natalia retreated, but the little pup followed her every footstep. To her right, a wooden staircase rose from a wide-open hallway. Ahead, a room overflowed with furniture, a large, overstuffed sofa, two matching leather armchairs, a huge TV in the corner.

Natalia froze in the doorway. This room was as big as the lunchroom at the orphanage. In a house? Their entire cottage in Suzdal could have fit into this one room.

"Do you like it?" Cecile beamed. "This is your home. Do you want to see your room?" She moved toward the wide staircase.

Overwhelmed, Natalia's mind screamed. *Nyet, Nyet.* This was wrong. Everything was too big, too bright, too new, too foreign. Momma Cecile was too loud. *She wants me to like her. To like everything. I can't.* The dog jumped at her feet, yipping in a shrill staccato. Everyone stared at her. She wanted to run, as fast and as hard as she could, run back to Nika. Her body began to tremble, and she felt a wetness dribble down her leg.

Cecile clapped her hands and pointed up the stairs, babbling. "Your room's up here. You don't have to share with anyone anymore. Do you like pink and green? We made a guess on colors for a girl your age. Fun colors … not for a baby, but a sweet girl like you."

Natalia's legs were wooden. She couldn't move. What if someone saw the yellow stream running down her leg and soaking her white ankle socks, filling her new shoes?

Momma Cecile pulled her up the stairs by the hand. Natalia felt the squish of the wetness in her shoe with each step.

Upstairs, Cecile led Natalia past the open doorway of a spacious bathroom, with gleaming white fixtures and a huge bathtub. "This will be your bathroom," Cecile nodded as they passed.

My bathroom? There was more than one? She wanted to run into *her* bathroom right then and slam the door behind her, to hide her shame of wetting herself like a little baby.

She let Cecile pull her down the hallway. They stopped at a closed door with bright pink and green wood letters. **N A TA L I E** adorning the door. Even though her English was limited, she knew that was not how to spell *Natalia*. The E should have been an A. Cecile opened the door and pulled Natalia in. The decor inside matched the letters with a big white bed with a comforter in huge pink and green polka dots, matching curtains on the wide window and a thick furry green throw rug beside the bed.

"See, Natalie, this is all for you." Cecile giggled with excitement.

Armand stood in the doorway watching, a hopeful look on his face.

"Nyet, Nyet, my name is Natalia!"

The little dog sniffed her wet ankle, then cowered in the corner, his tail between his legs and then scooted out of the room, and down the stairs.

They were the first words Natalia had spoken

since landing at the airport. It was too much. The people, the house, the smells, and the sounds. Her name. She hated it there. She would never call this home. Never. She collapsed on the fur rug on top of the plushy tan carpet, arms wrapped tightly around Ivan, her toy pigeon. *Nika, can you feel me hugging you? Come and get me.* The fresh stream of tears blinded her vision and wet the soft feathers of Ivan. She didn't even try to hold them back.

"Aw, baby," Momma Cecile said. "It's okay. Don't be afraid. We'll make you happy here, I promise."

Why did everyone make promises they couldn't keep? They didn't know how to make her happy. They didn't even *know* her.

"What's that smell?" Papa Armand said.

Natalia looked down at her ankles and the yellow stain on her socks. Would they be angry? Would they punish her?

Papa Armand noticed first. "It's okay, sweetie. I know you just got scared. Cecile, can you get her a clean pair of panties from her dresser. There's been a little accident."

He wasn't mad at all. Natalia grabbed the clean panties out of Mama Cecile's hand and rushed into the bathroom, slamming the door behind her.

"Maybe she needs a little time to herself. Natalia, is that what you want?" Papa Armand's voice was smooth and somehow calming. "Come, Cecile, let her be alone for a little while."

Natalia heard them exit her room.

"We'll be right downstairs, Natalie," Momma Cecile hollered through the bathroom door. "Take your time. Look around your room. Just leave your panties on the tub. I'll get them later. There're toys in the chest and new clothes in the closet. All for you. I'll come get y'all for supper."

Natalia finally breathed when she heard their voices fade away as they went down the stairs.

"I'm not so sure she needs to be alone," said Momma Cecile. "She's scared. Don't you think she needs us right now?"

"She does," Natalia heard Papa Armand say. "But first she needs to get a grip on her own feelings. Be patient. Baby steps. But our little girl is home at last."

I'm not home. I'm not.

Chapter Seventeen

Chalmette, LA.

March 2008

She hated it there. Even with the clean smelling sheets and the pretty curtains, all she wanted was to get home to Nikolai.

Natalia made a vow to herself to never speak English, no matter what. If they didn't understand her, they'd have to return her. Why hadn't she thought of that before? Remember what happened to Tasha? She'd even take a beating if they would send her back.

Natalia had to admit that it was hard to hate the pretty bedspread, the nice new clothes hanging in the closet, the shiny new toys she didn't have to share with anyone. And that little dog was so cute.

Papa Armand and Momma Cecile wanted her to call them "Mommy" and "Daddy."

"Nyet, I want to go home," she shouted in Russian.

Natalia found a black magic marker in the desk beside the toy box. She crossed out the E and added an A to the sign on her door. Beneath it she wrote her name in Cyrillic Russian, Наталья.

When Cecile came to get her for supper, Natalia braced for the anger she knew was coming. The anger that would send her home to Nika.

"Oh, Natalie." Momma Cecile cried when she saw the artwork. She grabbed the marker off the floor where Natalia had dropped it, uncapped. A black smear ran across the plush, taffy-colored carpet. "Look what you've done!" Cecile stared at the carpet and the handiwork on the door. "We don't write on doors—or stain the carpet!"

Papa Armand appeared in the doorway. "What's going on?"

"Look." Cecile waved at the floor and artwork. "That's permanent marker."

"Calm down, Cecile. Perhaps you shouldn't give six-year-olds permanent markers. You're scaring her. She didn't know."

Natalia jutted out her chin and crossed her arms over her chest. She knew … and had made her point.

"Supper's ready," said Papa Armand. "Let's go down. I'll see if I can get that stain out of the carpet and, well … it is her door."

Yes. It was Natalia's door.

"But—" Cecile started.

Armand shook his head and headed for the stairs. Cecile followed behind him, not looking back at Natalia.

Natalia waited in the doorway, undecided what

to do next. Refusing dinner was the plan, but her tummy was growling. Maybe she could eat a little bit.

Small, half-moon bugs floated in a thick red soup. Momma Cecile called it shrimp jumbo. The smell burned the inside of Natalia's nose.

"*Nyet*." She roughly pushed the bowl away, the contents spilling over the sides onto the tablecloth.

"Natalie, it's good. Try it," Cecile pleaded.

"Nyet." *And my name is Natalia.*

"How about a corn muffin?" Armand passed a plate heaped high with small golden cakes. Natalia had to admit they smelled delicious.

When she kept her arms crossed over her chest, Papa Armand set the plate down next to the bowl of shrimp jumbo.

Natalia's stomach grumbled so loud everyone at the table heard.

"That's one hungry tummy." Papa Armand smiled. "You have to eat something."

"Nyet." She shook her head. She eyed the yellow cakes and pressed her elbows into her tummy to keep it from making noise.

Momma Cecile and Papa Armand ate the rest of the meal in silence, glancing at Natalia every few minutes.

"Yum, this is sooo good, Mommy," said Papa Armand. He spread creamy yellow butter across a muffin. He handed it toward Natalia.

She shook her head. No, she would not take it, no matter how good it smelled.

"If you're not going to eat," said Momma Cecile. "You can go to your room."

Natalia pretended not to understand.

Cecile pointed to the stairs and spoke slower and louder, as if Natalia was deaf. "You-can-go-to-your-room."

Natalia jumped from the chair, bumping the table hard and spilling the glass of milk and ran up the stairs.

Curling on the bed, Natalia wrapped her arms around Ivan and twisted the key. "**Korobushka**" soothed her. *Can you feel me hugging you, Nika? Can you?* She could imagine the Church of the Nativity with its green bell-shaped roof along the winding Kamenka River. She pulled the snow globe from her suitcase and watched the white flecks snow down on the tiny cottage. Why couldn't she be a homing pigeon? She'd find her way home across the ocean to Nika. They'd go home to Suzdal, and Nika would be a priest and take care of her forever. She drifted off to sleep.

When Natalia awoke, Neptune was laying on the foot of her bed, curled in a fuzzy ball. The yellow cakes and a glass of milk sat beside her bed. She placed the snow globe beside the plate and eyed the muffins. She picked one up and took a small bite. The grainy texture felt strange in her mouth, and they crumbled between her fingers, leaving yellow crumbs all over the table and floor. But she ate every crumb, except for the pieces Neptune gobbled up from the carpet.

Armand tapped lightly on the door and opened it without waiting for a response.

Natalia watched him eye the empty plate. He didn't comment. "Would you like to come down and watch television with us?" His eyes were soft and pleading.

Be strong, don't give in, Natalia said to herself. *Pretend not to understand.*

He pointed to the TV in the corner of her room. "TV. Want to watch with us?"

"*Nyet.*" She stomped her foot.

He stared at her for a moment with a sad countenance. "All right, maybe another night." He backed out of the room, leaving the door ajar.

Natalia ran across the room and pushed it shut with a loud bang. When she turned toward her bed, there was Neptune, waiting patiently, his tail swishing across the carpet, his little head cocked to one side. "Oh, Neptune, I wish they wouldn't be so nice. They are making this so hard."

A week into the homecoming, Natalia still wouldn't speak or acknowledge her new parents in any way.

"Armi, she hates us." Cecile's exasperated tone spoke volumes.

"She'll come around. Maybe Miranda will have some thoughts."

"It certainly couldn't hurt. Perhaps her insight as a Russian child herself could help Natalie. Let's call her."

Miranda drove from New Orleans the next day. "Some children have a harder time than others adapting," she said. "But I have another idea. I'm going to do an experiment on you; are you game?"

Armand and Cecile exchanged glances. "On us? Okay, if it will help."

Miranda pulled a brown paper sack from the huge Hobo bag on her shoulder. "I'm going to blindfold both of you."

"Blindfold us, why?" Cecile asks cautiously.

"You need to trust me on this. It's an experiment on your senses. You'll understand better what Natalia is going through."

Natalie, Cecile thought but didn't correct Miranda. She sat opposite Armand at the kitchen table.

Miranda took two black scarves from the sack and secured them around their heads, completely blackening out all light.

When next she spoke, it was in Russian. "Esh."

Cecile had no idea what she was saying, so she sat still.

"Esh," she said slower and louder as if that would make them understand.

Butterflies flitted in Cecile's stomach. The experiment made her anxious.

With a click, Russian music filled the room, a strange minor key and singing they could not understand. Pretty, but unfamiliar.

Miranda took Cecile's hand and placed a cup into it. "Esh." Lifting her hand, Miranda raised it to Cecile's lips.

Ahh—food. Now she understood. Cecile smelled the contents of the cup. Her nose twitched. What in God's name was that?

"Esh." Miranda did the same for Armand. She spoke more forcefully and pushed the edge of the cup to his lips.

Cecile's heart was pounding, and she felt the trickle of sweat between her breasts. The music, the smell, Miranda shouting "Esh."

"Okay, okay, I get it." Cecile conceded.

Miranda pushed the cup against her lips again.

Tentatively, she tasted a spoonful of the liquid and winced. "Agh." She felt for the edge of the table and set it down.

Miranda removed the blindfolds. She tapped her iPod, and the music stopped.

Cecile looked into Armand's cup. It was half empty.

"This is the overload that Natalia—Natalie is going through," Miranda explained. "Think of the senses involved here: taste, touch, smell, sound. I couldn't reenact the sight, but with the blindfolds I could block out everything familiar from your view. Think of people that lose just one of their senses. If someone were to go blind or deaf, most would agree that person would need therapy to get accustomed to their disability. All five of Natalie's senses have been altered by coming here. Everything she sees, smells, tastes, hears and touches is different. It's going to take more than a week or two for her to adapt. She's going to mourn the loss of everything she ever knew—before she's ready to accept this as her new home."

She paused and let them absorb what she had said. "Think about giving her something she recognizes to ease her transition. You can't change what she sees, but you can change what she hears—starting with her name. Consider letting her keep her name, Natalia, at least until she's ready to become Natalie. That wouldn't be so hard to do, would it?"

Miranda was right. Cecile saw that now. Maybe someday, she'd want to be Natalie. But for now, she could be Natalia. Cecile could give in on this. She nodded.

"Now, food," Miranda said. "I don't expect

you to change what you eat or how you cook. But wouldn't it be fun to learn a few new recipes... Russian recipes?"

Armand pointed toward the cup. "This wasn't bad. What is it?"

"Borscht. It's a common Russian dish that is probably very familiar to Na-tal-i-a." She said her name slowly, emphasizing her point.

Cecile smiled. "I thought you were coming to change Natalia, not us."

"I'll talk to her, too. I know a little Russian, but my guess is that she knows more English than she is letting on. Per the notes from the orphanage, all the children were taught English along with Russian. I haven't spoken it in a long time, but I minored in it in college, since it was my native language. My adopted parents didn't understand a word of Russian."

Armand stood. "Want me to call her down? She hardly ever leaves her room."

"No," Miranda said. "Let me go to her. That is probably where she is most comfortable."

Miranda tapped lightly on Natalia's door. "Natalia? May I come in?"

Natalia started with surprise. Who was speaking in Russian? She cracked the door and recognized Miranda, the lady who brought them from the airport.

"Hello, Natalia. Do you mind if we talk awhile?" Her Russian was not perfect but good.

Natalia relaxed a little, opened the door and let her in.

Miranda sat gingerly on the bed, her legs swinging back and forth like a child. "Natalia, do you remember me?"

"Yes."

"I understand things aren't going so easy for you here."

Natalia stared down at the hot pink tennis shoes that lit up at the heels when she kicked them against the bed rail. "I want to go home," she said, her eyes filling with tears.

Miranda wrapped an arm around the child. "Natalia, Cecile and Armand want to make this your new home. And they want very much for you to be happy here."

Natalia wiped her eyes on her sleeve. "I'm afraid."

Miranda picked up the little bird and petted his soft feathers. "Who do we have here?" She turned the key and the music of "Korobushka" filled the room. "Aahh. I know this song." She smiled.

"That's Ivan. Nika gave him to me for my birthday. He's like the pigeon Dedushka had at home. I promised Nika I'd keep him forever."

"He's very nice." When she turned it over, she noticed ragged stitches across the stomach. "Oh, it looks like Ivan's had some surgery."

"Oh yes, Nika sewed him so his music box wouldn't fall out."

Miranda pulled Natalia off the bed and danced around the room, singing along with the music. Laughing, she lifted Natalia in the air, spinning around and around.

Cecile and Armand stepped into the room, smiling at the dancing. The music stopped, and Natalia scowled at them. They were spoiling all the fun.

"Can we dance to your music too?" Cecile

smiled.

"*Nyet*," Natalia said as Miranda set her down.

"Play it again, Natalia." Miranda encouraged. "Let's all dance."

"Nyet." Natalia climbed on the bed and tucked Ivan under her body.

Miranda sighed. "Baby steps," she said to Cecile and Armand. Miranda turned to Natalia and spoke in Russian. "I'm going to go now. But I'll come see you real soon, okay?"

Cecile walked Miranda to the door. "We'll have borscht for dinner for you. Maybe Natalia can help me make it. Will you help me, Natalia?" She looked back for Natalia's approval.

Natalia turned away without answering.

Chapter Eighteen

Chalmette, LA.

July 3, 2008

Natalia stared out the window at the patio below her window. The picnic table was covered in a yellow checked tablecloth, bright red and black Mickey Mouse helium balloons were tied to the backs of chairs. All for her seventh birthday party. Papa Lafayette and Grandmother Le Bieu were there. She hadn't had a birthday party since she was four years old. Should she be happy? It did look like fun.

"Come down, Natalia. Everyone's here for you." Cecile called up the stairs.

Natalia sat in her room, petting Neptune and ruffling Ivan's feathers. She had been in America four months. It was getting harder and harder to dislike her new parents. Mommy Cecile and Daddy Armand were being so nice. She could tell they really wanted her to fall in love with them.

Admittedly, she did love it when Daddy Armand pushed her on the swings. And Mommy Cecile always made a special effort to have her favorite chocolate ice cream on hand. And how could she resist little Neptune? He loved her unconditionally, whether she was good or bad.

No, she chastised herself. If she ever wanted to see Nika again, she had to make them send her home.

Natalia made her way down the stairs and out to the backyard where the celebration was already in full swing.

Papa Lafayette carried a huge pot of crawling things with pinchers. "Mmm mmm. We fixin' to get some good mud bugs." He was loud and spoke with an accent Natalia didn't understand most of the time. Papa Lafayette was nothing like her real Dedushka.

Natalie looked into the pot. What were those things? She sat at the long picnic table as far away from the boiling pot as possible.

Mommy Cecile said, "They're called crawfish," and threw some potatoes and vegetables into the pot with them.

Grandmother Le Bieu was scary. They said to call her *Mamère*. She called the ugly red things in the pot "mud bugs." She squeezed her heavy body out of the lawn chair and came over to Natalia. Her dress looked like a big tent, splattered with different color of paint. She wore thick beads of orange and green raindrops around her neck. She placed her hands on Natalia's head and mumbled something Natalia didn't understand.

Get away from me. Natalia shrieked and slipped from under her grasp.

"If you continue to misbehave," Mamère Le Bieu said, "the lou-lou or loup-garous will get you."

Mommy Cecile waved a finger. "Don't, Mamère. Don't tell her the boogey-man or werewolves will get her. You'll frighten her."

Natalia was glad when Daddy Armand took her hand and led her away from the women. His eyes were all lit up, and his smile was contagious. "Natalia, I have something very special for your birthday. Wait right here."

What could it be? Natalia stood planted in the spot. Whatever it was, she would not act happy. *Please let it be a Barbie doll house.*

Daddy Armand ran into the house and returned carefully cradling a large package. He placed his gift in front of her.

Wow. That was a big present. Natalia's tummy did a happy dance. *For me?* The package was wrapped in a huge plastic bag painted with red, blue, and yellow balloons.

"Go ahead, Natalia. Open it." Daddy Armand puffed out his chest, his eyes twinkling with excitement.

Mommy Cecile didn't look very happy. Why was that?

Natalia pulled on the red ribbon and let the plastic fall. A painted wooden horse with shaggy brown yarn bangs and tail, a padded seat and leather stirrups rocked on wooden arches.

Mommy Cecile's hand flew to her mouth.

"Do you like it, sweetie?" Armand squatted down in front of Natalia. "I made this rocking horse for your brother, Armand Junior, but now it's yours."

I have a brother, other than Nika? Natalia looked

around, confused. *Where is he?* The glassy look in Daddy Armand's eyes told her this was very important to him. She touched the smooth surface of the horse's neck and ran her fingers through the soft mane.

Daddy Armand pulled the rest of the plastic bag away. "Here, give 'em a ride? What do you say?"

Natalia wanted to ride that pony. *I could call it Masha, like our pony in Suzdal.* No, she couldn't do that. She had to pretend not to like it, not to like anything or anybody if she ever wanted to see Nika again. But it was such a cute pony. One little ride wouldn't hurt, would it? She climbed on top and leaned forward to make him rock. "Ahh." It was so much fun she laughed out loud.

Daddy Armand's grinned and clapped his hands.

"Come, Natalia, it's time for your birthday cake." Mommy Cecile acted like she couldn't wait to get her off the horse.

"*Nyet.*" Natalia said and rocked harder.

Papa Lafayette, with his bearded chin, winked at her. "Oh, CeCe, she can't rock forever. We haven't even eaten yet. It's her birthday. Let her be."

Everyone resumed their conversations, letting Natalia rock until her bottom was sore. Jumping off, she accidentally knocked it onto its side.

Mommy Cecile gasped, and Daddy Armand lunged for it, but not before it hit the ground.

"It's okay. It didn't break." Armand said with a nervous smile. "Good thing it was on the grass."

The birthday dinner of crawfish, potatoes and vegetables were a hit for everyone except the birthday girl. She picked at the potatoes and veggies, refusing to even try the crawfish.

When the cake was served, everyone sang "Happy Birthday."

"Make a wish" Papa Lafayette said. "If you close your eyes and make a wish, when you blow out the candles, your wish will come true."

Natalia closed her eyes and blew out the candles. *Let me go home to Nika. Let me see my real Momma and Papa, my real Babushka and Dedushka.* She knew that couldn't really happen, that her wish could never bring everyone back, but maybe her wish for Nika could come true.

"Next is her birthday spanking," said Mamère Le Bieu, clapping her hands playfully. "One spank for every year and one to grow on, seven, right?" She reached for Natalia, pulling her by the arm across her lap.

Natalia screamed and bolted from her grasp and toward the house.

"*Tsk, tsk,*" Mamère said as Natalia ran beside Daddy Armand. "Perhaps if I had a lock of her hair, I could cast a spell to make her behave."

"No black magic, Mamère," Armand scolded the Cajun voodoo queen.

The next day, the rocking horse was in Natalia's room next to the toy box when she awoke. What would make them send her to Nika? What could she do? Her hand swayed the pony back and forth on his shiny rockers. The big brown painted eyes stared back at her.

Pushing the pony into the hall, she stroked his back one more time. *I'm sorry, pretty Sasha. It won't hurt, I promise.* She pushed him off the top step. She watched as the sound of splintering wood echoed through the whole house when it tumbled down the stairs, the thin glossy neck split in half. The decapitated horse's head lay halfway down the staircase, the body cracked and splintered at the bottom of the stairs.

Her new parents came dashing out of their room, Mommy Cecile pulling a pink robe about her waist, Daddy Armand dancing on one foot, one slipper on, one clutched in his hand.

"Oh, God," Daddy Armand groaned. "Not the rocking horse. Why, Natalia? Do you have to break everything we give you? That was a very special gift." He stopped on the stairs and cradled the wooden head in his lap.

"That's it!" Mommy Cecile screamed. "I can't take it anymore. Natalia, you are grounded to your room. No TV, and you can eat all your meals alone today. Are you satisfied? Do you have any idea what you've done?"

"Stop, Cecile." Daddy Armand spoke softly. "She has no idea what she did. It has no special significance to her." He turned and looked at Natalia. He looked so sad. "Natalia, what do you want from us? What can we do to make you happy?"

She looked between them. "*Ya hochu domoi* (I want to go home)," she screamed and slammed the door.

Chapter Nineteen

St. Petersburg, Russia

August 2008

Nikolai sat on his lower bunk. She was gone. After everything he's said about wanting her to find a home and a family, now he could be honest. He hadn't wanted her to go.

"Please, Mr. Korkov, I need to speak to my sister in America."

"That's not possible, son. It was a closed adoption. She has a new home now. It's best to let it be, let her forget you."

"No, she will never forget me, nor I her. I need to know if she's happy. I need to tell her that it's okay. That I am fine. Please, Mr. Korkov, I'm begging you."

The caretaker considered for a long while. "I could get in a lot of trouble for this. It's against protocol. I'll have to see if I can find their number.

It won't be easy. You'll have to make a collect call. If they accept the call, so be it. If they don't, that's your answer. Understood?"

"Yes, yes. Thank you. You are a good man."

It took the director a few days to find the number in the system.

"Long distance collect to America please."

"Number please."

"10 + 1 + 504 555-6778."

Ring, Ring. Looking at his watch, he tried to do the math. What time was it in America now anyway? Four in the afternoon in St. Petersburg equaled eight a.m. in Chalmette.

"Hello?" A woman's voice.

The operator spoke. "Collect call from St. Petersburg, Russia. Do you accept the charges?"

Nikolai froze, his heart pounding so loud in his ears he could hardly hear. Would she take the call?

"Hello? Say again?" said Cecile.

"Collect call from St. Petersburg, Russia. Do you accept the charges?"

"Ah, yes, yes. I accept."

"Go ahead. Your call is connected." The operator hung up.

Nikolai breathed. "Ya, I mean yes, I am Nikolai. Natalia's brother."

"Oh my God! It's Natalia's brother." A woman's voice spoke to someone else in the room. That had to be her adopted mother.

"Nikolai." A man's voice this time. "This is Armand. Natalia's father. Is everything okay?"

"Ya, ya. May I speak with Natalia, please?" Please, please. He really needed to talk to her. Was she happy?

"Nikolai," said Cecile. "I'm not sure that's a good idea. Natalia's having a hard time adapting."

Nikolai didn't understand the word *adapting*. "Yes, please. Speak with Natalia now?" He waited. Someone muffled the phone as they talked among themselves. Were they going to hang up?

"Nika, is that you?" a small voice finally said.

Nikolai jumped up from his chair. "Yes, Golubka, it is me."

Natalia was crying. "*Ya hochu domoi.* (I want to go home.) Nika. Bring me home."

"Golubka, I had to hear your voice. Are you happy?" Tears coursed down his cheeks.

"I miss you, Nika."

"Nikolai," a male's voice came on the phone. "I don't think this is a good idea. Natalia is very upset. Goodbye, Nikolai. I'm hanging up now."

Nikolai stared at the receiver. The dial tone buzzed in his ear.

Cecile wrapped her arms around the little girl. "Oh, sweetie, I'm sorry. You can talk to Nikolai again real soon."

Natalia pushed her away. "*Ya hochu domoi!*" She sobbed. *How could they hang up on Nika? I hate them. I really do.*

"I don't understand, sweetie. Speak English please. I know you miss your brother. Tell me how I can make it better for you." Armand tried to put his arms around her, but she pulled away.

"*Ya hochu domoi!*" Natalia threw herself on the floor, pounding fists on the carpet until, exhausted, she curled into a ball. A cold little nose nuzzled in beside her and inched his way into her arms.

Cecile's groaned. "What are we going to do?"

"Call Miranda," Armand said, stooping and rubbing Natalia's back.

She flinched, pulling away from him, even as she wanted to curl up in his arms.

"We can't run to Miranda every time she has a temper tantrum," said Cecile. "We have to learn to cope with this on our own."

When the tears subsided, and her legs no longer felt like jelly, Natalia climbed the stairs. Neptune followed her, but she slammed the door, leaving him whimpering in the hallway. She dropped onto the pink shag rug, grabbing Ivan for comfort, turning the key, and hugging the toy close to her chest. *Can you hear me, Nika? Please, take me home!* She spied the snow globe on the bookshelf, crawled over and reached for it. She shook it, watching her cottage sprinkle with snow. Her chin trembled, and she wiped her eyes on the sleeve of her shirt.

Armand rapped on the door and poked his head in. "Baby, lunch time. Mommy made you potato soup."

Natalia loved Cecile's potato soup, but she wasn't going to eat it. They took her away from Nika. She hated them. At least she wanted to hate them.

Chapter Twenty

Chalmette, LA.

September 2008

Things didn't get better with time. Miranda came on numerous occasions and spoke with Natalia. They tried counseling, but the outbursts and tantrums only got worse. The drab-looking counselor met with Cecile and Armand while Natalia played in the other room.

"Tell me, Cecile, how are you holding up?"

Cecile drummed her thumb on her pant leg. "It's hard. She won't let us near her, emotionally or physically. Is it me? What am I doing wrong?"

"I'm sure you are doing everything you can. How long has it been?"

"Six months. Sometimes I think we are reaching her. Especially Armand. He can calm her down when she's having a tantrum better than I." *Because he's a natural, and I'm a failure. It's the curse. I know it.*

"That's not true, Cecile. She is warming up to you, too." He reached over and clasped his big hand around hers to still her nervous tic.

The counselor smiled. "That's not unlike natural parents, little girls love their daddies and little boys, their mommies. Think of it like their first love."

Cecile dabbed at her eyes with a napkin she dug from her purse. "What about maternal love? Isn't that supposed to be instinctual?"

"Are you saying you don't love Natalia, Cecile?"

"Uh, I don't know. I care for her, but I'm also terrified of her." She tried to make light of the situation.

The counselor frowned. "You're afraid of her? Is she violent?"

Cecile was relieved the subject had shifted to Natalia and away from her own feeling of inadequacy. "Sometimes. Usually more toward herself. I'm afraid she's going to hurt herself. But the other day I caught her with matches, trying to light them. She could've burned the house down."

Armand's head jerked up. "What? When did that happen?"

"Hmm, didn't you say her family died in a fire? She could have a misplaced preoccupation with fire." The counselor wrote on her pad.

Now Cecile was sorry she had brought up the matches. In reality, she was only trying to light the candles on the dining room table. She had made Natalia sound like a pyromaniac. "No, I don't think so, but I'll keep a closer eye on her."

"She's really not that bad." Armand explained. "She's just so sad all the time. My heart breaks for her."

"Has she been violent with you?" The councilor sat poised with a pen over her tablet.

He shook his head, but his eyes watched Cecile's reaction. "Tantrums, that's all. She threw a rocking horse down the stairs, but nobody got hurt. Except maybe my pride. I made it for my son who was stillborn."

"Hmm."

What was that supposed to mean?

The following week, Cecile and Miranda shared a pitcher of sweet tea around the kitchen table.

"Have you tried looking for support groups, either local or online of other adoptive parents?" Miranda suggested.

Cecile stared into the coffee cup she cradled in her hands. "Are there really groups like that out there?"

"Sure" Miranda said. "I can give you a name of a few groups I am aware of, and there are new ones popping up online all the time."

Cecile sighed. "Does that mean I'm not a terrible mother? That it's common to have a problem child not adjusting to adoption?"

"Of course, you're not a terrible mother. I told you in the beginning. Sometimes it just takes a little longer," Miranda assured her. She wrote some addresses on a notepad and passed it to Cecile. "Try these online sites. Just because they aren't local doesn't mean they won't be sympathetic to your plight. Even my parents needed help when they adopted me. I had some issues too. But *ta-daa.*" She spread her arms wide and grinned. "Look at me now."

Cecile giggled. "At least Natalia's in school now. Is it bad that I couldn't wait for September to get here?"

"No. How is that working out? Does she speak English in school?"

Cecile frowned. "The teacher says she does a little. It's only kindergarten, but doesn't that show that it's us that's the problem? Or me? It's me she won't talk to."

"She's talking to Armand?"

Cecile shook her head. "Well, no, not really. But she's better with him. Miranda, I'm really at the end of my rope. I feel like such a failure. Armi goes off to work at the refinery every day and expects me to handle everything. He wasn't here when Natalia bit my arm when I tried to get her out of the bathtub. And he wasn't here when Natalia pulled my good china plates from the cabinet and dropped them on the floor, watching them shatter with amused curiosity. He's missed most of the tantrums. She throws herself on the floor, flailing about and screaming at me in Russian, in grocery stores and shopping malls. He doesn't have to ignore the stares of other parents, wondering why I can't control my own child. I keep waiting for someone to call the police because they think I am kidnapping her."

"Have you talked to him about it?"

"Of course. But I'm not sure he totally believes me. He thinks she's his broken little bird. His words, not mine." Her fingers made air quotes.

"Cecile, it'll get better. Now that she's in school. You'll get a little breathing room, and she'll make friends. You'll see, it'll get better.

Cecile walked her to the door and lingered,

gripping the knob. *I hope she's right.*

Cecile googled "Families of International Adoption." Her heart expanded when she saw so many sites. She clicked on "Families for International Children" and discovered pages for both parents and children. It even had a camp for children that nurtured their native heritage. Another site, Adoptive Family Circle, had a group discussion forum for parents of Russian children. A flicker of hope settled in her chest. Perhaps there was still a chance to save this family.

Some of the sites referenced that many parents shared Facebook pages. Cecile had never been a big fan of Facebook. She always thought of it as a place that only young people talked about teen and tween problems. But she was willing to follow any lead to find some support.

That evening she cuddled next to Armand in bed. "Armi, Miranda gave me some sites for support groups to help us with Natalia. You won't believe how many sites I found on the internet. Some of the discussion groups said parents share their thoughts on Facebook. What do you think?"

He pulled her closer, kissing her temple. "Babe, do you really think we need that? Natalia's in school now. Maybe she only needs more time."

"You think so?" she said, disappointed that he didn't share her feelings. He didn't understand at all. *What about me?* "So, it's just me that's a total failure."

"You're not a failure, CeCe. We haven't reached her yet. Inside that little blond head is a little girl that needs to understand that we love her, and we're not going away."

Cecile stared into the darkness. She was so tired.

If only he was right. What if he was wrong? What if they could never reach her? What then? She fell asleep with her mind full of what if's.

Surfing the 'net became a daily obsession. Cecile connected with dozens of other mothers going through the same issues. Some of them never knew that their foreign adopted children could be such damaged goods, emotionally and sometimes physically handicapped. At least Natalia was physically strong, and Miranda had warned them about issues they could face. Natalia's incontinence had improved since she started school, and her temper tantrums were reserved for when she was alone with Cecile.

"I don't mean to be insensitive," one Facebook friend stated. "But there are alternatives if you can't handle her anymore."

"What kind of alternatives?" Cecile typed back.

"You can place her with another family... sometimes even a Russian family."

She stared at the blinking cursor, incredulous. "We can't give her away. She's our daughter, not a foster child."

"I understand," said Brenda, her new Facebook friend. "I don't mean to imply you would simply give her up. But sometimes it's better—for the child as well—to be in a more familiar environment."

Cecile could not believe what she was reading. "No, no. That's not an option. We need to work harder at helping her adapt. She's doing better since she started school."

":-) Good for you," Brenda typed. "File it for future use if you decide you need it. I know of families that might be willing to take her."

Cecile slammed the cover of the laptop. *What was this woman saying? That I should give her away?* No, no. We promised to take care of Natalia, to be her parents.

Chapter Twenty-One

St. Petersburg, Russia

October 2008

Nikolai saw no reason to stay at the orphanage with Natalia gone. Dimitri had left six months earlier. The odds of a family adopting a sixteen-year-old boy were slim to none. No one would stop him if he walked out and never returned. They had too many mouths to feed, and a boy his age was past the age of adoptability. He could join the throng of homeless youth on the streets of Russia.

There wasn't much to pack, a few clothes donated by the generous people of Suzdal and St. Petersburg, an Orthodox Bible, and the cap Babushka had knitted that he had carried in his backpack for two years.

At least he had one thing to be proud of. The cross was safely hidden away as security for Natalia's future. When the time was right, he'd tell her where it was and she could use it to support herself for as long as she needed, maybe forever. He'd keep his promise to Momma to take care of Natalia.

Dimitri's address was scribbled on a napkin. With no idea if he was still there, it was the only place Nikolai could think of going. He slipped on the knapsack. Should he escape through the tunnels? No, if he was going to leave, it was going to be as a man, walking away head held high, not like a varmint slinking through the dark tunnel.

It was dawn when he crossed the bridge off the island. He looked over his shoulder for a staff member to stop him, but no one was in sight. Electricity surged through his body. It was both terrifying and exhilarating. Although he'd been sneaking off the island for almost two years to work on the docks, it was different knowing he'd never be going back. The small income from the docks was not enough to live on. He followed Dimitri's direction down Canal Griboyedova, looking for his flat above a honky-tonk bar. As he walked the streets, the rising sun reflected off the yellow dome of St. Isaac Cathedral, temporarily blinding him with its brilliance. His heart seized at the thought of attending the Alexander Nevsky Monastery, a mere step away, but unattainable for so many reasons.

If only I could have remained pure ... if only God would forgive me ... if only Momma and Papa had not died in the fire. He shook his head. It was no use laboring over what was and what never would be. He needed to be a man and move on. Without Natalia. Without Momma and Papa. Without God.

Dimitri was one of the few youths that had a

roof over his head. How he made the money for the rent was debatable, and at this point Nikolai didn't really care. The flat smelled of vodka, glue, and dead cockroaches.

"Hey, what's up?" Dimitri squinted through slitted eyes. If he was surprised to see Nikolai, with everything he owned flung over his shoulder, Dimitri didn't show it. His buzz peaked as he slumped over the filthy torn sofa, and he picked at the stuffing poking from the arm, concentrating on the growing mountain of synthetic filament on the floor.

"Got anything to eat?" Nikolai looked around for a refrigerator or cupboard. The apartment was essentially one room with a commode plumbed into a closet.

"Box." Dimitri pointed to a crushed cardboard box. Inside, there was a box of crackers with small teeth marks scratched into the corner and a half empty bottle of vodka. Tiny black droppings peppered the bottom of the box.

Nikolai pulled a few crackers, inspecting them for bite-free pieces and dropped down on the bare mattress on the floor. Stale. He ate them anyway.

Dimitri's head bobbed on to the sofa cushion, either out cold or in a drug-induced coma.

I hope he doesn't die on me. That would suck. He'd have to find someplace else to live. For now, he needed something more substantial to eat. The last rubles from the docks jingled in his pocket. They would barely be enough to buy a small cup of soup. Nikolai wandered into the street. Before he made it a block, he felt something brush against his pants. Spinning around, he caught the small hand still extracting from his pocket.

Nikolai grabbed the young thief by the collar.

"Get your fucking hands off me." A child about Natalia's age cursed at him like a drunken sailor. Nikolai couldn't tell by the rags and wool cap pulled over most of the face whether it was a boy or girl.

"Look, kid. I don't have any more money than you do. Is this how you make it on the street, picking pockets?"

Without answering, the kid sniffed, took off down the street, and disappeared into the stairs of the train station.

Well, he was fast. Nikolai had to give him that.

On the next corner, a vendor was selling *obzhorchiki*. The smell of the fried black bread, fish, and cucumber made his mouth water but the few rubles in his pocket weren't enough. A woman with a small child placed orders for two *obzhorchiki* plus two *kompot*, a non-alcoholic drink made by boiling fruit in water. As the vendor turned to make change for his customer, Nikolai snatched the wrapper with the food from the booth and tore down the street ducking into an alley. His chest was on fire, cutting off his breathing. Huddled in the dark, he puked into the alley. It was official. Now, he was an orphan and a thief.

His heartbeat slowed, and he peered around the corner for the vendor. He was safe. Walking toward Dimitri's apartment on a different street, three small children lay together against a brick wall on a rag mat. The oldest, about ten or eleven, sat between the two younger ones with her hand out begging. He tossed the *obzhorchiki* toward them. Even the orphanage was better than this, but there was no turning back now.

Nikolai sat on the bare mattress on the floor.

His stomach grumbled. Dimitri still had not stirred. Nikolai leaned his head against the battered wall, and his mind drifted to another time.

Natalia's high-pitched laughter filled the air. "Hurry, Nika, it's time for the parade." She cooed at the silver pigeon perched on her shoulder. Dedushka was spreading bird seed in his lofts. When the three of them walked back to the cottage, Momma was singing lullabies as she baked the black bread. Babushka sat in her rocker by the fire with her red scarf tied under her chin. The beautiful town of Suzdal sang with church bells from the arched domes of the cathedrals as Papa loaded the little cart behind Sasha.

Dimitri woke with a start and retched all over the floor.

The spell was broken.

Chapter Twenty-Two

Chalmette, LA.

October 2008

It was a beautiful day for a trip to the park. Natalia walked Neptune on the leash until they reached the playground.

"Want to swing?" Daddy Armand's long legs strode toward the swings. He tied Neptune to a pole safely out of the way and lifted Natalia onto the wooden seat and gave it a push.

Natalia tried not to smile, but the wind raced through her hair. She tipped her head back, toes pointed toward the sky and became one with the trees, close enough to the leaves on the branches to see a little robin's nest nestled in a crevice of branches. If she closed her eyes, she could imagine she was high in the pigeon lofts in Suzdal with the real Ivan cuddled on her shoulder. She heard a laugh behind her. She and Dedushka were laughing about naming the pigeons. Excited, she opened her eyes and looked back. Confused, her face fell. It was Daddy Armand that was laughing, not Dedushka.

Nyet, Nyet, I want off. I have to stop. Stop – stop the swing. She let go of the chains.

Not noticing she had let go, Armand gave her another push.

Suddenly, there was nothing beneath her but air. Natalia landed face down in the dirt, her arm caught under her at a strange angle. *Whoosh.* She couldn't breathe.

"Natalia!" Armand screamed at the same time air returned to her lungs and she let out a blood curling wail.

"Oh, my God, Oh, my God!" screamed Cecile. Through the pain, Natalia saw Cecile run toward the swings to reach for her as the swing kept swaying and knocked Daddy Armand squarely in the back of his neck.

He flinched but didn't miss a beat as he lifted Natalia into his arms. "Quick, Cece, get the car. I think her arm is broken."

"Hurts, it hurts," Natalia cried.

"I know, baby, I'm so sorry. Daddy didn't mean to push you off. I didn't know you had let go. It's going to be okay."

"Nika." Natalia sobbed into Armand's shoulder, holding her left arm out at an odd angle.

Cecile raced toward the car. Neptune was barking and pulling on the leash, still tied to the pole. Cecile retraced her steps, loosened the leash, and picked up Neptune as Armand carried the screaming Natalia.

Leaving Neptune in the car with the windows cracked open, they rushed into the emergency room which was a whirl of activity. They waited behind curtain B for what felt like an eternity before a doctor finally saw her. Armand and Cecile circled the cot Natalia lay on, Armand wiping strands of hair off her forehead and apologizing over and over. Cecile stroked her good arm while Natalia whimpered in Russian. The orderly whisked her off for x-rays and confirmed her broken arm.

With her arm set, she came home the same day, okay but groggy from the medication. Cecile painted Natalia's cast pink to try to put a smile on her face, and Armand drew little birds all over it. But Natalia's eyes were clouded with a sadness they could not clear.

"Maybe we should let her talk to Nikolai again." Armand said. What else could they do to cheer her up? "Perhaps I was wrong not letting him talk to her. We should let them have weekly calls."

"I don't know," Cecile said. "How will that help her move forward? There's a reason the adoption agencies do closed adoptions. Clean break—fresh start—that stuff."

"Well, the fresh start doesn't seem to be working. I'm going to call the New Holland Orphanage." Armand reached for the phone.

The news was not good. Nikolai had walked out of the orphanage and not come back shortly after his phone call to Natalia.

"Didn't you call the police? You can't leave a child out there alone, can you?"

The director of New Holland sighed. "Mr. Boudreaux, there are thousands of children on the streets of St. Petersburg. The police can't take the time to search for one missing orphan. He was almost ready to age out anyway. He would have ended up there sooner or later."

Armand hung up the phone in shock. The Russian homeless children situation left a lot to be desired. New Orleans was not immune to having their share of homeless, but the idea of thousands of children living alone on the streets was incomprehensible.

Cecile had only heard his side of the conversation. "What is it?" she asked.

Armand hung his head. "He's gone."

Miranda, their pediatrician, and their pastor all told Armand and Cecile that Natalia was making progress, and that attachment issues were to be expected with adoption. She demonstrated some of the symptoms of RAD but not all. Was that supposed to somehow give them comfort?

Cecile knew that Natalia was not the only one with attachment problems. Try as she may, something was missing. Something deep in her heart. If she told Armand how she really felt, it would be an admission of defeat. Why did she feel so different toward Natalia than she would have with Armi Jr., Theresa, or Mariella? Or would she have? Would she have been a failure to them as a mother as well? She'd never know. It was the curse. She was never meant to be a mother. "Armi, how can you be so relaxed with this situation."

"Relaxed? Hardly," he answered. "CeCe, of

course, it's different with Natalia. And yes, this is more difficult than I expected. But different doesn't have to mean wrong. She's still adjusting to us. If anyone should feel bad, it should be me. I pushed her off the swing, for God's sake."

"That was an accident, and Natalia knows that. That's not it." She fought the impulse to rap her thumb on her leg. "It's not only Natalia. It's me. I keep trying and trying, but I am not connecting with her on the maternal level I should. Something's missing — the motherly instinct. What's wrong with me?"

"Time, CeCe. Give it more time."

Time wasn't going to take away the curse. She should go to Maimre.

Miranda suggested attachment therapy, which consisted of one-on-one classes to strengthen their relationship. Cecile joined a Mommy-and-Me Yoga class with Natalia. While other little girls quietly cuddled with their mothers in relaxation poses, Natalia sprinted around the room like it was a gymnasium. After the third session, the instructor suggested that perhaps this was not the right avenue for them.

After the cast came off, Armand tried swim lessons with Natalia. She hid in the locker room and refused to come out. Armand went in after her. She shrieked and fought him until he agreed to leave with no lessons.

The county social worker tried to work with them, both as a family and in individual sessions. Natalia showed no signs of remorse for her outbursts and instead saw the visits as an avenue for attention. She dragged the social worker around by the hand, pointing out things in the room and hanging on to her like a lost waif.

"This child appears to suffer from lack of attention. Are you giving her confirmation that she is loved?"

Armand almost threw the woman out on her heels. "Are you kidding me?" He pounded his fist on the wall. "Not enough attention? Our whole world is consumed with giving her attention."

"Take a break," Armand said to Cecile one Saturday. "We'll be fine. Buy yourself something, get a pedicure, or go to the library. Go, I've got this."

Cecile welcomed the respite, but checked her watch continually, wondering how things were going at home. It was nice not to deal with the temper tantrums or searching frantically up and down aisles at the grocer's when Natalia wandered away without a word.

"How did it go today?" she asked as she dropped the bags on the kitchen counter with a contented smile on her lips.

"Fine, she's up in her room." Armand sat at the desk going over the piling medical and therapy bills. "I tried to get her to join me for some Saturday cartoon time, but she wasn't buying it. I'll go up and get her. Let's go out for dinner, a family night out." He headed up the stairs as Cecile put the groceries away. His heart sunk at what he saw. "Oh, no. Natalia, why did you do that?"

What now? Cecile climbed the stairs.

In Natalia's room, Armand stood with his head dropped to his chest, a limp blue leg with stuffing falling out in his hand.

On the carpet, stuffing and blue material, a

button eye, and a droopy tail were scattered everywhere. Theresa's Eeyore doll. It had sat on the top shelf in Natalia's closet since he had it dry-cleaned. He thought that someday he would tell Natalia all about the three babies that came before her. How did she even reach it?

"Oh, Natalia. Why would you do a thing like that?" asked Cecile.

Natalia pointed to Neptune who jumped up and licked her face.

Armand crossed his arms across his chest. "You're going to blame this on Neptune? How do you suppose he got it down from the top shelf in the closet?"

She didn't answer. Not that anyone expected her to.

After the Eeyore incident, Cecile surfed the web, looking for some empathy from other parents also struggling with their adopted children. Her Facebook friend, Brenda, popped on the chat line.

"How're you hanging in there, Cecile?"

"Oh, Brenda. It's awful. Natalia's destroyed everything of value in the house, and no matter what we do, we can't get through to her. I can't do this anymore."

As soon as the words appeared on the screen, a flood of emotions washed over her. Was she really telling a perfect stranger that she was a failure at being a mother? She sobbed, her hands trembling over the keys.

"You still there?" Brenda typed. "Call me." Her phone number appeared on the screen.

Cecile punched the numbers into her cell phone.

She took a deep breath. It helped to be honest with her emotions. "Thanks, Brenda. When I try to talk to Armi about this, he tells me she just needs more time. I feel so helpless. And things are getting tougher between the two of us. She's tearing our marriage apart."

"Is she speaking English?"

"Not to us. Her kindergarten teacher says she speaks to her and the other children in English. But to us, she only speaks or, I should say, screams in Russian."

"Have you tried therapy?"

Cecile let out a bitter laugh and rapped her fingers against her jeans. "Yes. We've done Mommy-and-Me Yoga. Armand tried swim lessons with her. She had a major meltdown. We did family counseling. We've made no headway. The only person she connects with at all is our home study counselor from the agency. And that's only when she speaks to her in Russian."

"That's rough. Do you think that she'd be better off in a Russian home."

Cecile paused. This was the second time she'd brought that up. "I don't know. But I can't just give her away."

Brenda didn't respond.

"Brenda, are you still there?"

"Yes, I'm here. There's a chat room you might want to look at. On Yahoo. It's called Adoption through Disruption."

"What is it?" Cecile asked cautiously.

"A placement service for children that can't acclimate to their first family. They place the children with new families where they are better suited. Like in your case, a Russian family. It's called rehoming. You can post information about your child, and parents looking for children will respond."

"You mean they advertise their children? Sounds horrible. Is it even legal?" Incredulous.

"In some states, it's a misdemeanor to advertise, but it's essentially a private adoption. Nothing illegal about that."

"I don't know, Brenda." The conversation made her skin crawl. "I've got to go. I'll look into it." She hung up, disturbed that she was even considering it. Armand would never go along with something like that.

Could she really do that? Give away their child? That was insane. What kind of monster would Cecile be? But what if Brenda was right? What if Natalia would be happier with another family? Were they being unfair to Natalia, making her miserable because Cecile couldn't cut it as a parent?

A week later, she logged onto the Yahoo chat rooms and found *Adopting through Disruption*. The organization was impressive. Other desperate adoptive parents posted notes about children they couldn't care for. Those parents were exactly like them, beyond their limits. They shared how difficult it was to handle a child that didn't understand their language or suffered from emotional and psychological scars they hadn't anticipated. Cecile no longer felt alone. Some had it even worse, with children with physical disabilities they were not aware of at the time of adoption. All international adoption agencies were not as forthright as Hope had been. Unlike Natalia, some children had clear-cut symptoms of RAD.

Cecile breathed a little easier. *At least they prepared us, even if we're not handling it as well as we had hoped.*

There were new adoptive parents on the chat as well. Parents looking for children, many foreign born and speaking the languages of these children. Some already had an adopted child through Adopting through Disruption and were willing to take another.

No one judged. Finally, someone understood the endless attempts to make a home for Natalia only to fail at everything they did.

"Is this for real, a legit organization?" Cecile typed.

"This is a private adoption," someone responded. "There is no government or welfare department involved. Thousands of children have been rehomed through this or similar organizations. It is a win-win for everyone."

"What would we have to do—if we even considered it?"

"Through this site, you will connect with couples wanting to adopt a child like yours. Sometimes, if the distance is substantial, a facilitator will help transfer the child from one family to the other."

"Would we know where our child is going and with whom?"

"Certainly, you will select the family from the requests. You are free to check their backgrounds, whatever makes you comfortable."

"Is there a cost?"

"We don't sell children. That's illegal. But if there are transportation expenses, you would be responsible for the child and the facilitator's travel costs."

"How are the children legally transferred?"

"A notarized Power of Attorney is required to legally transfer the child to his or her new parents."

That was all? A Power of Attorney and a child was gone? This was wrong, so wrong. Cecile scanned the various posting for parents looking for children. There were six specifically asking about Russian-born children. One wanted only a baby. Three others asked for boys. That left two that had an interest in a six-year-old Russian girl.

She clicked on the first family bio. Katya and Rolan, no last names provided, ages thirty-six and forty-eight. Both born in Moscow, immigrated here in 1997.

"We have two boys of our own and one boy adopted through Adoption through Disruption. Have always wanted a little girl."

The attached photos revealed a stern looking couple, very European looking with no make-up and plain, conservative clothing.

She clicked on *Reply to this bio*. "Katya and Rolan, We have a six-year-old Russian girl that will not adapt to our family. Please contact us so we can speak in person. Cecile and Armand."

She left a phone number. Her pounding heart pulsed in her ears.

She clicked on the next family: Polina and Maxim, ages thirty-four each. "Russian couple seeking a little girl of similar ancestry. Unable to have children of our own. This is our first adoption."

The attached .jpg showed a professional photo of an attractive young couple handsomely dressed, staring lovingly into each other's eyes.

Cecile's heart skipped a beat. Their situation was so similar to their own. Was this the ideal home for Natalia? Young, eager, same language, childless.

She clicked on their *Reply* button and wrote a note comparable to the one she'd sent to Katya and Rolan. There was nothing else to do but wait for responses. She hoped her instincts were right, that Polina and Maxim were the right match.

It took less than four hours to receive responses from both families. Katya and Rolan's English was very limited. Cecile quickly became frustrated with the communication and left them a vague response.

Polina and Maxim's response was intelligent and witty. Polina was warm and easy to talk to. They explained that they were both college grad-uates from the University of Miami and lived in the Miami Shores section of Miami, in a primarily Russian neighborhood. They co-owned a Russian delicatessen with Maxim's parents. They were both natural-born citizens of the US, though their parents were Russian immigrants.

Cecile liked them immediately. They provided their last name and invited her to check their creden-tials online or with a private investigator.

They spent over an hour chatting about their life. They asked lots of questions about Natalia, showing genuine concern for what she was going through. Cecile was honest with her frustration in connecting with their daughter.

"The poor little thing sounds scared to death. Not that we are experts, but we've been told that some children can never adapt to a household totally different from theirs. How old was Natalia when her parents died?"

"Four years old. Then she was in the orphanage in Russia for two years. She really is a darling little girl. But she's so unhappy." Cecile choked on the words. It was hard to admit she failed her daughter.

"It's not your fault. We'd be very good to her. And we're patient. I understand how hard this is. We want you to be sure this is what you and your husband want to do."

Cecile hesitated. "I haven't discussed this with my husband yet."

Silence on the other end of the line. "Oh, you must both agree this is the right thing for you and the child."

"Oh course. We'll keep in touch. Thank you for being so kind."

Later, Cecile curled behind Armand in bed, spooning his body.

"Hmm. You want some of this?" He had laughter and anticipation in his voice.

"And if I do?" She licked his ear.

"Don't tempt me, woman, unless you are willing to go through with it." He rolled onto his back and pulled her on top of him.

When they finished making love, they lay in a sweaty pool, heaving with exhaustion and satisfaction.

"Babe, there's something I want to talk to you about?" she said softly into the darkness.

"Now? When I'm too spent to resist? You're a wicked woman." He tucked her under his arm.

"Yes. I think we need to consider that Natalia will never be happy with us."

She felt his body go stiff. "CeCe, what are you saying?"

"Maybe it's time to think of other options—for

Natalia."

"What options?"

"There's a place ..." Cecile said softly.

"What kind of place?"

"Well, it's really an organization. They call themselves Adoption through Disruption. The process is called rehoming. They place adopted children with new adopted parents."

Armi leaned on his elbow, looking down at her, the moonlight from the window casting a light across her face. "You can't be serious."

She sat up, pulling the comforter over her breasts. "I am, Armi. I can't do this anymore. And I don't think Natalia can either. She deserves better."

"Better than us? Are you saying we're bad parents?"

"Not you. You're terrific. But we're failing—no, I'm failing at this. I wasn't meant to have children. God was trying to tell us that when we lost the others." *It's the curse.*

Armand didn't speak. He fell against the pillow, staring out the window at the stream of moonlight.

Cecile waited ... and waited ... and waited. "Say something, Armi. What do you think?"

In the tense silence, the only sound was the whirling of the ceiling fan.

Armand wrestled with the demons in his head. Was Cecile right? Would Natalia be happier with another family, a Russian family? His heart broke at the idea. He loved Natalia, even if it was not reciprocated. Armand and Cecile talked about it for several nights in hushed whispers after Natalia was tucked in bed.

Finally, he agreed to look at the Yahoo chat room, *Adopting through Disruption*. He had to admit they were the first to understand what they were going through. It was comforting to know so many other families were out there going through the same thing. Even Miranda did not understand.

Cecile showed him the picture of Polina and Maxim Borgov and relayed all the information about them that she knew. Armand agreed to a Skype video chat with them.

"It's a pleasure to meet you." Maxim smiled into the camera. "Ask us anything. Honest."

Armand didn't smile at the camera. "Why haven't you gone through a traditional adoption agency like we did?"

Polina brushed a dark curl out of her eye and attempted a smile, but a deep hurt crossed her brows. "We did. Went through the home study, the Dossier, all of it. They found a child for us, and we went to Russia and met her. She was beautiful." A single tear escaped her glassy eyes. "But during the waiting period, a distant relative claimed her. We were devastated."

Cecile pressed her hand to her face. "Oh no. That's horrible. I was afraid that would happen to us too."

Maxim said, "We didn't want to wait another year, if we didn't have to. And someone told us about Adoption through Disruption. Like you, we were skeptical. Then some friends of ours adopted a beautiful little boy through them. It happened quickly and easily, and the child is happy and adjusted to his new family. It turned out wonderfully for everyone."

When they hung up from the video call, Armand

scoured the internet for information on Maxim and Polina Borgov. He googled them, checked LinkedIn. He paid for a complete background check on People. com. Good credit, no police records, US citizens, owned their own business. Everything they had said appeared to be true.

"What would we tell Natalia?" he asked Cecile. His heart ached from deep inside, almost worse than when they lost the newborns. "If we are really considering this, how do we make her understand? Should we have Miranda come talk to her, help her understand she'd be going to a Russian family?"

In the morning Cecile tried to reach Miranda. She was away on a two-week vacation with her parents in Scotland. It was either wait for her to get back or talk to Natalia themselves.

Chapter Twenty-Three

Chalmette, LA.

February 2009

Natalia sat in her room, playing with Ivan and the Barbie doll from the orphanage and the new ones in the toy chest. She let the Barbies ride on Ivan's back. He didn't mind, and he hardly let them fall when he flew over the bed and onto the window seat.

"If I were a homing pigeon like you, I'd fly high, right out that window into the sky and go to Russia," she said to Ivan. "Nika and I would return to Suzdal. And when we grew up, Nika would become a priest, and I'd give lectures in the church, just like Momma."

Cecile rapped on the door, and they entered, hand in hand. "Natalia. May we come in?"

"What are you playing?" Armand asked. His voice sounded funny, kind of far away.

Natalia pretended not to understand and threw

the Barbies in the chest.

Cecile sat on the floor beside Natalia and lifted her chin, so she had no choice but to look at her mother. "Sweetie, we want to talk to you about something."

Natalia didn't answer and pulled her face out of Cecile's hand.

Cecile sighed and retreated. "I know you're not happy here. Daddy and I have tried very hard to make you a part of this family. I wish we knew how to fix it for you."

You can't fix it. I want to go home to Nika. Natalia turned her back and twisted the key on Ivan's stomach.

"Natalia," said Armand. "We need you to understand. We found you a new family. A Russian family where you will be happy."

Natalia spun around and stared at Armand, and then Cecile. Did he say that she was getting a new family? In Russia? They were sending her home? She could see Nika? Maybe he would come and live with her and her new family before he went into the monastery. She jumped up and threw her arms around Cecile's neck, a huge grin spreading across her face.

Cecile, caught by surprise, fell backward onto the floor. "You understood that? You want to go to your new family?"

"Ya, ya. Thank you," Natalia said in Russian, then again in English, "Yes, thank you."

Both Mama Cecile and Daddy Armand had tears in their eyes. They didn't look happy, but Natalia danced around the room with Ivan. She was going home.

Chapter Twenty-Four

Chalmette, LA.

Feb. 17, 2009

It was decided. Darlene, the facilitator, instructed Armand to bring Natalia to Mobile, Alabama, where the disruption would take place. She'd fly with Natalia from there to Miami to meet her new parents, Polina and Maxim Borgov. "It's better that you don't make the exchange," she said. "A clean break is best for everyone. Once she is settled, you can check on her, even talk to her if you want, but give her a little time to get adjusted first."

Armand dreaded the hundred and forty-mile drive. What would he say to her when it was time to let her go? What was she thinking or feeling? Did she understand what they were doing?

When Cecile and Natalia joined Armand in the garage with her suitcase and backpack filled with

Natalia's things, his heart caught in his throat. They could still call it off. He wanted to say *No, we're not doing this*; instead, he silently lifted the suitcase into the trunk. He had the Power of Attorney, notarized with their signatures in his pocket and the thousand dollars in cash to pay the air fare to take Natalia and Darlene to her new parents.

Cecile strapped Natalia in the booster seat in the rear and slipped into the passenger seat up front while Armand slid behind the wheel. He looked through the rear-view mirror at their daughter. She looked so happy. Would she even miss them?

They pulled out of the driveway. Ten minutes down the road, Armand's cell phone rang.

"There's been a change in plans," the facilitator, Darlene, said curtly.

"What kind of change in plans? Don't the Borgovs want her now?" he whispered into the phone.

"There has been a change in the exchange site. You don't have to drive to Mobile. I had to make an unexpected trip to New Orleans. Bring her to me on Toulouse Street in the French quarter."

He slammed the car in park and leapt from the car. He walked out of ear shot of Natalia. "What's the meaning of this? It's a week before Fat Tuesday for God's sake. We can't bring a child down there in that mob of people." A flicker of hope fluttered in his belly. Good, this gave him a reason to back out.

"761 Toulouse Street in one hour or the deal is off. And I'll need two thousand now for the airfare." The line went dead.

Armand slammed his fist on the hood. There was no way he was taking Natalia to the French Quarter during Mardi Gras. It would be a zoo down there for another full week. Toulouse was right on the parade routes. Anything could happen to her. And now they wanted more money? The deal was off.

Cecile opened the car door and turned to look at Natalia. "Stay right here, sweetie. Mommy and Daddy need to talk." Did Natalia even know what she was saying?

"Armi," Cecile brushed her hand over her husband's arm. "What is it?"

He repeated what Darlene said. The look of relief was all over his face. He wanted to take their child home and forget all this nonsense.

"Polina and Maxim Borgov are waiting for their child. We can't change our mind now," Cecile reasoned.

Armand pinched his lips together for a minute. "She is not their child yet. I don't feel good about this. Something's wrong."

Cecile pointed to the cell phone in Armand's hand. "Well, let's call them then."

Armand thought about it for a minute. "Okay, I guess. I don't like this Darlene woman, but maybe if I talk to the Borgovs …"

He hit the speed dial where the number was saved and hit the speaker button.

Cecile looked back at the car. Natalia was humming along to the music box in her toy pigeon, tucked under her chin, cradled at her throat.

"Hello?" Polina answered on the second ring.

Cecile breathed a sigh of relief. "Polina? We received a phone call from Darlene that the exchange location has been changed. We were concerned that there was a problem at your end."

187

"No, no. We got the same call from Darlene. She said she was picking up Natalia in New Orleans instead of Mobile. She said she'll arrive three hours earlier this way, and you wouldn't have to drive to Mobile. We're very excited. Is everything okay there? Is Natalia all right?"

Cecile looked again at Natalia, who waved to her from the window. "Yes, she's right here. We were already in the car, ready to drive to Mobile when Darlene called. So… you still want her, right?"

Polina's enthusiasm was obvious. "Yes, oh my, yes. We have everything ready for her."

Armand hesitated. "Okay then. Are you sure everything is fine?"

"Armand, Cecile," Polina spoke softly into the phone. "We will love her, we promise."

Armand saw the tears well up in Cecile's eyes. He knew that she blamed herself for this. But it wasn't her fault. This was best for everyone. He kept telling himself that over and over.

"We know." Armand forced down the lump in his throat. "We want what is best for Natalia. We'll talk soon." He hung up and looked at his wife. "So, you think we should go through with this?"

"Yes," Cecile said. "You heard her. Darlene called them, too." She placed a hand on his arm. "It'll be fine, Armi. We'll get through the crowds, and Darlene will take Natalia to the airport. She'll be out of the throngs in no time."

Armand looked in the car window at the little girl, happily oblivious to any drama going on around her. He hung his head in defeat and dropped behind the steering wheel. It still didn't feel right. Why wasn't Miranda around to ask? He looked at his watch. It was technically not yet happy hour on Bourbon Street. Not that it mattered. The drunken brawling crowd of the French Quarter had been going strong for the two weeks leading up to Mardi Gras.

They stopped and withdrew another thousand dollars from their savings, then drove west, parallel to the Mississippi River. When they crossed the Claiborne Avenue bridge of the Intercostal Waterway, traffic came to a dead stop. The revelers extended for miles outside of the French Quarter. Luckily, the parade wouldn't start until after sunset. They'd be out of New Orleans by then.

They parked on Esplanade Avenue, the closest they could get to Toulouse Street. Walking was their only option. Armand pulled the small suitcase from the trunk and slung the backpack over his shoulder. Cecile took Natalia by the hand, and they weaved their way through the crowds of people. A costumed person, male or female, totally indistinguishable, jumped out in front of them dressed in an iridescent purple bodysuit with flowing gold sequined sleeves. The headdress and masque with huge ostrich plumes of matching colors made him look ten feet tall. He screeched something in Creole that even Cecile couldn't understand and proceeded to dance in a frenzied circle around them. Natalia shrunk against Cecile's skirt in terror.

"Back off," Armand shouted. To separate them, he stepped between the masquerader and Cecile and Natalie. "Move along before you regret it."

The reveler shrugged and continued down the street, jumping out at the next innocent bystander in the sea of outrageous costumes and masked merrymakers.

Cecile picked Natalia up in her arms. "It's all right, sweetie. They won't hurt you. They're having a big party."

Natalia pressed her eyes tightly shut and gripped tighter to Cecile's neck.

Cajun and jazz music blasted from open windows on every block. The combination of music, costumed throngs of people and smells of spicy food created a surreal calliope of sights and sounds.

761 Toulouse Street was two blocks from the parade route. The three-story building housed three apartments, one on each floor. Balconies with wrought iron railings ran the entire width of the front of the building on the second and third floors. Each floor's siding was painted a different color, reminding Armand of a triple layer birthday cake with different colored frosting.

Armand rang the bell for the lower-level property.

An obese, slovenly-dressed woman in cheap black polyester pants with frayed cuffs that dragged over dirty tennis shoes answered the door. A dirty T-shirt covered her rolls of fat but didn't quite cover the elastic waist band. She puffed heavily on a cigarette that dangled from her dark red painted lips.

Armand stepped back, "Are you Darlene?"

"Darlene who?" She blew smoke into his face.

"From the adoption agency?" Alarm registered in Armand voice.

"Never heard of her." The woman attempted to shut the door.

A top-heavy woman with a non-existent derriere stepped onto the balcony from the second story. Her startling white breasts, spilling from her bustier was the only contrast to her ensemble, all black, including stringy blue-black shoulder length hair. A black mask covered her eyes as she called over the railing. "Be right down." She disappeared through the glass French doors.

"You're late." The masked woman said as she sauntered down the stairs. "Our plane leaves in two hours for Miami, and we have to get through security. Did you bring the money and power of attorney?" She didn't even glance at Natalia.

Armand pulled Natalia close. "Are you Darlene? Traffic was heavy. Why the mask?" He turned to Cecile, his eyes pleading with her. "I don't like this," he whispered.

Darlene gave a short laugh and snorted through her nose. "It's Mardi Gras, haven't you heard?"

"Well, I'm not giving my daughter to someone I can't even identify. This is a mistake." He turned to leave.

"Don't want the disruption? Suit yourself." Darlene shrugged and lifted the mask and tossed it on the steps. It revealed a homely, nondescript middle-aged woman.

Cecile shook her head. "We've talked about this, Armand. This is best for everyone, especially Natalia."

"Look," he said. "I know what we agreed, but this is crazy. Look at her. We can't give Natalia over to someone like this."

Darlene waited, pulling another cigarette from her pocket and lighting up from the butt of the last one.

Armand knelt in front of Natalia. Her deep blue eyes penetrated his soul. He inhaled her scent, touched her soft cheek, and ran his hands through her soft hair. "Natalia, I don't know how much of this you understand. Do you want to go live with another family… a Russian family?"

Natalia nodded. "Yes."

Armand resigned. "Okay, we want you to be happy." He looked at the facilitator with pure disdain. "We'll be checking with the Borgovs real soon." He hugged the child again. "Natalia, we'll call, email, and send letters. And if ever…ever you need us, you can call us. Here is our number." He tucked a piece of paper with their contact information into her backpack. "We'll mail the rest of your things to you after you get settled. All those things in your room … they are still yours. I promise." He pulled her into his arms and held her tight. He tried to fight the tears, but they coursed down his face.

Natalia patted his shoulder and offered her cheek for a kiss.

Cecile knelt beside them and tapped her husband on the shoulder. He released Natalia so Cecile could say her good-byes. She kissed Natalia on the cheek, then gave Natalia one last quick squeeze before standing up. She couldn't speak, the lump in her throat choking her. She sobbed quietly, trying unsuccessfully to hide her emotions.

"Ahem. Sorry to break this up, but we really do need to get going." Darlene gathered Natalia's things, flinging the backpack over her shoulder and extended her hand. "The money?"

Reluctantly, Armand handed her the envelope with the cash and the Power of Attorney.

She stuffed the envelope into her bag. "Come along, Natalia. Your new mommy and daddy are waiting for you." A cab arrived, as if on cue, and Darlene ushered the child into the back seat.

"Thank you, Papa. Thank you for sending me to Nika." The cab pulled away before Armand could answer.

She called me Papa for the first time. She thought they were sending her to Nika in Russia. Oh God, what would she think when she found out she was only going to Miami?

Feb. 20, 2009

Three days passed, and they hadn't heard a word from the Borgovs. Cecile tried to convince Armand that they had made the right decision. "She'll be happier in a different home, with Polina and Maxim, and grandparents that speak her language, understand her ways. We tried, Armi. We tried everything to make her happy, and nothing worked."

The Borgovs's phone number was pinned to the cork board next to the phone. Darlene said to give Natalia and her new family a few days to acclimate, then they could call and speak to them.

The television rattled on with reality show contestants nobody cared about. Armand sat across the room from Cecile, a cavern of tension between them.

"Armi," Cecile said. "We did the right thing. She'll be happier."

He looked up from the paper he only pretended to read. "We should have checked to make sure she arrived safely. It's been three days. Even if we can't talk to Natalia yet, why couldn't they have called us and let us know that she's okay?"

"Let's call them," Cecile said.

The line rang four times. Cecile almost hung up when Polina answered with a scratchy "Hello?"

"Polina. I know we aren't supposed to call yet, but we're worried sick about Natalia. Is she doing all right?"

"What?"

"Natalia. Is she doing all right?"

Polina's voice cracked. "Cecile, Natalia is not here."

"What do you mean? Is she with Maxim or his parents?" She sank into the nearest chair before her legs gave out.

"No, I mean she never came. We received a call from Darlene shortly after we talked to you. We were getting ready to leave for the airport. She told us that you changed your mind. I could tell you were upset, but we couldn't believe you would do that to us. We've been devastated."

Armand grabbed the phone. "Polina, what's the meaning of this?"

"She's not here." Polina cried into the phone. "She's never been here."

Armand jumped to his feet. "My God! Call the police. That woman stole Natalia."

Chapter Twenty-Five

Chalmette, LA.

Feb. 20, 2009

Armand hit the speaker button as he dialed.

"911. What is your emergency?"

"A woman took our daughter," Armand said, the panic rising in his voice.

The dispatcher was calm. "A woman? Your daughter? How old is your daughter, sir?"

"Six. She's six years old."

Cecile hovered over the phone by Armi's side. Hurry! Why couldn't Armi make them hurry?

"Sir, are you sure she's not at a neighbor's or asleep under the bed? Children do that all the time, you know."

"No, no, she stole her." His eyes bore into Cecile's.

She knew this was all her fault. This had been

her idea.

The dispatcher's voice echoed through the speaker phone. "Sir? Mister? What's your name?"

He ran his hand through his thinning hair. "Boudreaux, Armand Boudreaux. You must find her."

"Mr. Boudreaux, we will send a patrol car. Address please?"

Cecile couldn't keep silent any longer and leaned closer to the phone, "Amber Alert. Can't you put out an Amber Alert?"

"Mrs. Boudreaux? Let's get all the details first. Your address please?"

Dear God. Didn't they understand? They had to find her.

"Sir, ma'am, your address?"

"23 Bl-Bl-Blanchard Drive in Ch-Ch-Chalmette." Armand stuttered. "Please hurry."

Cecile hadn't heard that stutter from him since being stuck in the attic during Katrina. It only raised its ugly head when he was nervous.

"I'm dispatching a car right now. You say a woman took her? Did you see her take your daughter?"

Cecile tried to wrap an arm around Armand's shoulder, but he pulled away, turning his back to her.

"Yes, yes, we left Natalia with her."

Under the veil of panic, she sensed a boiling anger. He hated her. She knew it.

The voice of the dispatcher instantly changed. "I'm sorry? Like a babysitter? I don't understand. How long has your daughter been missing?"

"Three days. Darlene was supposed to take her to the Borgovs in Miami?"

"Three days!" Her calm voice now had an edge

to it. "Your child has been missing three days, and you're only now reporting it?" Her voice crackled with ice.

"N-n-no. It's not like that." Armand wheezed out. "We d-d-didn't know she was missing until right now. They t-t-told us to wait before we called. Oh, my God!" He ran a sweaty hand down his face.

Cecile knew how bad it sounded.

The dispatcher stayed on the phone until the officers arrived. They repeated the entire situation to the patrol officers.

"The agency sounded legitimate," said Cecile. "They've had hundreds of international children rehomed into better suited families." She sat on the edge of a sofa, rapping her thumb on her leg.

Sergeant Devoe scratched his jaw. "Who is this woman you left your daughter with?" He pulled his glasses down and looked over the rim at Armand.

"Darlene… Darlene… What's her last name, Cecile?" Armand turned to her. His eyes were glassy and wide eyed, but somehow vacant, as if he'd already lost his daughter.

"I don't know. She was the facilitator for the disruption." Cecile's voice didn't sound like her own. It came out shrill, and she whimpered uncontrollably.

"Excuse me? The what?" the officer said.

"The disruption. That's what the adoption agency calls it when they rehome a child to new parents," Cecile stammered.

"What's the agency name, ma'am?" Lieutenant Benoit, a female officer sat beside Cecile on the sofa, patted her hand and offered tissues from her pocket.

Cecile blew her nose and dabbed at her eyes. "ATD, Adoption through Disruption."

Sergeant Devoe wrote in his small steno pad. "Adoption through Disruption? Is that an international agency? I've never heard of them. We'll investigate them."

"Can we see the adoption papers?" Lieutenant Benoit asked.

Cecile and Armand eyes met. "We gave them a Power of Attorney releasing Natalia to her new parents," said Armand. He handed a copy of the paper to the Lieutenant.

Sergeant Devoe sputtered, a spittle of saliva lingering in the corner of his mouth. "That's it? A Power of Attorney? Don't tell me you gave them money too."

Armand hung his head, unable to meet the officer's stare. "Two thousand dollars—travel money for Natalia."

Officer Devoe baulked at the answer. "Two thousand dollars." He leaned on his elbows. "Let me get this straight. You paid some lady you had never met to take your daughter? And you signed away your rights to her... like a dog?"

"That's enough, Sergeant." Lieutenant Benoit frowned at her partner. "Cecile, where did you say you took Natalia to meet this Darlene lady?"

"New Orleans. 761 Toulouse Street. She left in a cab with her. They were to fly from Louis Armstrong to Miami with Natalia where the Borgovs were picking her up."

"We have several problems here," said Sergeant Devoe. "We don't have jurisdiction in Miami. First, we'll check out Toulouse Street, the cab companies, and the airport. But if they transported a minor across state lines, it's now a case for the FBI. We'll call them.

But I think there may be another problem since you willingly signed a POA giving away your rights to your daughter."

"No. The POA gave the Borgovs custody, not Darlene. It's right there on the Power of Attorney." Cecile said. "Darlene never delivered her. She stole her. You must do something."

"Mrs. Boudreaux, we'll do what we can. We'll contact the Missing Persons Bureau to issue an Amber Alert. The FBI will be in touch with you. What about this Borgov family? How can you be sure they don't have her? What do you know about them?"

Cecile ran into the bedroom and returned with the papers she printed about Polina and Maxim. "Here, we checked them out. We ran a background check on both. They have no criminal records, and everything they said about themselves checked out. We've already spoken to them. Darlene lied to them, too. She told them that we changed our mind. They don't have her."

Lieutenant Benoit asked, "Do you have a recent picture of the missing child? Can you describe what she was wearing?"

This was all too TV-drama. She was not just a missing child. It finally settled in Cecile's heart. *She's Natalia, our daughter.* Cecile handed Lieutenant Benoit a picture of Natalia from her sixth birthday party. "She had on a denim jumper and pink shirt. She had her toy pigeon with her. She takes it everywhere."

Lieutenant Benoit stared at the pretty little girl with blond pigtails and round cheeks. In her arms was a gray toy pigeon clutched close to her face. She was not smiling. "This was her birthday? She doesn't look very happy for a birthday girl."

"That was the whole problem." Cecile said. "Nothing we did ever made her happy."

Armand nodded. "She did smile — once, on the rocking horse I gave her for her birthday."

"Yea," Cecile sighed. "Right before she pushed it down the stairs, breaking it in two. After all your work making it for Armi, Junior."

She smiled one other time, when they told her she was going to a new family. Where was she now?

Armand and Cecile waited for the FBI to arrive. Armand was coming unglued. It was like a horror movie in slow motion. "I-I th-th-think we should call M-m-m-Miranda. Maybe she'll know what to do. Is she home from vacation?"

Cecile couldn't do this anymore. She crouched lower in the corner of the sofa and didn't answer.

Armand punched the numbers into his phone. "Miranda? It's Armi, Armand Boudreaux."

"Oh, hi, Armand. How's our girl doing?"

"Umm … we have a p-p-problem, Miranda."

"Do you need me to talk to Natalia again? We really need to get her speaking English."

He swallowed hard, forcing down the lump in his throat. "It's not that. W-we don't know where she is?"

"She ran away? Oh, gosh. Did you call the police?"

"They've already been here. The thing is… we rehomed her… or so we thought."

He heard her suck in her breath. "Armi, did you get involved with those adoption disruption groups? Please tell me you didn't give Natalia to those people."

Shivers ran down his spine. "You know them?"

"Somewhat. I've heard of couples that used them. I don't want to scare you. Some cases worked out okay, but…"

"B-but what, Miranda? Tell me." Armand paced nervously between the kitchen and the living room.

"They aren't all what they appear. I think their original intentions were good, but they don't screen the applicants very well and sometimes…"

"Sometimes what?"

"I've heard that sometimes the children get placed in…questionable circumstances."

He turned and puked into the kitchen sink.

Cecile appeared in the kitchen, wrapped in an afghan, and reached for the phone before he dropped it on to the floor. "Miranda, can you come over? Tell us everything you know. The FBI are coming soon. Maybe you can help."

"I'll be right there. Hang in there. We will find her."

Chapter Twenty-Six

Chalmette, LA.

Feb. 21, 2009

When a man and a woman in dark suits rang the bell before dawn the next morning, Cecile had returned to her corner of the couch and finally dozed off while Miranda and Armand were on their third pot of coffee, trying to figure out what to do next. The male agent was about Armand's size, over six feet tall with a Marine style buzz cut so close to his head it was impossible to distinguish any hair color. Armand guessed him to be slightly younger than himself. The woman stood almost as tall, looking lean and muscular in her black pencil skirt and conservative pumps, and possibly older than her male counterpart.

The agent flipped open his badge case to show his identification. "Morning, sir. I'm Special Agent Simon Wolfe, and this is Special Agent Joyce Rayne from the FBI New Orleans field office. May we come in?"

"Yes, of course." Armand showed them into the living room.

Cecile pushed herself vertical on the sofa. "Sorry, excuse me while I freshen up." She hurried up the stairs to brush the morning breath out of her mouth and run a comb through her bedhead.

"I'm Armand Boudreaux. That was my wife, Cecile." He extended his hand. "And this is Miranda Fisher, our adoption counselor. Thank you so much for coming. Please find our little girl."

Agent Wolfe furrowed his brow. "Perhaps you should start from the beginning." He glanced over at Miranda and back at Armand. "Maybe I have the facts wrong. I was informed you believe the *agency* took your child away."

Miranda reached out to shake Agent Rayne's hand "Perfectly understandable. I'm their counselor from Hope International. They adopted Natalia from Russia through my agency." Agent Wolfe's hand was strong and enveloped her small one in his. Miranda felt the flush that spread across her cheeks. Why was she blushing? She pulled herself together and said, "The woman that took Natalia supposedly worked for Adoptions through Disruption."

"Please sit down. Can I get you some coffee?" Armand gestured to the two armchairs in the living room. "We're worried sick. Have the New Orleans police been able to find out anything?" His hands shook; he debated whether it was from nerves or the fourth cup of coffee. At least he wasn't stuttering.

Agent Rayne spoke. "The property at 761 Toulouse Street is vacant. Child abductions are out of the jurisdiction of the NOPD. That's why we're here."

Cecile came down the stairs, not quite refreshed as her eyes were still swollen and puffy, but her face was scrubbed and her hair pulled into a ponytail. "It's all my fault. I talked Armand into this. I was at my wits end. I couldn't take it anymore." She dropped to her knees on the floor and buried her face in her hands.

Armand gently lifted his wife from the floor and deposited her on the sofa, next to Miranda. His eyes met Agent Wolfe's. "It was a mutual decision. We thought we were doing the right thing. Natalia was... difficult. No, more than difficult. She was hostile, aggressive, and sometimes violent. We tried for almost a year to reach her.

"Then we heard about this agency that placed adopted children in new homes where they could adapt better. In our case, Natalia is from Russia, and the Borgovs are a childless couple of Russian descent. We checked them out. Everything seemed on the up and up. Good jobs, no police records, established in their community in Miami. Maxim's, that is, Mr. Borgov's family, emigrated here from Russia and owns a Russian deli in Miami Shores. We were sure Natalia was going to loving people that understood her better than we do."

The agents took notes as Armand talked but did not interrupt him.

Armand shook his head and dropped his chin to his chest. "I had a feeling something was wrong when Darlene changed the location for the disruption, where we were to meet her. Then when I saw her, I felt even more apprehensive. But the Borgovs were waiting for Natalia. I should have listened to my instincts. We made a mistake, a terrible mistake."

"Walk us through how you found out about this organization."

Cecile lifted her head and spoke in a tired monotone. "It's all online. I'll show it to you. I followed it for months before we made any decision. Then we interviewed several parents before we agreed on Maxim and Polina Borgov."

Armand sensed what the agents were thinking. Things too horrible to say out loud. Did they suspect Armand and Cecile of killing their child — or selling her? Did they think Natalia was buried in their backyard? As parents, they were certainly suspects in Natalia's disappearance. They weren't bad people. Really. Armand had to make them understand.

"Let's talk about this woman. Darlene, correct? Tell us about her," said Agent Raynes.

Armand ran his hands down his face and paced the floor. "We're wasting time here. Shouldn't we be doing something to find Natalia? Now it's four days. Four days."

"Yes," Agent Wolfe said. "Let's talk about that then. Sit down, Mr. Boudreaux. Why did you wait so long to report her missing?"

Armand sat on the edge of the seat, feeling ready to pounce. "Oh, God. We've been through all this with the police." He ran his hand through his hair. "We're wasting time."

"Humor us, Mr. Boudreaux. We need to hear it in your words. Sometimes going over it again will trigger a clue to help us find Natalia."

Cecile answered. "The agency, that is, ATD said it was best to give the new family and Natalia a few days to get to know each other before we called them. We were trying to do the right thing for her ... not make it any harder than it already was."

Armand nodded. "By the third day, I couldn't wait anymore. We were going crazy wondering how she was ... if she was happy with the Borgovs. So yesterday, we finally called."

"That's when they told us that Natalia never arrived." Cecile said. "Darlene told them that we'd changed our mind. They were so devastated they didn't call us either. They had already lost one child during the waiting period."

Agent Rayne looked puzzled.

Miranda nodded. "In international adoptions, after the paperwork is all completed and the child is assigned to a family, the courts require a ten-day waiting period to give any next of kin a chance to object to the adoption and step forward to raise the child. That's what happened to the Borgovs in their first adoption."

Armand, Cecile, and Miranda spent the next three hours repeating everything over and over what they had already told the local police. The agents were polite but thorough in the questioning. Armand, though, understood he and Cecile were suspects in Natalia's disappearance.

"Do you have any reason to believe this is a kidnapping for ransom?" Special Agent Wolfe suggested.

"If it is, they picked the wrong people," said Armand. "We don't have any money. I'm the drilling manager at Murphy Oil, and Cecile hasn't worked since..." He glanced at Cecile. He'd almost said *since our other babies died.* How would that sound? He quickly changed it to "...since Hurricane Katrina.

It took our entire life savings to get Natalia from Russia."

Agent Wolfe met Miranda's stare. "Miranda, tell us what you know about these disruption agencies. Are they legit?"

"Well," she stammered, clearly embarrassed by being caught staring at him. "I believe the original intent was honorable. The adoption system is not adequately equipped to handle adoptions that go wrong. At Hope, we spend a lot of time preparing families for the possibilities of troubled children, but not all agencies do that. Lots of parents end up with children with severe disabilities or RAD kids."

"RAD kids? What's that?" Agent Raynes poised her pen above her notebook.

"RAD stands for Reactive Attachment Disorder. These children have spent their entire lives in orphanages; they are institutionalized. Don't get me wrong. The caretakers at the orphanages are doing the best they can. But when there are eighty, ninety, sometimes even a hundred children in these institutions at one time, the best the staff can do is clean, clothe, and try to educate them. Many children have never been hugged, never known love. And sometimes, no matter how hard you try, that can't be overcome."

"Oh, God. That's horrible. Is Natalia a RAD child?" asked Raynes.

Was she? Armand watched Cecile stroke the scruffy little head of Neptune that rested in her lap.

Miranda hesitated and gave Armand a weak smile before looking up at Agent Raynes. "Natalia was orphaned at the age of four. So, we didn't think she would be as affected by the two years she was in the New Holland Orphanage in St. Petersburg. But her symptoms indicate that it could have been more severe than we originally thought. She can be very aggressive. She never speaks English to Armand and Cecile, even though according to her records from the orphanage, she was taught English and spoke it quite well. I'm afraid Natalia is a bit of a puzzle to all of us."

Agent Wolfe crossed his arms over his chest and glared into Armand's eyes. "So, because of her behavior, you were going to give her up to strangers?"

"I know how pathetic that sounds." Armand says. "But unless you've lived through it, you can't imagine how horrible it is. It wasn't simple things like temper tantrums, although those certainly were common, but Natalia seemed so miserable. We were failing her. She deserved to be happy, and we couldn't make that happen."

Armand glanced at Cecile, who wiped fresh tears from her face with her hand.

"We're not monsters. We're not." Cecile pleaded. "We wanted her to be happy, and if that meant giving her to another family, well, we decided we would do it."

"Getting back to this agency, Adoption through Disruption. How are the children transferred?" Wolfe asked.

Cecile gulped down her tears. "Parents post information online in chat rooms and in forums; about their child; age, sex, nationality, physical or emotional issues, and new parents connect with matches for the child they are looking for. Then a facilitator transfers the child from one family to another. We gave them a Power of Attorney and money for airfare."

"So, they advertise their children for sale."

Agent Wolfe reclined in his chair, shaking his head. He didn't hide his disgust well.

"No, it's not like that. We didn't sell Natalia," protested Cecile. "We thought we were placing her with a new family. We only paid the airfare for Natalia and the facilitator, Darlene. Nobody forces anybody to do anything. Polina Borgov said she knew another couple that received their child from ATD, and it worked out wonderfully for everyone. The child is happy and well-adjusted. That's why they chose to use them."

"Can't we put Natalia on an Amber Alert?" Armand pleaded. "Maybe someone saw her. What about the cab driver? There must be something we can be doing instead of sitting here talking."

Agent Rayne nodded. "We did that already. The New Orleans Police Department contacted the NCMEC, the National Center for Missing and Exploited Children. Natalia's already been added to the database of missing children. The alert will be broadcast within the hour. We also have our own task force, VCACITF—The Violent Crimes Against Children International Task Force—within the Bureau that deals directly with child abductions. We'll set up a base here. Is there a room here we could use as a home base?"

"Of course." Armand stood. "Will my office work?"

"Thank you, sir," she responded. "That will be sufficient. We would like to look at your computer if that's okay."

"I guess. May I ask why?" Armand asked, but he knew. They wanted to see what kind of people they really were.

"We'd like to look at the correspondence you had with ATD and with this facilitator, Darlene," said Agent Wolfe.

Cecile gestured to the office. "Oh, sure. That makes sense. Most of it was through the Yahoo chat room, not private emails. Will that be a problem?"

"Not for our computer people. They can decode conversations through chat rooms, emails, or forums. Even if they were deleted from your hard drive."

"We also have Darlene's cell phone on our caller ID when she called to tell us the location had changed. Can't you put a GPS on that?" Armand asked.

"Of course," Agent Wolfe said. "But chances are it was a disposable phone if she was up to no good. Can we have that number?"

Armand showed them the display on his cell.

Chapter Twenty-Seven

St. Petersburg, Russia

February, 2009

With Dimitri evicted from the apartment for failure to pay his rent, the two boys joined sixteen hundred other homeless children and drifted into living in the labyrinth of the streets of St. Petersburg. For a while they stuck by one another in an abandoned basement they shared with seven other street urchins. One day, Nikolai returned from the docks to find the police rummaging through the debris. There was no sign of Dimitri or the others. He huddled in the alley until they were gone. Slipping into the basement, Nikolai realized that his few belongings were gone. His heart sank. What would he do now? All he had left he carried on his back. Things looked more hopeless with each passing day.

Nikolai walked the streets looking for

somewhere to sleep, dodging in and out of train stations and alleyways until he was chased from each place by other homeless who feared he was intruding on their turf. He wandered for three days, falling asleep on benches and under bushes in Alexander Garden. He lost track of time and days. The last of the money from his paycheck had run out. He couldn't show up for work smelly and filthy. The foreman was adamant about not hiring the homeless. Without a residence, Nikolai would lose his job.

"*Psst.* Nikolai, here." Olga, one of the others from the abandoned basement, waved him into an alley.

He hadn't seen Olga in several days. The skinny teenager's greasy brown strands poked from a threadbare knit cap. She wore a ripped bomber jacket, much too big for her and on her feet, one torn tennis shoe and one man's loafer. Under the jacket, a tight knit dress barely concealed her skeletal frame.

"Here, I saved this from the police." She handed him the black Bible he had left on the crate next to his tattered blanket.

Nikolai palmed the small leather cover. "Thank you, Olga. I couldn't find anyone. Do you know where Dimitri went?"

"The police, they took him away. He was too stoned to run, and they found stolen wallets on him. At least he'll get a meal and a roof over his head for a while." She managed a smile through broken, rotting teeth. A nasty looking bruise was turning yellow on her left jaw.

"Where are you staying?" Nikolai asked.

"Come on. I'm heading to the shelter on Borovoj. They might still have some food and beds left."

A Maltese cross hovered over Borovoj Street, 112 B. A social worker with gray braids twisted on her head introduced herself as Helga. Did they need a hot meal? No drugs and no alcohol. Those were the rules.

"Yes, please." Nikolai stared at the wood floor. Charity was so demeaning.

Nikolai took a bath and washed his clothes. He forced himself not to gobble the hot potato soup. After a good night's sleep, he'd go back to work. If his job was still there and if word of his homelessness hadn't leaked to the foreman. Nikolai's registration papers had been taken during the raid. He couldn't get hired anywhere else or be allowed healthcare without them.

They gave Olga a matching pair of shoes and a pair of jeans she slipped under her dress. Nikolai noticed she was very pretty once she washed the grime out of her hair and body.

"How long have you been on the street?" he asked.

She shrugged. "Dunno, most of my life, I guess. Never knew my parents. My dedushka gave me to a family in Pushkin. The papa raped me, so I ran away. Been out here ever since. At least on the streets, I choose who I'm going to fuck."

Nikolai cringed. "Why don't you go to the orphanage?"

"No papers." She raised her chin and waved her hand. "Besides if I'm lucky, I can get into shelters like this. I'm my own boss. Nobody tells me what to do."

Nikolai didn't share Olga's optimism. The next day he went straight to the docks, grateful the foreman was nowhere in sight when he picked up a hose and started hosing out the first of a hundred containers.

"Hey, that's my hose." A tall thin man with hollow cheeks towered over him.

"Sorry, I must be on the wrong row." Nikolai mumbled. It was the right place, but he wasn't about to admit it. Moving over a few rows, he looked for an unused hose near some empty containers.

"Boy, what do you think you're doing?" The foreman bellowed at him "You've missed three days of work." He eyed Nikolai closely.

Could he tell he was homeless?

"I know. I'm sorry. I've had the flu. But I'm okay now. What row do you want me on?" Nikolai crossed his fingers behind his back.

"Nyet. I had to replace you."

"How about someplace else? I'm a good worker. You know that." Nikolai hated begging.

"Let me see your papers again." The man stretched out his hand.

Don't panic. Be polite. "Umm, I don't have them with me. I'll bring them tomorrow."

The foreman shook his head. "No papers, no work. Bring them, then we'll see if there's any work for you. Until then, get lost." He turned and walked away, his wide girth disappearing behind a five stack of multi-colored containers.

Chapter Twenty-Eight

Chalmette, LA.

Feb. 21, 2009

They had to notify the family. Cecile called her father in Butte La Rose.

"We'll be right there," said her father. "What can we do to help?"

"I wish I knew," Cecile said.

"I'll make a gris-gris for Natalia," said Mamère Le Bieu.

More voodoo. Black magic had caused all of this to happen.

"No gris-gris, Mamère," said Cecile.

Armand called his parents in Washington D.C. When he finished giving them the short version, his father asked to speak to Special Agent Wolfe.

"What for, Dad?" Armand did little to hide the agitation for his parents.

"Put him on the phone, son. I'll take care of this."

Armand hit the speaker button. "It's my father. He'd like to speak to you."

"Special Agent Wolfe, speaking."

Cecile could hear her father-in-law's voice booming into the receiver. "Yes, yes, of course. Do you know who I am? I'm Senator Boudreaux. I want you to extend all resources to find our granddaughter. If it's money they want..."

Agent Wolfe maintained his composure. "Senator Boudreaux. There's been no request for ransom. We're fully equipped to handle the situation and are doing everything we can to find your granddaughter."

Armand interrupted. "Dad, there's nothing you can do. Really, thanks for your concern. I'll keep in touch." He hit the *end* button. "Sorry about that. He can be a real pain in the ass sometimes, but he means well."

Wolfe's lips turned in a slight smile. "Understood. Everyone deals with stress in a different way. Some must exert their authority to get a sense of control over an otherwise-unacceptable situation."

The FBI traced the source of the chat room for ATD to a host site out of Atlanta, Georgia. VCACITF were unable to link any illegal activity to the group. In some states, it was a misdemeanor to advertise children looking for new homes on a website, but for the most part, all was legal, if not ethical. Researching the message boards, they discovered that anywhere from two to ten new children were advertised each week.

Not all the stories had sad endings. There were

dozens of posts of successful disruptions, with jubilant families praising ATD for bringing together parents and children in a perfect match. The loosely-managed organization showed a conspicuous lack of involvement in the actual transaction, a clever way to avert the law. Except for using a facilitator to assist the families in the physical transfer of the child, ATD was not a party to the actual choosing of the families that "rehomed" these children. The Power of Attorney was strictly between the parents with no reference to ATD. Any responsibility for background checks or investigative work into the character of these new families was placed entirely on the original adopted family.

Cecile pleaded with Armand, who was up pacing again, to stop and sit with her on the sofa. She needed his strength. "What about Darlene? Have you found anything out about her?"

"We don't have much to go on. The phone was, as expected, a disposable and untraceable. The Louis Armstrong airport checked for any woman traveling alone with a child leaving the day of the disruption and every day since. Over thirty single women traveling with a child have passed through the gates since Monday. None of them match the description of Natalia and a woman with dark hair."

"Maybe she was traveling with someone else, to look like a couple." Cecile rapped her fingers on her leg. "Or maybe she was wearing a wig?"

"Possibly, but every child's face was scanned to compare the picture you provided. No matches. We have reason to believe that Natalia is still in Louisiana somewhere."

Cecile looked at Agent Raynes. "That's good,

right?"

"We're hopeful. But if here, she's most likely not being placed with a loving home. Foul play's involved," Raynes said.

Armand's tanned face paled. "What are you thinking? Please, give it to us straight."

"VCACITF has been following two different child trafficking rings here in New Orleans. One focuses on teens and preteens, ages eleven to seventeen, for child prostitution. These children typically get sold to Mexico or Thailand."

"Natalia is only six," Cecile said.

"Yes, but the other group focuses mostly on prepubescent children between the ages of three and ten. This is a child pornography ring, and we suspect these children are being held against their will."

"Omigod!" Cecile fell against Armand's shoulder.

"If Natalia is with one of those groups, the problem is finding them. One of our agents has been posing as an online customer for two years—but we haven't been able to find the children yet. Wherever they're keeping them, they take the photos and upload them to an encrypted site. Paying customers buy the code to convert the innocent looking photos to the child pornography hidden encrypted underneath."

Cecile was aghast. She fought the urge to hurl. "Two years! There are children that you've been watching for two years and not been able to save?"

"Not the same children. Typically, each child is only on the site for a few weeks or months."

Was that because they didn't live that long? Otherwise, what became of those children? If they were going to save Natalia, time was of the essence.

At least, the FBI finally appeared to believe them that they didn't do any harm to Natalia. That wasn't exactly true. They willingly handed her over to these monsters.

"What are you going to do?" Armand pleaded.

"We doubt that Darlene was acting alone. Someone in the ATD organization got greedy and realized that selling children to these groups was far more profitable than exchanging a child between two honest families. Our plan is to infiltrate the ATD. We'll plant one of our undercover agents as a facilitator. If our UC agent can 'facilitate' a sale of a child to this porn group, we might find Natalia among the children. Our mole, who's buying the porn, is also watching for Natalia to show up on that site. So far, no sign of her."

That was one silver lining, right? If she wasn't on the porn site, then she might still be okay. Dear God, let her be okay.

"Wouldn't your undercover agent need to know the lingo in the adoption disruption world?" Miranda asked. "Not unlike the FBI with its menagerie of acronyms, the adoption arena has its own language that would be unfamiliar to the average person or even law enforcement. Perhaps I could act as the facilitator."

Agent Wolfe shook his head. "No, our undercover agents had extensive training to get their UC certification. We never allow civilians to go under cover. These people can be extremely dangerous. This is a million-dollar business."

"There must be a way I can help," Miranda said. "These people don't know me personally, but they could easily check me out on the Hope International website. It would be a believable story … if I was disillusioned with Hope because I couldn't help couples disrupt in failed adoptions."

Her eyes met Armand and Cecile. "It's not so far from the truth. Perhaps if I could have helped you … Natalia would be in a happy home now, safe and sound."

Cecile reached out and touched Miranda's arm. "It's not your fault. You've done more for us and Natalia than anyone else in the world."

Agent Raynes tapped on the computer and opened the website for Hope International. "What would it take to switch out your photo with one of our UC agents? Could you teach enough of the lingo to our agent to make her pass as you?"

"The photo would be easy. I could give her a crash course on the lingo. It's hard to know how knowledgeable these people would be. But if there was a way for me to communicate with her, like with a wire or something … or is that too TV drama?" She smiled at Agent Wolfe as she spoke, a faint blush creeping up her neck.

Wolfe returned her smile. "Well, real life is pretty far from TV drama or John Grisham novels, but our UC agents do wear a wire sometimes."

Agent Raynes was still reading the bio of Miranda on the website. "Let's get UC Agent Julia Stone down here. She's close to the same age as Miranda and speaks Russian and Romanian. She might be able to be our facilitator. It's a long shot, but it's all we've got at this time."

"Done," said Wolfe, staring at the photo of Natalia in his hand. "And our poser will keep watching for Natalia to show up on the porn site. If they've got her, it won't be long before they'll want to exploit this beautiful little girl."

The thought of Natalia posing naked on some sick website made Cecile physically ill. She gagged on the muffin she was trying to force down.

Cecile let Miranda rinse out the coffee cups and put them in the dishwasher. They were alone in the kitchen while Armand walked Neptune and the agents discussed their strategies in the office.

Cecile raised an eyebrow at Miranda. "Do I detect a bit of chemistry between you and Agent Wolfe?"

Miranda coughed and wrapped her arms around her middle. "Is it that obvious? Talk about inappropriate timing. I'm sorry."

"It's okay. He's very professional. I don't think he likes me or Armand very much, but when he talks to you, his entire demeanor changes."

Miranda picked up a sponge and wiped down the counter she'd already cleaned several times before. "I don't know what's gotten into me. I don't go gaga over men. I don't have time. Besides, I'm sure he's only using his tactics to get me to talk. He can't possibly be hitting on me, can he?"

"Why not? You're single. My guess is he's single. No harm, no foul." Cecile gave Miranda a quick shoulder squeeze. "It's kind of nice to see something positive in all this hell."

Chapter Twenty-Nine

Chalmette, LA.

February, 21,2009

Undercover Agent Julia Stone arrived within an hour. She had the same straight, light brown hair as Miranda. Make-up could add the freckles that Miranda tried unsuccessfully to hide. Agent Stone spoke better Russian than Miranda and was an avid student.

"To understand how difficult some of these children can be, let me tell you a little history," Miranda began. "In 2006, Peggy Sue Hilt of Manassas, Virginia, was sentenced to twenty-five years in prison after being convicted of fatally beating a two-year-old girl adopted from Siberia. More recently, Kimberly Emelyantsev of Tooele, Utah, was sentenced to fifteen years after pleading guilty to killing a Russian infant in her care. These are parents that are so distraught from trying to handle these special needs kids that they resort to terrible measures. I don't believe either one of these women were born killers."

"I remember reading that about the Utah woman on the news. What's so terrible about these children that their adoptive parents resort to murder?"

"Many children that have been institutionalized for most of their life have RAD, Reactive Attachment Disorder. Although there are varying degrees, these kids can range from being introverted and nonresponsive to being extremely violent. Unfortunately, many parents aren't prepared for the children's conditions. And the symptoms don't always manifest right away. They tend to get worse with time, not better."

"Why would another family be willing to take these kids on if the adopted parents can't handle them?" asked Agent Stone.

"That's a very good question. Some have already been through this with another child and have learned how to cope. Others think that since they speak the native language of the child, they'll be able to get through to them. Some can; some can't."

Agent Stone glanced over at Cecile. "Is Natalia one of those children?"

Miranda shook her head. "We didn't think so, but she was showing more signs of it. I personally don't think she is. Since I speak Russian, I am the only one she would talk to. She told me repeatedly that she wanted to go home to Russia to be with her older brother. I think she was acting out in the hopes they'd send her there."

"Is that what she thought we were doing?" Cecile cried. "Sending her to Russia?"

Miranda patted Cecile's hand. "I wasn't here, so I can't speak for her, but it's possible she misunderstood you and thought so."

Cecile folded into Armand's arms. "I betrayed her. She'll never forgive me, even if we get her back."

Armand gave her a little squeeze. "Let's concentrate on finding her first, then we'll deal with all of us learning to forgive."

Agent Stone continued to question Miranda. "What other things could come up that I need to know?"

"Another major disadvantage of some of these internationally adopted children, especially in Russia and Romania, is Fetal Alcohol Syndrome. FAS causes central nervous system damage. This can create poor memory, attention deficits, and bad impulsive behavior. While many of their symptoms are similar to RAD kids, their prognoses for recovery are bleak. These are permanent defects. You need to understand what these parents are going through if you are going to assume the role of their savior—because that's how they will view you. And the ATD may ask if the child you are transferring has RAD or FAS.

"When parents get to the state where they are considering rehoming the children, it's a critical point in their lives. It is either find these children a new home, or the parents will end up on the news with Peggy Sue Hilt and Kimberly Emelyantsev. Desperate times call for desperate measures."

"I see now," said Stone. "And in desperate times, some of these children get picked up by slimebags such as child traffickers and pornography rings. That's where I come in."

"Here's the plan," Agent Wolfe said. "Agent

Stone—or I should say Miranda?— will contact the ATD people through the Yahoo chat room." He turned and faced Julia Stone. "You'll express frustration in not being able to help a particular family from Hope International that needs to rehome their child. Understanding the breaking point these parents are at, you'll attempt to become a facilitator for ATD in the hopes they will lead us to the pornography ring."

Agent Stone stood up and hugged Miranda. "Together we'll get these bastards. Let's do it."

Cecile hoped it would work. There was a lot of "ifs" to this plan, and time was running out to find Natalia. Where was she? Was she hurt? Hungry? Being abused? Unspeakable scenarios ran through Cecile's head.

Feb. 22, 2009

The process was slow and disheartening. Agent Stone spent hours communicating with ATD before anyone responded. The next day, they got a hit with a private instant message.

"We've checked you out on Hope International's website," someone typed into the IM. "Why are you switching sides?"

"I'm not," typed Miranda with Agent Stone sitting by her side. "I still work for Hope. But they can't help my couples whose adoptions didn't work out. I want to do more to help them."

"What role do you see playing with ATD?"

"I'd like to do what I do now but with your organization. Find new homes for these children."

Agents Wolfe and Raynes cautioned them to take it slowly. "Ask them if they need another facilitator. Emphasize that you speak Russian and Romanian and can communicate with the children."

Miranda followed their lead.

No response. Everyone stared at the screen, watching the cursor blink incessantly.

"Damn!" Wolfe pounded his hand on the desktop. "We spooked them. They're not going to bite."

"Hold on," Miranda said. "Be patient. They're thinking."

Agent Wolfe pressed his face toward the computer screen, inches away from Miranda's. She could smell his woodsy aftershave.

"We don't have time," he said. "Natalia's been missing for five days now."

The screen came to life. "Can you travel?"

Miranda typed back. "I can. Do I pay my own travel expenses?"

"No, the disrupting families will pay your airfare and any other expenses you may incur. Do you have a family now that is looking to disrupt?"

Of course, they didn't have a child to transfer. Miranda looked at Agent Wolfe. "What do I say?"

"Tell them *yes*. We can't lose them," Cecile urged her.

Miranda typed, "I do."

"What is the age of the child? Have them post a profile on our site. We may be able to find a home for the child."

Miranda shook her head and looked at Agent Stone in a panic. "Now what do I do?"

UC Agent Stone told her to make up a profile. "Tell them you'll pass the information along to the family. We'll need a different email address to pose as the family. They might be able to trace it to the same server. Our tech guys can handle that. Wait a day before you post it. Use a family you are familiar with. Use all their information exactly, except for their names. That way you won't get caught in a lie. But use a prepubescent child. We want to trace them to wherever they took Natalia."

"Okay," said Miranda. "I have a child in mind. But I wouldn't want to post any pictures of her."

"We'll pull some photos of children from the closed files of NCMEC. They can't hurt those children."

Cecile had to ask, "Why is that? Why are their cases closed?"

"Those children were found, Mrs. Boudreaux." said Raynes.

Did that mean that they were found dead? Cecile didn't want to know the answer.

Armand paced the floor, and Cecile curled up on the sofa. They'd have to wait another day. A car pulled in the driveway. Cecile's father and sister hurried from the car. Mamère Le Bieu followed close behind in a flurry of colorful kaftan and a wild turban.

Yvette raced into the room and wrapped her arms around her sister. "My sweet CeCe. You must be frantic."

Cecile shook her head and crumbled in her sister's arms. Her father joined in the embrace. "We don't have any idea where she is," said Cecile between sobs. "Are the boys with you, too?" She hoped not. She couldn't handle them right now.

"No," Yvette said. "I left them with their dad. Have you found out anything yet?"

Cecile blew her nose and told them what Agent Wolfe had said about the child pornography ring.

"Who knows what kind of horrible things they are doing to her."

"Ah, baby," her dad said. He didn't have any words of comfort.

Mamère Le Bieu wandered into Natalia's bedroom. She came out with her hands full.

"What do you have there, Mamère?" Armand inquired.

"Some strands of her hair from her hairbrush, this little shirt that was in the hamper, her pillowcase where she rested her head. I'll make a gris-gris doll. I find da' chile."

Armand rolled his eyes. "Mamère, with all due respect, I don't think your voodoo will bring Natalia back to us. That's what the FBI is here for."

Dark eyes flashed at him. "Don't scoff what you dun' understand. I find her." She went about her business making the doll, using the child's objects to invest her gris-gris magic into the doll.

Cecile knew it was time to make sure Armand knew the truth. She pulled Armand into their master suite and shut the door. "I've got to tell you something, Armi. Something I've hidden from you. It's the reason Mamère's potions won't work." Cecile sat on the edge of the bed and dropped her head into her hands.

Armand ran his hands through his hair, pacing the floor. "CeCe, I don't believe that mumbo jumbo. I know why her potions won't work—they're only superstition."

She grabbed his arm and pressed hard until he looked her in the eye. "Listen to me, Armi. We'll never have a child, and it's my fault. I've told you this before, but I need to explain why I'm cursed."

"Jesus, CeCe. We have a child…we have Natalia. And I'm getting tired of all this."

Cecile wanted to look away in shame, but she locked her eyes on him. "The reason the spirits won't let us have a child is because I killed one when I was fourteen."

Now she had his attention. He froze. "What the hell are you talking about?"

"I met a boy. We were fooling around, and things got out of control. I got pregnant. I couldn't have a baby at fourteen. I couldn't tell my parents or Mamère. I went to a priestess in Jefferson Parish. She gave me a potion to make me lose the baby. The spirits have cursed me for what I did. We're never going to get Natalia back alive."

Armand pulled away from her and crossed the room in three wide steps. He spun back around to face her. "Stop! Stop with this nonsense. There are no curses. I wish you would have told me, but it's not making any difference now. Did Dr. Teekell know about the abortion? Is there some damage that was done that prevented the live birth of the others?"

"He knew. I refused to give him permission to tell you, HEPA laws and all. He said it had nothing to do with losing the babies. But I know it's not physical, it's mystical. The curse."

Armand walked across the room and gripped her shoulders, gently shaking her. "No, CeCe. You did not cause this, and there is no curse. You'll see. We'll get her back alive."

Cecile wished he was right. Losing Natalia had broken the wall Cecile had built around her heart. If the spirits gave Natalia back to them, Cecile would spend the rest of her life helping this broken child adapt. Whatever it took, she'd do anything, short of ever letting her out of her sight again. And in the process, maybe Cecile would heal as well.

Chapter Thirty

Chalmette, LA.

Feb. 23, 2009

Agent Raynes was glad Armand and Cecile were occupied with their family, even if it was a strange conversation of voodoo dolls and gris-gris magic. So much for life in New Orleans. They had news.

"Miranda?" Agent Wolfe motioned for her to step away from the crowd so he could speak privately. "We've got some information. I wanted to tell you first. It's not pretty. Our mole made a match with Natalia on the porn site."

"Oh, no." She weaved, suddenly unsteady on her feet. When he reached out to stabilize her, his touch sent a shiver down her spine. She pulled her arm away. "How bad is it?"

"The good news is we at least know for sure who has her. The bad news is the 'viewers' like new faces—and bodies. The photographers pace it out with teasing photos that get increasingly more graphic."

"Should we show the pictures to Armand and Cecile?"

"I think we must be honest and tell them about it. Whether they want to see the photos can be their choice."

"Oh, God, I hate this. What about UC Agent Julia Stone posing as a facilitator? We need to find the location of those babies fast."

"You two stay on that. See if you can get them to give you or Agent Stone a disruption to place. That's the only way we can follow them to the site. I'll tell the Boudreauxs about the photos."

Miranda and Stone logged back on the chat room, sending hints of what they wanted, hoping to get a private IM.

Pulling Armand and Cecile aside from her parents, Agents Wolfe and Raynes repeated what they knew about the photos.

Armand steeled himself for the worst. "Tell me first. What am I going to see?"

"The first ones are usually pretty tame," said Agent Wolfe. "It's a tease for more graphic ones to come. She's on all fours, dressed in white ruffled panties, her back to the camera but her head turned to look at the camera. Nobody else in the photo."

Cecile went into denial mode. She waved her hands and vigorously shook her head. "Well, that can't be Natalia. She doesn't have ruffled panties. It must be another poor child."

Raynes sat next to Cecile and wrapped an arm around her.

Wolfe's eyes met Armand's across the room.

Armand gave a slight shake of his head, then asked quietly, "Can I see the pictures?"

Wolfe nodded. The two men went into the office where Miranda and Agent Stone were sitting at the computer. He opened his personal laptop and punched in the codes to bring up the site.

Armand's hand flew to his face. On the screen, Natalia stared at him, her eyes unfocused and a forced smile upon her lips. Her little behind with the ruffled panties filled most of the screen.

Armand reached for a waste basket and puked into it.

Wolfe handed him a handkerchief from his pocket.

"Those sons-of-bitches. If they lay a hand on her, I swear I'll kill them with my bare hands." Armand pounded his fist into the wall, cracking right through the drywall.

"I understand how you feel, and we'll get them. At least now we know who has her." Wolfe patted Armand on the back.

"We've got something." Agent Stone smiled. "They've agreed to give me a disruption. With Miranda's help, I've got my first delivery tomorrow night."

"What's the scenario?" asked Raynes.

"There's a couple in Corpus Christi with a Russian girl with FAS. The child's a real handful. She has set the house on fire twice and smashed their cat's head in with a rock. She's a perfect fit for the porn site. It would be faster and easier than finding a real set of parents for her. They'll keep her drugged up enough that she won't be any trouble to anyone."

"Great," said Wolfe. "Well, not great for the parents or that kid, but good for us. When and where is the disruption supposed to take place?"

"They told the parents to bring the child to the Houston airport with the POA and two grand. I, or I should say Miranda, is to pick up the child at 8 p.m. and take the 9:15 p.m. flight to New Orleans and deliver her to her new parents." Agent Stone beamed. "Then, bingo—we got 'em."

"Did they give you an address, or is someone meeting you at the airport?" Agent Wolfe asked.

Agent Stone shook her head. "They said they'll give me the address by phone once I arrive with the child."

"What do I do?" Miranda asked.

"You and Agent Stone will both fly to Houston. We'll book the flights separately from different IP addresses, in case they're smart enough to trace the reservations … which I doubt. Stone will wear a wire in case they ask her questions she can't handle. We'll be waiting for you at Louis Armstrong, and we'll tail you to the delivery location."

"What time does the flight get into Louis Armstrong?" Armand asked.

"It's an hour and fifteen-minute flight so it should land at 10:30 p.m. Hopefully, the child will be too exhausted to be any trouble," Miranda said, clicking on the reservation through CheapFlights. com.

Cecile heard the commotion and joined everyone in the office." You found her? Is she all right?"

"Not yet," said Miranda as she wrapped an arm around Cecile. "But by tonight, we should have her location. With a little luck, we could have Natalia home by tonight."

Armand gave Cecile an *I-told-you-so* look.

"Let's not get ahead of ourselves," said Agent Wolfe. "There are a lot of things that could go wrong. If they suspect that the FBI is involved, they'll dump that kid anywhere. And who knows if the disrupting parents will even go through with it."

"I want to go with you." Armand said to Agent Wolfe. "I want to be there when you catch those bastards."

Wolfe shook his head. "No can do. We'll have an entire task force at the airport when Miranda and Agent Stone get off the plane with the child. We can't involve civilians. But we can do this … you can stay in the surveillance van when we follow them to the delivery point. You can listen to all the exchanges on the radio. Once we find your little girl and have secured the perps, we'll let you come in and get your child. You can carry her out."

Mamère Le Bieu stepped into the office. "I have some information for you."

"Not now, Mamère. The FBI has a real lead," Cecile said.

"I've seen her. She's in a dark hole."

Cecile tried to direct her out of the room. "I believe you, Mamère. But we need more than that. I don't suppose you got an address with that vision?"

"You're mocking me, CeCe. You know I have the gift."

Cecile didn't say what she was thinking. Then why didn't the gris-gris she wore around her neck for years keep her from losing all those babies? Her potions didn't work then, and they wouldn't work now. Instead, she said, "I'm sorry, Mamère. We are really stressed."

"There's a boy in there with her, an older boy."

"That's good information. I'll tell Agent Wolfe." Cecile sighed and walked into the other room.

Chapter Thirty-One

Houston, Texas

Feb. 24, 2009 - Fat Tuesday

Miranda sat three rows behind Agent Julia Stone on the flight to Houston. She bounced her knee. Her seatmate, a man with thinning hair and thick coke-bottle glasses smiled. She pressed her hand on her leg to steady it.

"You seem nervous. First time flying?" he asked.

"Oh, no, I have an important meeting coming up. Sorry if I bothered you," Miranda said.

"Job ... or a man?"

That was rather personal. Was he trying to be friendly, or was he hitting on her? Better squelch that idea right now. "Man," Miranda said with a smile. "I think he's going to propose." Where had that come from?

The man leaned away from her, closer to the

window. "Oh, well, I guess congratulations are in order."

"Thanks." She laughed. "He's gorgeous; tall, dark, and handsome; cliché, right? But he is."

A voice echoed through her earbud. "Was that Agent Wolfe you just described? You still have your speaker on the wire." Stone chuckled from three rows ahead.

Was it that obvious? Did everyone see that she was attracted to him? Did he? Well, if she did have a boyfriend, he would definitely be her first pick.

The plane taxied down the runway. "Testing," Stone said. "If you can hear me, cough."

Miranda went into a coughing fit, and an old lady across the aisle handed her a bottle of water. "Thank you," she mumbled.

Both women followed the crowd to baggage claim, the disruption point. Sweat trickled between Miranda's breasts.

Standing at the rotating conveyor belt, a couple in their forties stood with a dark-haired child, tethered with a child's lease. Miranda recognized the look of despair in their eyes and the sense of failure they felt.

The child was sullen but calm. She exhibited all the physical signs of children with FAS. Her head was unusually small, eyes too far apart, upper lip thin and flat. She was wearing glasses strapped around her head.

Miranda gave a discreet nod to Agent Stone who approached the parents. "Mr. and Mrs. Colson? I'm Miranda Fisher. And this must be Katie."

Miranda could hear the conversation with the parents. "Good," she said into the wire. "Smile at the child, but don't touch her."

"How do you do?" they said in unison.

Mrs. Colson's lip trembled. "Will she be going to a good home that knows how to handle her? We don't know if we're doing the right thing. There's nobody to help us."

Miranda saw the woman's eyes glisten with tears.

"They never told us she was special," said Mr. Colson. "We thought we had enough love in us to cure her." He stroked the child's head.

She jerked away.

"Tell them there is no cure for FAS," Miranda said.

Stone repeated what Miranda said. "It's a difficult situation. No one's blaming you for the disruption. Do you have everything?"

The tears were flowing openly now down the adoptive mother's face. "Yes, it's all in here." She handed Stone an envelope. "You might need these too. If you put one in a soda, they'll dissolve." She handed the agent a bottle along with the other end of the child's leash.

Agent Stone looked at the bottle. "These are animal tranquilizers," she stated so Miranda could hear.

The woman nodded without commenting.

Miranda watched as Agent Stone knelt, trying to get Katie to look at her. "Honey, I'm going to take you on a plane ride now. Okay?"

"Easy ... that's good. Soft quiet voice," Miranda said into the mic.

Katie rolled her neck and looked at the ceiling. "Pane."

Stone smiled. "That's right, airplane. Do you want to say good-bye to your mommy and daddy?" She gulped down her own emotion.

Mr. and Mrs. Colson dropped to their knees in front of their child. "Mommy and Daddy will always love you, Katie-bug," said Mrs. Colson. "I- I-I'm sorry." She gave Katie a quick kiss on the cheek and a hug, then stood and hurried away. Mr. Colson held the child until she squirmed to get out of his arms. "Be good, Katie-bug. We love you." He handed a small suitcase to Agent Stone and jogged away to catch up with his wife.

Miranda watched from the other side of the carousel. Her heart broke for the couple and the child. Thank God, they were intervening, or this child would end up exploited and abused her entire life.

"My name is Miranda," Agent Stone said to the child. "Let's go get on that plane." She reached for Katie's hand, hoping not to use the leash.

"Aaaaahhhhh!" Katie twisted away and tried to take off in the opposite direction. The leash kept her from going far but jerked her back, and she fell onto her bottom.

"It's okay. She's not hurt," Miranda said.

"Katie, Katie. You're not hurt." Agent Stone tried to soothe the child. "We need to get on the plane. Let's go." She tried to pick her up, and Katie smacked her hard across the face.

"Stay calm," Miranda spoke into her wire. "Sit down on the floor with her. Don't touch her."

Agent Stone followed Miranda's instructions as she rubbed her cheek.

People passed by and stared. One grandmotherly woman asked. "Dearie, can I do anything to help?"

Stone shook her head. "No, thank you. We'll be fine."

"Wait until she stops crying," cautioned Miranda. "Don't lose your patience. Remember the Russian lullaby I taught you? Sing it softly, like you're singing to yourself. Pretend you don't even notice she's there."

"*Bayu-bayushki-bayu, Ne lozhisya na krays,*" Agent Stone sang softly, her eyes half closed.

The wailing slowed to a whimper.

Stone sang the song again.

Katie moved closer and placed her fingers on Stone's lips. Both women's eyes met over the child's head.

"Can we get on the plane now, Katie?" Agent Stone said quietly.

The little girl stood up and offered her hand. They walked silently down the corridor and boarded the plane for New Orleans.

Miranda followed and settled in a seat six rows ahead.

Agent Raynes received a call from the poser. Another photo was up on the site. She pulled her laptop and logged in. This shot of Natalia had her naked on a big bed. It looked as if someone had shot the photo while she slept, her pigeon close to her neck. Fortunately, she faced away from the camera so only a small part of her round bottom was exposed. A hand with hairy knuckles clutched her inner thigh.

"Don't show this to the Boudreauxs," Wolfe said. "We're so close to catching these bastards; there's no point in adding flame to the fire. It could only jeopardize the mission."

Raynes agreed and logged off the site, nauseated by what she had seen. Despite the fifteen years she had been with the agency, crime involving children still made it hard to stay objective and focused on the mission. Some things you never got used to.

Chapter Thirty-Two

French Quarter, New Orleans, LA.

Feb. 24, 2009 – Fat Tuesday

At the Louis Armstrong airport in New Orleans, an entire task force of agents waited for the 10:30 flight from Houston. No one was sure if someone from Adoption Through Disruption would show up and take the child, leaving the agents no choice but to move in and possibly lose the trace on the location of the children.

In a utility van outside the airport, Armand and Cecile sat with four vested and armed FBI agents. The atmosphere was tense.

Katie fell asleep minutes after takeoff in Houston and never stirred for the hour and fifteen-minute flight. When they landed, Agent Stone tried to lift her into her arms without waking her. The child opened her eyes in alarm, apparently not remembering who she was with. The agent started singing quietly, and the child cuddled up in her arms and went back to sleep. A flight attendant helped her with the carry-on bag and offered to get a steward to help her.

Miranda stepped up. "May I help you, ma'am?"

"Why, thank you. My daughter is getting to be quite a load, but it's late and she's so tired." Agent Stone smiled at Miranda.

"I'll wheel your bag along with mine. Is your car in the lot?"

"Yes, that's very nice of you. I'm in B lot."

"What a coincidence. So am I." Miranda took the handle to Katie's bag and headed down the concourse.

They reached the parking lot without incident. Miranda left the child's bag with Agent Stone and proceeded to her car in the next section. From then on, she could only listen and advise from a distance. What was the range on the wire? Would she lose her in the crowd or on the road?

"Mommy?" Katie said, partially awakened by the harsh streetlamps as Agent Stone settled her into the car seat.

"It's okay, Katie-bug." Stone was glad she'd remembered what the Colsons called the girl. She waited in the car for her cell phone to ring. She hummed the Russian lullaby to stay calm. Ten minutes—no call. Fifteen—still no call.

"Can you still hear me?" Miranda's voice asked in Stone's ear.

"I can hear you," the agent sang back.

"What should we do if they don't call?" Miranda had no idea where to take the child or how to find

Natalia.

"I suspect they're desperate enough for the child that they'll call—eventually. They may be trying to make us antsy or are exhibiting a good deal of caution."

At 10:52 p.m. Stone's cell phone rang.

Miranda, lulled asleep herself by Agent Stone's humming, startled at the sound in her own ear.

Miranda could only hear one side of Stone's phone conversation. "Yes, and I have a very tired little girl. Where are her new parents? And who are you?" Stone sounded irritated.

"I don't know. Who are you again, and how do you see me? If you're here, why don't you take the child to her parents? I've made the disruption. I'm tired, and I want to go home."

The voice on Agent's Stone's cell gave her an address and hung up.

"Let me make sure I have this right," Miranda repeated the address into her cell, so Agent Wolfe understood. "She's to take the child to 871 St. Peter Street in the French quarter."

"Hmm, change in venue. Got it. We'll be there. Good job, Miranda," Wolfe said.

Within ten minutes, over twenty FBI agents had the property at St. Peter Street surrounded, not that anyone could tell. It was Fat Tuesday, and Mardi Gras was in full swing. The streets were full of people in crazy costumes and feathered masks. Some agents were in costume, reveling on the corner. One posed as a king cake vendor, selling the sweet yeast bread with cinnamon and icing. Others positioned themselves in the wine store across the street and in the abandoned property next door. Jazz and Cajun music blasted from every window; color and motion and deafening noise rising from the crowds made hearing cues from the other agents almost impossible. The only plus to the scenario was that the narrow one-way street would make a get-away difficult when the agents moved in on the perps.

"Why can't you bust in right now and get Natalia? Why do we have to wait for Agent Stone and the other child?" Armand rolled his shoulders in the cramped quarters of the van. Cecile sat beside him rocking and biting her nails.

"We need to make sure it's not a legitimate family, waiting for their new child. Hang in there, Armand. We're almost there."

Everyone in the van got stealthily quiet to listen in on the wire-tap Stone was wearing.

Agent Stone couldn't get her car through the throngs of people, so she parked in a garage ten streets over. She hitched the sleeping Katie on her hip and lugged the roll-along behind her. She spotted the address, a typical New Orleans shotgun house with three stories. The tall, narrow windows were secured with hurricane shutters giving it the appearance of a vacant property. The second story sported a wrought iron railing across the front and the third floor had small square windows with no balcony. She pushed her way through the crowd. The noise woke the sleeping child who clung tightly to Stone's neck.

"It's okay, Katie-bug," Stone whispered into her ear. "We'll have you out of here in no time. Hold on to me. I've got you."

She rang the bell. No answer. She pounded hard

on the door, realizing it was probably impossible to hear the bell.

A busty woman with long blue-black hair opened the door a few inches and peered out. A cigarette hung from her mouth, and she smelled of bourbon. She offered no introduction. "This the kid from Texas?"

Darlene, if the Boudreauxs's description was accurate.

"Who are you?" Stone said. "You don't look Russian. Where are the Popas?"

Darlene snorted. "What's it to you? You did your job. Gimme the kid, and then I'll give you the cash."

Agent Stone hesitated.

Agent Julia Wolfe spoke into the wire. "She has to give you permission to enter."

Stone nodded. "Well, I'm not leaving this child on a doorstep. If you want the child and the money, you're going to have to let me in."

Darlene debated for a few seconds before she opened the door wide and allowed Agent Stone to enter.

On cue, the agents swarmed in, some costumed, others with bullet-proof vests printed with FBI across the front and back. "FBI," they shouted as they entered.

Agent Wolfe jerked his chin toward Stone. "Get the child out of here."

Julia hurried out with the child still in her arms. A door on an inconspicuous van opened. Armand, Cecile, and Miranda were waiting inside.

"That poor baby," Cecile cried when she saw the now-crying child.

Stone handed the little girl to Miranda and headed into the house.

Inside the house, Darlene bristled. "What's the meaning of this? You can't come in here."

"Step aside." Agent Raynes held a gun on the woman while agents dashed past and systematically searched each room. Unless they found evidence or the children, they couldn't arrest her.

Stone entered one room that was set up with complex photography equipment, light modifiers on tripods and professional cameras with large zoom lenses. Rayne recognized the setting from the last photo of Natalia. A large bed was set against a backdrop. The other corner had a second set with children's play equipment.

"FBI, open up," they called before bursting through each closed door. So far, no children. They reached the third floor. No children. Had the perpetrators moved them or were the kids kept in a different location? Stone doubted that. It would be too difficult to move them from one location to another without raising suspicion. She called out. They had to be there someplace. "FBI! Kids, if you can hear me, call out." She strained to hear a noise over the revelry going on out in the street. Nothing.

Where were they? She looked up in exasperation. The ceiling was too low, even for these old houses. There had to be another floor. Where was the access? Seeing no seams anywhere in the sheet rock, she checked each closet. A piece of plywood had been nailed to the closet ceiling in one bedroom.

"Here," she cried.

Wolfe and the others joined her and pried the board off the ceiling, revealing a hole and a bare light bulb. He pulled the chain on the light bulb and heard a moan. Pulling a dresser over to stand on, he poked his head in the hole. The stench caused him to pull away and gag. In this tiny space, less than four feet high, eight large dog crates were lined between the rafters. The floor of each had a ragged blanket. Inside six of the cages where children, naked and laying in their own feces and urine. They all appeared to be drugged … or dead. There wasn't enough room to stretch out, so each child was curled in a fetal position.

"I got 'em," he called down to Stone and the other agents.

Raynes crawled up into the hole with him while another agent secured Darlene with handcuffs. "Check their pulses." She tried to reach the children, but her fingers were not long enough to fit through the wire mesh. She rattled the padlocks on a crate. "We have to find something to open these." Curled in a ball in the third cage was Natalia, her toy pigeon tight to her chest.

Agent Wolfe spoke into the radio communication going to the van. "Armand, there are metal cutters in the van. Natalia is here. Bring us the cutters."

Armand's head spun until he located a red toolbox. He sprang from the van, the cutters in his hand. His eyes wide with fear, he raced through the narrow house. "Where? Where's Natalia?"

The agent holding the gun on Darlene pointed up the stairs. "Third floor, follow Wolfe's voice into a closet."

"Here. In here." Stone's voice came from the second bedroom.

Armand climbed on the dresser and poked his head through the hole. "Oh, God. Are they alive?"

"Cutters. Give me the cutters." Wolfe reached his hand toward Armand who stared, unmoving.

"Armand!" Wolfe shouted. "Cutters!"

Armand snapped out of it and handed them to the agent.

Wolfe went to Natalia first, cutting the lock off the door. He reached in and put his fingers to her throat. The sound from the street drifted away, and time stood still as he felt for a pulse. "She's alive!" The perps had probably not planned on dead children, but Wolfe was sure nobody was checking weight levels against the drug dosages needed to keep the children subdued.

He lifted Natalia from the cage and handed the naked child through the hole to her father.

Tears flowed down Armand's cheeks as he stepped off the dresser.

An agent removed his jacket and wrapped it around the child. "Thank God," he said, patting Armand on the shoulder.

Raynes and Wolfe released the rest of the children, handing them down to Agent Stone, who laid them on the filthy bed. The other children, three girls and two boys, all between the ages of three and nine were alive. Three ambulances forced their way through the crowds. The paramedics took over, doing what they do best, saving lives.

Cecile joined Armand and they rode in the ambulance with their daughter. "Oh, baby. Natalia, can you hear me?" Cecile pleaded.

Natalia opened her eyes and looked directly at her. "Mommy?"

Armand and Cecile looked in amazement. She called her *Mommy*. Then they laughed. They put their heads back and shouted for joy.

The task force of agents and Miranda stood in front of the old French provincial house while Agent Wolfe brought out Darlene. Miranda could hear the contempt in Agent Wolfe's voice when he read Darlene her rights. Where were the others? There were no other adults in the house. His disappointment showed. Miranda knew he'd wanted to get them all. They'd convince Darlene to talk, then find the others. More importantly, the children had been found, and they were all alive.

They cuffed Darlene and put her in a squad car.

"You did good." Miranda smiled at all of them, especially Stone and Raynes, and then her gaze settled on Agent Wolfe."

Their eyes fixed on each other. "So, did you," he said. "We couldn't have done it without you."

The adrenaline rush evaporated from her body, and her knees went weak.

Agent Wolfe swept her up into his arms. "Whoa, are you okay?"

She blushed, feeling the strength of his hard body against hers. "I am now, Agent Wolfe."

He leaned in and brushed his lips against hers.

She hesitated for a millisecond, then responded with urgency, pressing her open mouth against his.

Everyone applauded.

"I think you can call me Simon now."

Chapter Thirty-Three

Chalmette, LA.

Feb. 25, 2009

Cecile breathed a sigh of relief when the doctors examined the children at the hospital and assured them that Natalia had not been raped or sodomized.

"Natalia is one of the lucky ones," the doctor said. "Thankfully she was rescued before any permanent harm could be done. We'll continue with a home child therapist, but since she was drugged most of the time, there's a good chance she'll have no memory of this as time passes. We want to keep her overnight, but then you can take your daughter home."

Some of the other children were not so lucky. There were signs of sexual abuse. Miranda worked with the New Orleans police and the FBI to find the parents that had rehomed their children. Once the children were out of physical danger, they would be returned to their parents with the promise of help from psychologists and therapists. For the parents, there would be intervention for dealing with the traumas of adoption and children with special needs.

They would not press charges against the parents. The Colsons had little Katie, and now, with the help they desperately needed, their lives with Katie could be enriching and successful.

Cecile couldn't believe the difference in Natalia. She was behaving like an entirely different child. She craved affection from them and spoke candidly in English.

"I'm sorry I was bad," said Natalia. "I only wanted to go home to Nika. Tasha was bad, and her new family sent her back. I thought if I was bad too, you'd send me back."

Cecile held her daughter on her lap, stroking her soft blond head. "Oh, sweetie. Why didn't you talk to us?" Her heart burst with love. Why had loving her been so difficult before? It felt so natural now.

Natalia shrugged and nestled in her arms as Neptune vied for space on Cecile's lap. He licked the child's face until she giggled and pushed him away. "Can I talk to Nika?"

Armand and Cecile exchanged glances. "Nika left the orphanage. We've already tried to call him. But once you feel strong enough, we'll go to St. Petersburg together and find Nika. How does that sound?"

Natalia beamed. "Thank you, Mommy and Daddy. I love you."

March 3, 2009

Cecile's parents and Mamère Le Bieu waited somewhat impatiently to see their granddaughter

253

after she came home. When they received the green light, a true Cajun cook-out was the venue for the celebration.

"Look," Natalia held up a squirming crawfish between her fingers as she beamed at Grandma Lafayette. "Mud bugs!"

Grandpa Lafayette sprayed beer through his nose. Mamère Le Bieu shook her head as she looked over at her son as Cecile and Armand doubled over in laughter.

"Careful you don't get pinched." said Cecile to Natalia. "Want to help make the shrimp etouffee?"

Natalie dropped the crawfish in the outdoor cooker and followed her mother into the house. In a big skillet, Cecile melted butter and stirred in flour until it was golden brown. She let Natalia drop in the chopped onion, peppers, and celery.

"Step aside so you don't get burned," Cecile cautioned as she poured in the water that sizzled in the pan. The steam filled the room.

"I can't see you." Natalia giggled.

"Wait one second. It'll clear. There, now drop in the shrimp. Slowly," Cecile cautioned as she added the all-important Tabasco sauce.

Natalia beamed up at her, stirring the mix with a big wooden spoon. "I like cooking with you, Mommy."

Mommy, Cecile smiled. How long had she waited to hear that precious word.

Armand came through the door and planted a kiss on two cheeks. "So, what are my two favorite girls doing in here?

"We're making shrimp-toothy," Natalia said proudly.

"Close enough," said her daddy.

When the sun went down, the celebration a big hit, a sleepy Natalia happily climbed into her bed, snuggled up next to her toy pigeon, a constant companion through one little girl's lifetime worth of trauma.

Mamère Le Bieu tucked her in as she told her the Legend of Evangeline. "Evangeline and Gabriel were in love. The English Governor of Canada issued an ultimatum to the Acadians to swear allegiance to the British Crown and give up their Catholic faith or be exiled. Evangeline and Gabriel refused and were separated on their wedding day. They were herded onto separate ships, forced to leave the country and all their possessions behind without any regard to family ties.

"Upon her arrival in Louisiana, Evangeline learned that Gabriel was in the Attakapas district. She began her journey there, but soon found that Gabriel, in a grief-stricken state, had left the region. She began a lifelong search for her lost love as she wandered through the American frontier. She eventually gave up her search and joined the Sisters of Mercy in Philadelphia, dedicating her life to the service of others. Years later, she found Gabriel who was on his deathbed and died in her arms. She died soon after."

Natalia fell asleep to Mamère's soothing voice telling of lost love and reunion in the bayous of Louisiana.

With the child asleep, Mamère Le Bieu joined the adults outside around a fire. She pulled the gris-gris doll from a large pocket in her kaftan. "I told you we would find her." She stroked the doll. "In a hole.

Did they find the boy, too?"

Armand didn't want to argue with his step-grandmother, the voodoo queen of New Orleans. "Yes, thank God, we found her in time. It wasn't exactly a hole, Mamère; it was an attic."

"Did you go through a hole to get her?" She smiled.

"Yes, I guess, we did. And there were two boys, so your gris-gris came true."

"Of course, it did," she said, then paused. "There is still another boy in a hole."

Armand groaned. There were probably thousands of children in something you could interpret as a hole if you really wanted to stretch it that far.

Chapter Thirty-Four

St. Petersburg, Russia

April 10, 2009

The flight to St. Petersburg had an air of excitement. Natalia bounced in her seat, and Cecile had to get inventive with lap games to keep the girl occupied. Cecile kissed the top of Natalia's head as she fidgeted in her lap. *Thank God, we found her. How could I ever have questioned my ability to love this child? We owe it to her to find her brother.*

Armand read through the material he had gathered on the internet about the thousands of street children in this huge metropolitan city. They lived in abandoned basements, in train stations that ran under the city, even in sewers. It was unfathomable that a country could totally ignore this massive problem. Several articles interviewed the street urchins that chose the streets to living at home with alcoholic and abusive parents. One heartbreaking story of a six-year-old boy said his parents took him downtown, told him to stay put, and walked out of his life never to return. He'd been on the streets ever since. Armand shivered. *Did we do that by handing Natalia over to Darlene? Even if a little different?* He shivered at the similarity. What if they couldn't find Nikolai? The streets were a dangerous place. He could be dead. How would he explain it to Natalia?

They chose a more affordable hotel this time around. They'd had to take a home equity line of credit to pay for the trip. A hotel shuttle picked them up at the Pulkovo II International Airport and quickly had them at the Nevsky Hotel Grand. The historic building, ancient and baroque on the exterior, was unassuming and contemporary inside. Their suite contained a king size bed and, behind a half wall, a sofa bed for Natalia. The furnishings were clean but austere.

"Can we go find Nika now?" Natalia asked hopefully.

"How about we settle in at the hotel and have some dinner, and we'll get started first thing in the morning?" Armand said. "We could all use a good night's sleep from that long flight."

Cecile was stacking clothes in the wardrobe. "I think our first stop needs to be at New Holland Orphanage."

A look of worry crossed Natalia's face. "Are you going to give me back because I was bad?"

Cecile wrapped her arms around the child. "Of course not. We're never letting you go again. The caretakers or the other boys there may have an idea where to look for Nikolai."

"Oh, okay. I don't like that place."

"Understood," said Armand, "but if they can help us find Nika…"

"I'll do it." Natalia jumped up and down, twisted the key to the pigeon's music box and danced around the room.

Cecile felt Natalia stiffen and grip her hand a little tighter as they approached the bridge to the New Holland Orphanage.

"It's good to see you again," said the director they had met on their first visit with Anastasia, the social worker with Hope International. "Is there a problem with our placement of Natalia?" A frown crossed her plain face, and she looked down at the child cowering behind Cecile's skirts.

"Oh, no, not at all," said Cecile. How would they feel if they knew about the past year and the eventual disastrous disruption? "We're trying to find her brother, Nikolai."

"Yes, of course," the woman said with obvious relief. "As I told your husband on the phone a few weeks ago, he left on his own accord, and we haven't seen him since."

Armand said, "We had hoped you might be able to give us some clues on where to look for him."

"Let me call Mr. Korkov. He was the caretaker for the boys' wing where Nikolai stayed. One moment, please."

They waited in the lobby as wide-eyed children sized them up.

Armand leaned over and whispered, "Do you see any of your friends, Natalia?"

She shook her head. "I didn't have any friends."

Mr. Korkov, his shoulders stooped, shuffled into the lobby. He looked tired and disinterested in anything going on around him. Cecile supposed that years of working in a depressing place like this would want anyone want to mentally block it out.

"I heard that Nikolai was working at the docks hosing out containers," he said. "It's also possible that he is with Dimitri, his friend who left six months before him. But I have no idea where Dimitri is either. Damn kids don't know when they have it well off. Better a warm bed here than on the streets God-knows-where."

The director returned with copies of a recent photo of Nikolai so they could hand them out to the street children in the hopes that someone would recognize him. "Good luck. I hope you find him."

Cecile handed one photo to Natalia.

"Hi, Nika," she said, fingering the picture of the boy with straight brown hair, round dark eyes and a navy cap sitting on the back of his head. "Babushka made that hat for him—before the fire."

Cecile's heart ached for her daughter. No wonder they call it a broken heart. It physically hurt her to see Natalia in pain.

Armand knelt, pulling Natalia into his arms. "You've had one hard time, haven't you, baby? But we're here to make it all better. Now let's go find your brother."

Armed with photos, their next stop was the docks. The problem was the Port of St. Petersburg was the largest in all of Russia, encompassing miles and miles of docks. With limited communication due to the language barrier, they finally located the FCT, First Container Terminal, on the Neva River. Six foremen later, they were directed to a barrel of a man with beady eyes. "Yes, he worked here. I fired him."

"Do you know where he lives?" Cecile asked.

The man looked at her blankly.

Natalia stepped in front of Cecile and repeated the question in Russian.

The foreman looked down at the hopeful little girl.

"He is my brother, and he is lost," Natalia pleaded.

He shook his head. "No, I don't know where your brother is. I'm sorry." Softly, in broken English, he spoke close to Armand's ear. "He didn't show up for work for three days. I had to replace him. Probably sniffing glue like the rest of them good-for-nothing kids. I'm sorry."

Cecile and Armand exchanged a look over Natalia's head. This could be bad. If he was doing drugs, God knows what condition he would be in or where he would be.

Armand thanked the foreman, and they headed back to the streets. The director of the orphanage had given them a list of shelters that fed the homeless. Maybe someone would recognize him.

No one at the Nochlezhka tent house recognized the picture of Nikolai. Most of the children turned away, refusing to look at the photo. Were they protecting one of their own, or were they jealous that Nikolai may have escaped and they hadn't?

As the day came to a close, everyone was tired and cranky. Natalia whined and lashed out at Cecile. "I want Nika. You said you would find him."

Cecile picked up the exhausted child and cradled her on her lap on the train ride to the hotel.

"We're trying, sweetheart. Let's get some dinner and a good night's sleep, and we'll try again tomorrow." What if they couldn't find him? What would she say to Natalia?

Chapter Thirty-Five

St. Petersburg, Russia

April 11, 2009

Olga had taught Nikolai how to pick pockets in the market at the Church of the Spilled Blood. Thousands of unsuspecting tourists converged on the market for a spending frenzy upon their departure from the huge cruise ships that came into port every few days. Most were easy pickings, women with large open handbags flung casually over their shoulders, men with fat wallets that barely fit into their hip pockets.

Nikolai shared his rewards with the younger children that had begun to follow him around, their tiny hands stretched toward him.

Olga scoffed at him. "Robin Hood, when are you going to learn? Everyone must take care of himself out here. You can't feed them all."

"No, but I can try," he said with a smile. "What

if one of those were my little sister? I hope someone would give her a hand."

"You have a sister? Do you know where she is?"

"Yes, she is in America with a nice family. They adopted her while we were at New Holland."

She sneered. "But they didn't take you, huh? Left you to rot there."

Nikolai shook his head. "Shut up, Olga. It wasn't like that. I was already too old. It only matters what happens to Natalia. I promised Momma I would make sure she was safe—and I did."

Olga sniffed on a plastic bag of glue. Her eyes glazed, and she pulled her jacket closer around her as the stink from the sewer faded from her consciousness.

Nikolai pulled the heavy iron cover over the manhole and settled onto the dry ledge above the human waste. Olga's head dropped into his lap as he fell asleep.

April 13, 2009

To cover more ground in their search, Armand and Cecile decided to split up. On suggestions by the hotel clerk, Armand headed toward Gostiny Dvor while Cecile and Natalia headed the other direction toward Nevsky Prospect and the market near the Church of the Savior

"Natalia, sweetheart, why don't you leave your pigeon here today?" Cecile attempted to lift the toy out of the child's hand.

"No," shouted Natalia, hugging the toy close to her chest.

Cecile sighed. "Okay, but I hope you don't lose

it. I have enough to carry if you get tired."

Natalia stomped her foot. "I won't lose it. And I'm a big girl. I'll walk."

I thought we were over this behavior. Cecile stamped down her own feelings of angst.

They walked for hours and hours, checking in every alley and peeking into basements. Every street urchin reacted the same way, saying they'd never seen Nika before. If they knew, they weren't telling.

Stopping to get something to eat at the Park Giuseppe restaurant, Cecile and Natalia waited on the sidewalk for a table.

"Stand still, please, Natalia. It'll only be a few minutes."

Natalia turned the key on the music box on her toy pigeon and danced to the "Korobushka" as passersby smiled.

A few meters behind them, a boy was picking pockets of patrons waiting to get into the restaurant. He paused when he heard the music. His heart skipped a beat. Natalia's song. He sent a silent prayer to let her know he was thinking of her. The music drew him forward.

There, dancing on the sidewalk, a little girl with yellow pigtails twirled around and around with a toy pigeon pressed to her cheek.

"Natalia?" Nikolai shouted in disbelief.

Cecile and Natalia turned to see a tall teenage boy rushing toward them.

Natalia dropped the toy and rushed into his arms. "Nika, Nika. We've looked and looked for you."

Tears streamed down his face. "Golubka, is it

really you?"

Cecile picked up the toy and joined the children in a group hug.

"Nika, this is Mommy, my American mama. We came with Daddy to find you."

Nikolai stood, giving an awkward bow to Cecile. "Thank you for taking care of my sister. I am most grateful."

Cecile noticed he was almost as tall as Armand. "We love her very much. It's nice to meet you." She kissed him on his gritty cheek and fought the urge to spit the dirt out of her mouth. "Nikolai, we're staying in the Nevsky Hotel Grand. Will you come with us there? Armand will be so glad to meet you."

Nikolai looked down at his ragged clothes and his dirty hands. His face flushed. "I...I don't know if they would want me there."

"Nonsense." Cecile said. "You are with us. Where are your things? We'll go and get them, and you will stay with us."

"Yes, Nika. Yes, you will stay with us." Natalia jumped up and down in front of him, squeezing both of his hands.

"Um, I don't have anything." The flush deepened at his collar.

"Nothing?" Cecile said, aghast.

Nikolai pulled the small black Bible from his right hip pocket. "I have this," he said. "It is enough. But I must let my friend know where I am. We kind of look after each other."

"Sure, shall we go with you?"

"No," Nikolai said quickly. "I'll meet you at the Nevsky Hotel Grand in an hour." He didn't want them to follow him to the manhole he and Olga had called home for the last few weeks.

Cecile caught the body language that he was ashamed of wherever he lived. "Okay. But promise Natalia you will come."

Natalia frowned at her brother. "Nika, don't leave me again. I want to go with you."

Nikolai crouched on his long legs and looked his sister in the eye. "Golubka, I must do this alone. But I promise I will meet you at the hotel." He pinched her cheek. "And hold on to that pigeon. We never would have found each other without it." He gave her an Eskimo kiss, rubbing his nose against hers.

Reluctantly, Natalia allowed Cecile to lead her to the train station to return to the hotel. She waved at Nikolai before he disappeared behind a corner.

Cecile phoned Armand on his cell and explained excitedly about the reunion. "Can you believe it? We found him, or rather, he found us."

"Thank God for that music box. I'll see you at the hotel."

Nikolai raced to the manhole in the hopes of finding Olga, still sleeping it off from selling herself on the streets the night before. "Olga. Wake up. Natalia is here."

"What are you talking about?" Olga pulled herself to a sitting position. She had a fresh new bruise on the side of her cheek.

"What happened to you? Are you all right?"

She waved his concern away. "It's nothing. A john didn't like my rules. No condom, no pussy. What about Natalia?"

"She's here. In St. Petersburg with her American parents. I'm going to the Nevsky Hotel Grand to see them now."

"Look at you. They'll never let you in." She dropped her head on the makeshift pillow of her bomber jacket. She winced as her cheek met the fabric.

Nikolai looked down at his clothes. "I'm going to the Borovaj Street shelter. Maybe they can give me some clean clothes and let me take a bath."

"Yeah, yeah. Good luck." She started to nod off. "Hey, man, maybe you'll get to go to America with them. You deserve it. You're Robin Hood. Nice knowing you, kid."

Nikolai hesitated in the rancid smelling hole they called a home. Was she right? Would this be the last he would see of his friend? He fought down the lump in his throat. "Yeah, who knows? Take care now. And don't take anymore shit from them johns, okay?"

"Mmm," she mumbled as he slipped the heavy cover over the hole before sprinting toward the shelter.

At the shelter, Nikolai excitedly explained about the lucky encounter with his sister and her new parents. They offered him clean clothes and let him shower. The clothes weren't a perfect fit but were a huge improvement over the smelly things he'd slept in for the past few weeks.

Armand paced the floor of the hotel suite while Cecile bathed Natalia and dressed her in the prettiest dress she'd brought.

"What do we do from here?" Armand asked his wife. "We haven't thought this through. How can we go about adopting him if he's no longer at the orphanage? Can he go back with us so we can start the process? Maybe we should talk to Anastasia from the Hope Agency here in St. Petersburg."

Cecile brushed out Natalia's golden locks and pinned them out of her eyes with a pink barrette. "Let's wait and see what Nikolai wants to do. We don't even know if he wants us to adopt him."

"Oh, yes, Nika will want to come, especially when I tell him how nice you are." Natalia beamed at Armand.

The front desk called from the in-house phone. "Mr. Boudreaux, a young man of questionable intentions is here asking for your room number." He whispered into the phone, "He looks like a street urchin. Should I send him away?"

"No, kindly send him up to our room, please."

"Um, of course, sir." The desk clerk huffed into the receiver.

"He's here! He's here!" Natalia jumped up and down. She raced to the door and ran down the hall to the elevator.

Nikolai stepped off on the correct floor and was immediately assaulted by a little girl jumping into his arms. "Whoa, Golubka," he said with a laugh. He hugged her tightly to his chest. "Show me which room to go to."

Armand and Cecile stood in the doorway, arm-in-arm, witnessing the reunion of the siblings. Armand thought about how differently this could have turned out. If Natalia had not been found. If Nikolai had not been found. Two lost children — safely back in each other's arms.

"Nika, this is my daddy," Natalia said proudly as the two approached the open doorway where

Armand and Cecile waited.

Armand's heart swelled with emotion. *My daddy.*

Nikolai switched Natalia's hold to his left arm so he could extend his hand. "It is a pleasure to meet you, sir," he said stiffly.

"The pleasure is all mine. I'm Armand Boudreaux. And I know you already met Natalia's mother, Cecile. Please come in." He waved them into the suite.

"Thank you, sir." Nikolai came to a stop a few steps into the doorway, Natalia still clinging to his neck. He had never been in a room this nice. The sitting area had a sofa bed, two lounge chairs, a desk, and a television. Beyond it he could see a spacious bed with a soft billowy down comforter and stacks of fluffy pillows. This was a far cry from sleeping in the sewer or Dimitri's rat-infested apartment or even the bunks of the orphanage. Somewhere in a distant memory, there was a little red cottage with comfortable rooms and warm cozy fireplaces.

"Sit down, please," Cecile urged the boy.

"Thank you, ma'am." He sat gingerly on the edge of one of the lounge chairs.

"Okay, how about we go for *Armand* and *Cecile* instead of *sir* and *ma'am*." Armand offered with a smile, trying to put the boy at ease.

Nikolai forced a return smile. "Okay, sir...um ...Armand."

"How about Mommy and Daddy?" Natalia asked.

Everyone smiled but had no response to that. It was too early to make those kinds of decisions.

"So, Nikolai," Armand said. "How long have

you been away from the orphanage? We tried to call you again, but the director said you had left, and he didn't know where you went."

Nikolai stared into his little sister's eyes. "I didn't see much reason to stay after Natalia left. I knew I was too old for anyone to want to adopt me. I thought it would be better on my own."

"Was it?" Cecile asked.

"Not exactly. I shared an apartment with a friend for a while, but after we got evicted and I lost my job at the docks, things went downhill. But it was too late to go back. I get by." He tried to sound optimistic, but there was no way to paint a pretty picture of being homeless.

Cecile reached across the table and stroked his arm. "I'm sure it was very difficult. You are a brave boy to do that. Are you going to school?"

Nikolai looked at his shoes. "No, ma'am, I mean Cecile. My papers were stolen." He didn't want to admit that the police had taken his papers when they raided the abandoned basement he was living in.

Armand offered a solution. "Nikolai, we'd like to bring you to America with us. We're not a rich family, but you could go to school and have a roof over your head."

Natalia clapped her hands. "And be with me."

Nikolai gave her an Eskimo kiss with his nose. "I promised our mama before she died that I would take care of Natalia. And I did that when you adopted her. I know she is in a good home. But I have also secured a future for her."

Armand and Cecile exchanged glances. "I don't understand," Cecile said.

He turned to Natalia. "Bring me your pigeon. I

want to show you something."

Natalia jumped down off his lap and collected the toy pigeon from the bedroom. She handed it to her brother.

He turned it over and picked at the stitching under its belly.

"Nika, you're tearing him!" Natalia cried.

"It's okay, Golubka, we can stitch it up. There is a surprise inside for you."

With the stitching loose, he slipped his fingers under the music box and lifted out a small Orthodox cross, about seven centimeters tall, pure gold, and encrusted with diamonds, rubies, and emeralds. The light from the window caught the gems and reflected prisms of light on the walls.

"Pretty," exclaimed Natalia, running her fingers over the stones.

Cecile and Armand gasped. "Omigod!" Cecile said. "Where did you get that?"

Armand frowned. "Please don't tell me you stole it."

"Not exactly. I found it in the catacombs under the orphanage on New Holland Island, wedged into the wall of the tunnel. I don't know, but I think it must be incredibly old."

"Yes, I would say so," Armand said. "May I see it?"

Nikolai handed the cross to him. "I thought that if it was worth a lot of money, Natalia could sell it if she needed to support herself. But maybe you could use it now to take care of her. It's not for me. It's for Natalia."

Armand examined the cross closely, trying to decipher the inscription on the smooth back.

"Nikolai, I believe this is very, very old. But I don't think it would be right to sell it. I think it should be returned to the church. Maybe you should take it to the monastery."

"But it was meant to take care of Natalia." Nikolai objected.

Cecile nodded. "I agree with Armand. This doesn't belong to any of us. It belongs to the Russian Orthodox Church."

Natalia pressed her little hands on her brother's downtrodden cheeks. "It's okay, Nika. The church can have it. Mama and Papa would have wanted you to give it to them...and then, maybe they will let you be a priest."

Nikolai smiled at her. "It's not that easy, Golubka."

"You want to be a priest?" Armand asked.

"Well, I did when I was a child. I thought God was calling me to the priesthood. But that was before … well, before I understood that it was only a child's dream."

"No, no, Nika. You must be a priest!" Natalia turned and looked at her parents. "God called his name. That's what Babushka said."

Armand set the ancient artifact on the coffee table between them. No one spoke for a minute, all staring at the cross.

"Well, first things first." Cecile broke the silence. "How about we get some dinner at a nice restaurant to celebrate Natalia and Nikolai's reunion. Then tomorrow, we can decide if the cross goes back to the church or to the police. But it is not ours to keep."

Everyone agreed. Over dinner, Natalia told Nikolai about her abduction, but her memory of it was so confused from the drugs that her tale had more to do with the scary people with masks during Mardi Gras. Armand and Cecile were relieved that was the extent of her memory.

Chapter Thirty-Six

St. Petersburg, Russia

April 13. 2009

Armand offered Nikolai a pair of his pajamas to use for the night. A little large in girth, but the length of the long pants was fine. Nikolai offered to sleep on the floor, but Natalia had a fit, wanting him to share the pull-out sofa bed with her.

Nikolai was exhausted, but the excitement of the day kept him from dozing off. He lay under the warm covers with Natalia spooned next to him, her toy pigeon tucked under her chin. The clean scent of Johnson's baby shampoo wafted in the air close to his nose. Her soft little body reminded him of the first time he held her in his arms.

He was ten years old. Mama had come home from the hospital with a little bundle in her arms. She was sleeping, but when Mama placed the tiny thing in his arms, she opened her blue eyes wide and stared up at him. People in the village all wanted to see the little gift that had blessed the family after so many years of trying. But Papa would not let them into the house, afraid a germ would take away their miracle child.

Natalia had been Nikolai's shadow from the moment she learned to walk. Then she discovered Dedushka's homing pigeons. From then on, he had to share her affection.

He finally drifted off to sleep with a smile on his face.

After a good breakfast, they headed off to the St. Petersburg Theological Academy. The austere monastery loomed behind tall iron gates. The yellow brick building beckoned Nikolai, and his heart skipped a beat at the sight. If only he had stayed pure. *If only…*

They pushed the intercom at the gate. A deep voice answered. Of course, neither Armand nor Cecile understood what the voice said.

"We have an artifact to return to the Church," Nikolai said in Russian.

They waited. No response from the black box. Then a young clean-shaven postulate dressed in a simple black cassock, a large Orthodox cross hanging from his neck appeared at the gate. "May I help you?" He stood solemnly on the other side iron barrier.

Nikolai hesitated, and then retrieved the cross from his pocket. "I found this. I'd like to return it." He showed it to the priest through the iron bars. He hoped the priest would not take it and walk away without letting Nikolai explain.

The deacon's eyes grew wide with wonder. He

retrieved a key from hidden pockets in his cassock and opened the gate so they could enter. "Follow me, please."

The small entourage followed him through the beautifully landscaped grounds leading up to the yellow brick building. Humbled to be on the Holy grounds of this sanctuary, Nikolai stumbled as he walked.

"Forgive me if I was rude," the deacon explained, addressing Nikolai, who he surmised was the only one that understood his language.

Nikolai gave a slight bow and spoke in Russian. "It is I that must beg forgiveness. We should have telephoned for an audience."

They followed the young man into a large room with sparse but elegant furnishings; two sofas facing each other in front of a large fireplace with two grandiose straight-backed chairs with red velvet cushions, a grand piano in a corner, and a floor-to-ceiling wall of ancient books.

"Please be seated. Archbishop Peterhof will be with you shortly." He quietly backed out and closed the massive double doors.

Nikolai paled. *Father in Heaven. The archbishop! Please don't let me pass out.* He wiped clammy hands on his trousers. He closed his eyes and took some deep breaths. His mouth felt like cotton, and he gripped the arms of the chair to resist the urge to run.

Natalia, oblivious to her brother's anxiety, jumped from the sofa and wandered over to the piano. She ran her fingers across the keys.

"Natalia," Cecile scolded. "We don't touch things that don't belong to us. Come over here and sit down, like a nice little lady."

The child's lower lip protruded, but she did as she was told.

They waited about ten minutes. Nikolai tapped his hands on his trousers. What on earth would he say to the archbishop? Why couldn't they give the cross to one of the deacons?

When the door opened, the deacon held the door for the archbishop. He was younger than Nikolai expected. Gentle eyes smiled above a full brown beard and mustache. Also dressed in a black cassock, but with a tall black pill-box hat and a much larger pectoral cross hanging from his neck.

Everyone stood.

"Father Peterhof, this is the family with the cross," the deacon said in Russian.

Armand extended his hand first. "Thank you for seeing us." He looked toward Nikolai to answer, but the boy was dumbstruck.

"It is my pleasure," the bishop answered in perfect English as he accepted Armand's outstretched hand. "Welcome to God's school. Please be seated."

Everyone sat after the bishop had taken his seat in one of the velvet chairs, everyone except Natalia. She wandered over to the bishop and stroked his brown beard.

"Natalia, come here," Cecile hissed.

The bishop smiled at the little girl and lifted her onto his lap. "And who do we have here?"

"I'm Natalia," she said proudly, still stroking his beard. "Your beard is soft. Like Dedushka's."

"Really?" The bishop entertained the child. "Where does your dedushka live?"

Natalia frowned and looked like she was about to cry. "In heaven." She slid off his lap and took a seat between Armand and Cecile on the sofa.

Nikolai fought to find his voice. "Our parents and grandparents died in a fire in Suzdal."

"I'm sorry to hear that. So, these are not your parents?" Archbishop Peterhof nodded toward Armand and Cecile.

Armand answered for him. "We adopted Natalia a year ago and live in America. Nikolai has been living here in St. Petersburg."

"Son, Deacon Alexy tells me you have a cross of some significance to the Church?"

Nikolai stood and walked on wobbly legs to the bishop. He withdrew the cross from his pocket and placed it in the man's open palm.

The bishop lifted it to the light and turned it over to scrutinize the engraving on the reverse. "Tell me, Nikolai. Where did you find this?"

Feeling unworthy to stand above the archbishop, Nikolai knelt before him. He started slowly, trying to find the words to describe living in the orphanage, how he and Dimitri used the tunnels to find broken pieces of armor and pottery in the catacombs, how he had wanted a gift for Natalia.

His words flowed faster and faster as he lapsed into Russian and explained getting lost on Christmas Day in the tunnels, how he found the artifact while feeling his way along in the dark and how Dimitri had rescued him.

The bishop listened without interrupting, allowing the boy to find the words he struggled to articulate. "And why has it taken this long to come to the decision to bring it here?"

Nikolai's face contorted in pain, and he threw himself prone on the floor. "Forgive me, Father. I hid it, and it was just yesterday that I disclosed its whereabouts. It was meant to be Natalia's savings. I promised Mama that I would take care of her. I have sinned, Father."

The bishop reached down and lifted the boy by the shoulders. "My son. It is not up to me to forgive you, but our Heavenly Father. But your intentions were good to take care of your sister. If this was indeed in the catacombs of New Holland Island, this could be priceless … perhaps from the time of Peter the Great himself."

Nikolai tried to hold back the sobs that choked off his breathing. He began to hiccup uncontrollably. "Sorry, sorry," he mumbled between each hitch.

Natalia stepped toward her brother and patted him on his back as he kneeled in front of the bishop. "It's okay, Nika. When you become a priest, it will all be better."

Archbishop Peterhof raised his eyebrows until they almost disappeared under his tall black hat. "What's this? Are you studying for the priesthood, my son?"

Nikolai shook his head. "No, Father. It was only a dream when I was a young boy."

"Nika, that's not true," protested Natalia. "God called him. I must have been sleeping because I didn't hear the phone ring, but Babushka said he called Nikolai to be a priest."

Everyone chuckled at the child's vision of God's calling.

Nikolai tried to explain how, before the fire, their parents had worked at the twin churches in Suzdal their entire lives and how there had been a time he felt God's calling. But those dreams were dashed when all the money their parents had saved for the seminary was used to bury them.

The archbishop stroked his beard. "Did you serve in the church prior to your parents' death?"

Nikolai nodded. "I was an altar boy and sang chants during Mass for five years. But none of that matters now. The money is gone, and I am unworthy."

"Nikolai, how long has it been since you have been to confession?"

Startled, the boy turned away, ashamed. "Not since I left New Holland."

The bishop fingered the cross in his palm. "Nikolai, if this artifact is indeed from Peter the Great, it is priceless. It would take the vote of the synod, but I would be willing to present to them the opportunity for you to attend the academy as reward for returning the cross to the Church. Do you still believe God has called you?"

Tears streamed down Nikolai's face. He nodded. "If God would grant me absolution for my sins."

Cecile and Armand had sat silently through this conversation. "We have asked Nikolai to come to the United States with us. But he says he no longer has his registration papers," Armand said.

"What would be your desire, Nikolai? To attend the academy or to go with your sister to America?"

Nikolai looked at his little sister, who for once, didn't beg for her own way. "If God would have me, I'd like to be a priest so I can help the homeless children on the streets. I've tried to help, but ..."

The bishop's face lit up. "Are you the one they call Robin Hood? I have heard of this boy that steals from the tourists and buys food for the street urchins. Is that you, Nikolai?"

"Yes, Father."

"Son, you know it is wrong to steal, but your intentions are good. I believe that God will forgive you if you take confession and unload your burden to Our Father."

Nikolai raised his head. "Do you really think so?"

The priest placed his hand on the boy's head. "Take it to Our Father, son. He will forgive you."

They all attended Mass with the students of the Academy. In the confessional, Nikolai poured out his heart, bearing his soul from the moment with the shopkeeper when he earned the cash for the toy pigeon on his knees to the last pocket he picked before hearing Natalia's music box.

After Mass, the archbishop told them that he would have the cross evaluated for authenticity. It would take a few days. Could the Boudreauxs please stay in the country until the results were in? If the cross was not authentic, he would do what he could to get Nikolai new registration papers so he could go to the U.S. with them. But if it was authentic, he would like to offer Nikolai admittance into the St. Petersburg Theological Academy.

They agreed they would extend their VISAs and wait for the results. Nikolai went with them to the hotel again.

Armand suggested. "What would you kids think about taking a trip to Suzdal while we wait for the results of the artifact?

Nikolai and Natalia exchanged huge grins.

"Yeah!" Natalia said. "We can show you where Mama and Papa worked. And the pigeon lofts. Nika, do you think the pigeons are still there?"

"I don't know, Golubka, but it would be fun to find out."

Chapter Thirty-Seven

Suzdal, Russia

April 15, 2009

With several days to wait until the results of the authenticity of the cross would be revealed, the four boarded a train for an eight-hour ride to Moscow, then another two and a half hours on a bus to Vladimir City, where they rented a car to Suzdal. In all, the trip took fourteen hours, stopping in Vladimir to eat and stretch.

Nikolai recalled the reverse trip they'd made on the orphan train, not knowing where they were going or what life would bring them. *I was such a child then, hardly more mature than Natalia is now.* Three years had changed so much. At seventeen, he was almost an adult, and God willing, his dream of the priesthood could become a reality. He had truly been to hell and back.

The countryside around Suzdal resembled a picture postcard. Before they entered the city, Cecile was awed by the skyline of domes and steeples, and windmills. "Omigod, what a beautiful place."

Nikolai could feel the grin spreading across his face. He sat a little taller in his seat and an excited flutter tickled his insides. He hadn't known if he would ever see this place again. It was a sight for sore eyes.

"Look, Nika." Natalia giggled, waving her arms. "Mama and Papa's churches." Before them they saw the small winter Church of the Nativity of St. John the Baptist with its elegant green bell tower and the larger summer St. John the Baptist Church with its multiple spires.

"Your parents worked there?" Armand asked. "We know so little about your life before coming to the orphanage."

"Yes," Nikolai exclaimed. "Mama gave lectures inside, and Papa was the groundskeeper. A melancholy look clouded his eyes for a moment. "They loved working there. Can we see where our house was?"

Cecile spoke above Natalia's head. "Do you think that is a good idea? It could be upsetting."

Nikolai turned to his sister. "Golubka, would it make you too sad to see where our house was?"

She shook her head. "It's okay. Can we find the pigeon lofts?"

Nikolai looked at Armand, who nodded. "We can try." He gave directions down the narrow road. Where the cottage once stood had been cleared of debris and a field of rosehip and wild strawberries bloomed in an array of pink and white blossoms.

A lump formed in Nikolai's throat. "God has

claimed this land, like he claimed Mama and Papa, Babushka and Dedushka."

Armand parked the car, and they walked through the wildflowers to the spot that had taken the lives of their family. They joined hands, and Nikolai led them in a prayer, giving thanks for their past life and asking for guidance for the future.

Armand and Cecile were overcome with emotion, as was Nikolai, but Natalia embraced the past and future with childish optimism, twirling, her face tilted up to the sky, taking in the warm spring sunshine.

"Can we find the pigeon loft now?" She jumped up and down, pulling on Nikolai's arm.

They crossed the old wooden bridge over the Kamenka River, through the meadow and up the small knoll.

Natalia spotted the stilted buildings first and rushed ahead. "Ivan, Ivan. Are you here?" Before she reached the first rung on the ladder, she heard the cooing of dozens of pigeons. She climbed up and disappeared through the little door.

Cecile and Armand were slightly out of breath by the time they caught up with their daughter at the foot of the lofts.

Nikolai smiled at them, "That's my sister. She's half pigeon."

Natalia emerged from the loft, a steel gray pigeon with an iridescent green neck, perched on her shoulder. With the exception of looking slightly older, she was the epitome of the photo Cecile carried in her purse. "See, Nika, Ivan is here. I told you I would fly home someday... and I did."

Yasha Borelov was late getting to the lofts to

feed the pigeons. He saw a family talking and laughing at the foot of the lofts. "Nikolai?" Yasha called. "Is that really you?"

Nikolai turned to see his boyhood friend, now fully grown with a shadow of a beard across his chin. "Yasha, my friend. It is me," he answered in Russian, slapping his friend on the back.

They conversed, typical teen-age boys jousting with long arms and pointy elbows. After Nikolai explained who Armand and Cecile were, Yasha switched to English.

"Sorry to be rude. We were just catching up. I'm still taking care of the birds," Yasha said proudly. "Ivan and Gerta are going to win the homing contest. They fly home Thursday. Will you be here to see them return?"

"I don't know." Nikolai looked toward Armand for direction.

Armand shrugged. "Fly? Tell me more."

Yasha stretched out his arm, and Ivan jumped on to it. "I've been training them for over a year now. They are thoroughbreds, descendants of the czar's homers. You see, homing pigeons use low-frequency sound waves to navigate to their lofts. We will release them in Vladimir and the first ones to make it home wins. Thirty-four and half kilometers. There is a purse of seventeen thousand rubles."

Cecile's eyes got wide. "That's five hundred dollars, am I right?"

"Yes, it is a very big deal. Is that how you say in English?" Yasha laughed.

"We just came from Vladimir. Yes, we will stay and watch for their return. There is much to see in this beautiful city."

Yasha packed up Ivan and Gerta in carrying crates, and they followed the path to town. With a promise to meet him at the lofts in two days, Nikolai laid out a plan to show Armand and Cecile around town.

They visited the Monastery of Saint Euthymius with its high red stone walls and joined the throngs of people at the Torgovaya open-air market. They made the precarious climb to the top of the bell tower at the Resurrection Church and were rewarded with wonderful views of Suzdal's gold-domed skyline.

"If you become a priest, Nikolai," Cecile asked gazing out at the beautiful rural countryside, "Would you want to come back here?"

Nikolai thought for a moment, and then shook his head. "I think I'd like to stay in the cities and help the street children, if that is God's plan."

Armand draped an arm around the boy. "You will always be welcome to come to the U.S. with us, but you will make a fine priest. So, they called you Robin Hood, huh?" He tussled the boy's hair.

The boy smiled at him. It was nice to have the camaraderie of a father. He was convinced Natalia was in good hands, that they would love and protect her always.

Nikolai wanted to thank the Butkovskys, the old couple that took them in after the fire, but they were saddened to find that Mr. Butkovsky had passed away the year before. Mrs. Butkovsky invited them in and offered them warm black bread and *medovukha*, a Russian type of cider made from honey. She fussed over Natalia, pleased to see the little girl happy and healthy.

They stayed in the Hotel Pushkarskaya Sloboda,

a large white complex with beautifully appointed rooms, and a huge rustic banquet table of solid wood several inches thick where the guests dined together. Armand and Cecile enjoyed the plethora of languages from tourists all over the world, intrigued by how most understood at least a little English.

On the day the pigeons were to return, they gathered at the lofts with several dozen onlookers to watch for the birds to appear in the sky. Yasha knew exactly how many minutes it should take them to make the trip. Squinting into the western sky, they saw a fleck heading their way. One lone bird, with white undersides to his wings, circled around the heads of the judges as if to show off before lighting on Yasha's shoulder. Ivan! Everyone cheered. It was another half hour before the next bird landed. Gerta was nowhere in sight.

Everyone applauded Yasha for his skills at training his birds and winning the prize for the fastest flight. But his joy at winning was shadowed by the disappearance of Gerta. There was always the danger that someone would shoot the birds or that they would get injured or lost along the way. Gerta had never been this late before on the test runs.

Everyone agreed to watch out for her, but she could be anywhere along the route. Nikolai rode with Yasha in his car as they tried to follow the route, but the roads did not go in a straight line the way birds fly. Then Yasha's cell phone rang. A man claimed he had Gerta. She had identification on the little collar she wore around her leg. She had abandoned her flight to settle with a flock of city pigeons in a park at a town halfway between Vladimir and Suzdal. The man recognized the tag on her leg as identification and was amazed at how the domesticated bird perched on his shoulder with little encouragement.

Tasha thanked the man and said they would be there shortly to pick her up, if he would be so kind as to keep her inside so she did not fly away. He agreed.

The excitement of the homing race behind them and with Gerta safely in her loft, it was time to say good-bye to their friends and take the long trip to St. Petersburg. Nikolai's future rested in the results of the cross.

Chapter Thirty-Eight

St. Petersburg, Russia

April 20, 2009

The same deacon led them to the waiting room for Archbishop Peterhof's appearance. When the archbishop entered, Nikolai kneeled and kissed his hand.

"Stand, my son. That is not necessary. Please, everyone be seated. I have news."

Nikolai tried to suppress the butterflies flitting around in his stomach. He brushed sweaty palms on his pant legs.

"The synod was very impressed with your finding, Nikolai. I have a story to tell you.

"Peter the Great ruled from 1672 until his death in 1725. During his reign, he modernized Russia and transformed it into a major European power. He had very modern ideas about improving the economy with European ideals instead of Asian. He built New

Holland Island for shipbuilding and introduced Russia to trade relations with European countries. For those reasons, he fought wars, aristocrats, and the Church.

He changed the face of Russia in five years. He started relations with other aristocratic families. One of the changes he made was having women accompany their husbands to social functions."

The priest smiled and continued his story. "In 1703, Peter met a beautiful servant girl named Marta, and shortly after took her as his mistress. In 1705, she converted to Orthodoxy and took the new name of *Yekaterina Alexeyvna* (Catherine Alexeyevna). She kept Peter company on many military excursions, and Peter married her secretly in 1707.

"It is said that he had a cross designed for his wife, a much smaller and daintier version of one he wore himself. It was encrusted with jewels and had an inscription to her on the reverse." Archbishop Peterhof pulled a photo from his cassock. He turned it to face his guests.

Cecile's hand flew to her mouth.

Armand leaned in to get a closer look.

Nikolai froze in place.

"Look, Nika," Natalia squealed. "That lady is wearing your cross."

The archbishop smiled and continued, "Catherine was a beautiful and compassionate person, and one of the few people that could calm Peter from his bouts of rage and epileptic seizures. At one critical point in Peter's leadership, surrounded by overwhelming numbers of Turkish troops, Catherine suggested that before surrendering, Peter use her jewels and those of the other women to bribe the

Ottoman grand vizier Baltacı Mehmet Pasha into allowing a retreat.

"It is said that jewels throughout the land were collected, but she had a special place in her heart for this piece. She instructed her servant to hide the cross instead of including it in the bounty for the bribe.

"The bribery worked, and Mehmet allowed the retreat. Peter credited Catherine for saving the country and married her again, publicly, at Saint Isaac's Cathedral. They had twelve children, only two of whom lived to adulthood.

"The cross was never seen again. As you can tell from this painting of Catherine that Peter had commissioned, she is wearing the cross I now hold in my hand."

"It is real," Nikolai said breathlessly.

The bishop smiled. "Indeed, it is, my son. This artifact came from the very neck of Catherine the Great. It is priceless. We are most grateful you chose to return it to the Church instead of selling it. Most likely, no one would have ever understood the value of this piece."

Nikolai stammered, "Does that mean that I can attend the seminary?"

"The synod is very specific on its rules. A candidate must have completed secondary school, which I understand you have not. Is that correct?"

Nikolai's heart sank. "Yes Father, I have not been to school since I left New Holland."

"And there are more requirements," the bishop continued. "A candidate must also show experience in the church life, have a recommendation confessor, and be practiced in discipline and purity."

Nikolai's shoulders hunched over. "I have not

served in the church since before my parents' death, and I have no one to recommend me. And I am not pure. I'm sorry."

"Sometimes there can be exceptions," the priest spoke softly.

"What?" Nikolai's head jerked up.

"The synod has made a very unusual decision. With a recommendation from your local priest in Suzdal and on your reputation as Robin Hood, you have demonstrated your God-given talent to serve others. You will be admitted into the Academy once you complete your secondary education, which we will secure within the confines of the dormitory."

Armand and Cecile had been silent while the priest spoke, but Armand's enthusiasm bubbled over. "Are you saying that Nikolai is accepted?"

"Yes, I am pleased to say that Nikolai is accepted once he completes his secondary education, and we are waiving his tuition fees."

"Oh, that's wonderful. I'm so happy for you, Nikolai." Cecile beamed and jumped up to hug him.

"Yay, yay!" Natalia clapped her hands and danced around him. "Nika is going to be a priest."

Archbishop Peterhof raised his hand. "There is one more thing. Because of the immeasurable value of this artifact, we would also like to offer a stipend that would cover Natalia's college education in the future." He handed a check to Armand.

Armand looked at the check in his hand. His mouth dropped open. The number of zeros were more than he had ever seen in his life. The amount exceeded any tuition he could fathom at the best Ivy-League school in America. "I don't know what to say, Father. Thank you hardly seems adequate."

Cecile leaned over her husband's shoulder and looked at the amount. "Omigod!" She sprang from her chair and wrapped her arms around the surprised priest.

He gingerly patted her back. "You are most welcome, my child. Take good care of this little girl."

"Oh, we will. We surely will."

They stood at the gate of the St. Petersburg Theological Academy saying their goodbyes. Natalia clung to her brother one last time. "Nika, I wanted you to come to America with me, but I know God says you should stay here. I'm going to miss you."

"I'm going to miss you, too, Golubka, but we will call each other and Skype. It'll be like I am right next door. We'll always have each other." He rubbed her nose in an Eskimo kiss.

"What's Skype, Nika?"

"It's a way to see each other and talk on the computer. I'll be able to see your face and you can see mine. We'll always know each other is okay."

"Will you ever come to America to see me?" Her lower lip pouted.

"Hey, stop that," he teased her. "A pigeon could land on that lip. Of course, I will come."

She giggled.

Cecile knelt at eye level with her daughter. "I'll tell you this. We'll all come back when Nika gets ordained to help him celebrate. How does that sound?"

Natalia hugged her mother. "Okay, I love you, Mommy. Let's go home now."

They had all learned an important lesson. There are many faces of family.

Acknowledgments

Suzdal, Russia is a beautiful town. For more information on the city, visit **http://www.travelall-russia.com/suzdal/**

To hear music from Natalia's toy pigeon "Korobushka" (or "Коробушка" in Russian), go to **http://www.youtube.com/watch?v=3ve5p-0Q4tY**

The orphan train in this story is fictitious. New Holland Island in St. Petersburg, Russia, has never been an orphanage. For information on this historic site, visit **http://www.saint-petersburg.com/ buildings/new-holland/**

Chalmette, Louisiana suffered great loss from 2005 Hurricane Katrina. References to the devastation are a combination of factual data obtained online and my vision of what it would have been like to live through such a disaster. The Murphy Oil Company did have a breach in their tanks following the storm, but any negative connotation is false and used for artistic drama.

Rehoming or adopting from disruption is real.

You can find forums and mailing lists devoted to the topic across the internet — everywhere from Facebook to, until recently, Yahoo Groups." Reuters. More information is provided by Reuters at the end of this book. It is my hope that, with proper education and enlightenment, we can stop the black-market transfer of children through rehoming.

The United States of America is now closed to International Adoptions in Russia, by order of the Kremlin. St. Petersburg, Russia has tens of thousands of homeless children living on the streets. To see their stories, go to **http://www.youtube.com/watch?v=D-F1RMeSOeps** sponsored by Doctors of the World©.

RAD, Reactive Attachment Disorder, is a serious problem for children and adoptive parents with international adoptions. If you believe your child suffers from RAD, visit **http://www.reactive-attachment-disorder.info.**

The premise to this story is to bring to light the trauma of both adopted children and their parents in international adoption. I am an advocate for adoption, whether domestic or international. For information on adoption or help if you are a parent struggling with your adoption situation, contact **http://www.adoption.com.**

Information on rehoming children

provided by Reuters

Rehoming or adopting from disruption is real. You can find forums and mailing lists devoted to the topic across the Internet — everywhere from Facebook to, until recently, Yahoo Groups.

A report by Reuters on the practice of online private adoptions describes a couple, Todd and Melissa P*****, who attempted to "disrupt," or end, their adoption of a Liberian teen. When they handed her over to a couple they met online, the couple, who had faked documentation attesting to their parenting skills, took the teenager and fled.

The term *rehoming* is a term typically used to weed out pet owners by requiring those seeking an animal to pay a *rehoming fee*. But as Reuters points out, to rehome a small child, sometimes all you need is an internet connection and a transfer of guardianship — the human equivalent of a bill of sale.

The similarities to pet adoptions are eerie. Even more eerie is the similarity to the days of the Depression and other historical hard times, when parents who felt they could no longer afford to take care of their children would simply abandon them or offer them up to Orphan Trains heading West for greater opportunity. Even after the foster care system was put into place in the 20th century, families who wound up without resources to care for their children often found themselves at loose ends and placed their children in informal childcare — the most notorious case arguably is the abuse and murder of teenager Sylvia Likens at the hands of her unofficial foster family.

Many disrupted adoptions proceed through correct channels, like the Interstate Compact on the Placement of Children (ICPC); but Reuters found so many instances of what amounted to black market child trading that Yahoo Groups eventually shut down numerous adoption disruption mailing lists on its servers.

Time reported in 2010 that the estimated number of failed adoptions from Eastern Europe and Russia was around 4,000 since 1990. But this fails to consider illicit adoptions and other means of child transfer. After several notorious public incidents of failed Russian adoptions — one woman put her seven-year-old adopted son on a plane back to Moscow — many countries tightened restrictions on U.S. adoptions. Russia banned them altogether.

But such restrictions don't always make it easier for families to disrupt their adoptions safely. "We recently accepted the placement of a baby girl and later found out her older brother was coming to our home as part of a package deal," writes one woman on an adoption forum at About.com. "We spent many sleepless nights and thousands of dollars in legal fees trying to explore our options for an adoption disruption." In the U.K., the rate of disrupted adoptions is almost 20 percent, while in the U.S. it can range from 3 percent to a staggering 53 percent, with the likelihood of an adopted child ending back up in care increasing with the age of the child. One of the most frequently cited reasons for failed adoptions is the negligence of social services who may not inform prospective parents of child histories that often include emotional or physical abuse. Many adoptions are disrupted before they are ever finalized.

Still, the ease of contacting and arranging a private adoption is appealing. Tim Stowell, the parent who created the now-deleted Facebook page Way Stations of Love, described it to Reuters as "a clearinghouse" for parents wanting to locate children in need of new homes. But the lack of oversight opens such adoptions up to predators as well. Reuters points out that one man involved in one such illicit internet adoption was later arrested for child pornography.

Adoption.com recommends increased therapy and possibly even residential treatment for a child before deciding that an adoption has failed. Legitimate services for adoption disruption, like All Blessings, will at the very least require a case study period in which to do a home study and background check.

But as long as you can find and offer kids for adoption on the internet on sites like Craigslist; the trafficking of re-orphaned children may be a harsh reality that's here to stay.